"Things seem to have changed between us,"

Denver said.

April fought to c⋯⋯⋯⋯. "Changed?"

"What happened l⋯⋯⋯⋯ was a mistake. I just hop⋯⋯⋯ won't let it cause any bad feelings between us now."

Pain knifed through her. "I had forgotten all about it," she said stiffly. "It was so long ago I hardly remember it at all."

His eyes seemed to lose their warmth. "Okay," he said quietly. "I just wanted to get that straight."

She gave him a tight nod, then looked away before something in her face gave away her thoughts.

If he only knew how many nights she had lain awake, wishing she could feel again the hot vibrant fury of passion she'd felt that night with him.

If he only knew that, even now, her body ached to recapture what she had given up for the sake of her son....

Dear Reader,

Once again, we've rounded up the best romantic reading for you right here in Silhouette Intimate Moments. Start off with Maggie Shayne's *The Baddest Bride in Texas,* part of her top-selling miniseries THE TEXAS BRAND, and you'll see what I mean. Secrets, steam and romance…this book has everything.

And how many of you have been following that baby? A lot, I'll bet. And this month our FOLLOW THAT BABY cross-line miniseries concludes with *The Mercenary and the New Mom,* by Merline Lovelace. At last the baby's found—and there's romance in the air, as well.

If Western loving's your thing, we've got a trio of books to keep you happy. *Home Is Where the Cowboy Is,* by Doreen Roberts, launches a terrific new miniseries called RODEO MEN.THE SULLIVAN BROTHERS continue their wickedly sexy ways in *Heartbreak Ranch,* by Kylie Brant. And Cheryl Biggs's *The Cowboy She Never Forgot*—a book *you'll* find totally memorable—sports our WAY OUT WEST flash. Then complete your month's reading with *Suddenly a Family,* by Leann Harris. This FAMILIES ARE FOREVER title features an adorable set of twins, their delicious dad and the woman who captures all three of their hearts.

Enjoy them all—then come back next month for six more wonderful Intimate Moments novels, the most exciting romantic reading around.

Yours,

Leslie J. Wainger
Executive Senior Editor

Please address questions and book requests to:
Silhouette Reader Service
U.S.: 3010 Walden Ave., P.O. Box 1325, Buffalo, NY 14269
Canadian: P.O. Box 609, Fort Erie, Ont. L2A 5X3

HOME IS WHERE
THE COWBOY IS

DOREEN
ROBERTS

Published by Silhouette Books
America's Publisher of Contemporary Romance

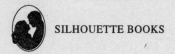 SILHOUETTE BOOKS

ISBN 0-373-07909-5

HOME IS WHERE THE COWBOY IS

Copyright © 1999 by Doreen Roberts

This edition published by arrangement with Harlequin Books S.A.

® and TM are trademarks of Harlequin Books S.A., used under license.
Trademarks indicated with ® are registered in the United States Patent
and Trademark Office, the Canadian Trade Marks Office and in other
countries.

Printed in U.S.A.

Books by Doreen Roberts

* Rodeo Men

DOREEN ROBERTS

lives with her husband, who is also her manager and her biggest fan, in the beautiful city of Portland, Oregon. She believes that everyone should have a little adventure now and again to add interest to their lives. She believes in taking risks and has been known to embark on an adventure or two of her own. She is happiest, however, when she is creating stories about the biggest adventure of all—falling in love and learning to live happily ever after.

To Lynda Curnyn,
my wonderful editor.
This story is as much hers as mine.

And, as always, to my beloved Bill—
my own special hero.
Thank you for your generosity of spirit,
your never-failing loyalty and understanding.
I love you.

Chapter 1

Denver Briggs was not having a good day. Usually he managed to keep his emotions under wraps, but for once he let his frustration get the better of him. He slammed out of the office door and, for good measure, aimed a vicious kick at the chutes on his way out of the arena.

The phone call had rattled him, and his irritation was due more to his own reaction than to anything April had said. He didn't like to be reminded of the effect his sister-in-law had on him. He hadn't planned on being around her anymore for that very reason. Now it looked as if he didn't have any choice.

The familiar smell of sawdust and sweaty animals helped soothe his frazzled nerves, and he had it all under control again by the time he emerged into the full force of the sun's light.

It was unseasonably hot for June in Oregon. The dry, dusty heat hit him in the face, and he pulled the brim of his Stetson lower to shade his eyes.

The last thing he needed right now was trouble. He'd had a good season so far, and he sat pretty high in the standings for bull riding. If he could keep it up, he'd easily make the national finals in December. This could even be the year he realized his dream of making the world all-around championship.

In order to do that he needed his concentration—the needle-sharp reflexes that meant the difference between sticking on the back of an angry bull for eight mind-numbing seconds or scrambling in the dust to escape the vicious horns.

What he didn't need was to get embroiled in his sister-in-law's problems. It looked very much as though that was the way things were brewing.

He ignored the bold, coveting glances from female fans still leaving the grounds, as he strode purposefully across the parking lot and threaded his way among the trailers, pickups and campers clustered at the far end.

A thick stand of firs shaded the vehicles from the sun. Even so, the heat stung his fingers when he twisted the door handle of the camper he shared with his travel partners.

The cooled air fanned his face as he went through the door, and the two men inside turned toward him. Cord, seated closest to him, gave him a slow, searching look. Understanding the question in his friend's dark eyes, Denver gave him a reassuring nod.

Cord McVane never did waste much time with words. He preferred his own company to just about anybody, with the possible exception of his two travel partners.

Jed Cullen, the third member of the team, sat in a swivel chair opposite Cord, leaning forward with his big hands thrust between his knees. "Well? Is she coming to get him?" he asked, as Denver took off his hat and threw it down on the bench behind him.

Denver gave a quick warning shake of his head and

glanced at the boy who sat hunched by the window. His grimy face looked as sullen and uncompromising as only a defiant ten-year-old's could. He didn't even glance up when Denver said gruffly, "You'd better get washed, Josh. Your mom's gonna be here real soon. She won't be happy to see you looking as if you'd been dragged through a hedge by a mad heifer."

Josh's lower lip jutted out, and he started swinging his leg. His heel thudded against the upholstered bench in unmistakable rebellion.

Denver stared at his nephew in silent frustration. For once he was out of his depth. Angry bulls and ornery men he could match any day. When it came to women and kids, well…that was a different story.

There had been a time when he could forget his troubles in the arms of a woman—a sort of mutual hello-goodbye thing, without complications. Now he didn't even bother to do that. Women, he'd long ago decided, were better off not messing with the likes of him.

As for kids…they were unknown territory. He didn't have one smidgen of an idea how to handle them, especially one who looked as miserable as his young nephew.

Luckily, Jed didn't seem to have that problem. He uncoiled his lanky body from the chair and held out a hand to Josh. "How about you and me going for an ice cream, pardner?" he suggested in his characteristic drawl. "We can stop in the men's room while we're about it."

Denver let out his breath in relief when Josh, after a moment's hesitation, flung himself off the bench and out the door.

Jed grabbed his hat and followed the boy, lifting his hand in farewell. "Be right back."

The door closed behind him, and Denver sank onto the bench with a groan.

"She give you trouble?" Cord asked, sounding sympathetic.

"No, she was too shook up for that. I just hope she doesn't think I encouraged the boy."

"That's the trouble with women when they get agitated. Just won't listen to reason."

"Not April. She's the most levelheaded woman I know."

Cord grunted. "Not too many women keep their heads when they lose their young-uns. I'd rather face a demented bull any day than take on a woman defending her young."

Denver closed his eyes and leaned back. He knew better than to argue with Cord about a woman. That was one subject the three men usually avoided.

"Still, must be tough on her since your brother died," Cord murmured.

"Real tough. Josh took Lane's death pretty hard. That's why April's having trouble with the boy now. He misses his dad a lot."

"You've gotta miss him, too."

It was a statement more than a question, and Denver didn't bother to deny it. He still found it impossible to believe that Lane was gone. His big brother, the one he'd always looked up to, worshiped and idolized…the invincible one who was supposed to always be there if he needed him.…

His throat closed up and he swallowed hard. He hadn't seen much of Lane in the past ten years or so. Not since his brother had married April. He'd kept in touch with them all through letters and phone calls, gifts to his young nephew at birthdays and Christmas, and the occasional flying visit. But he never stuck around, always giving the excuse of having to hit the road to make the next ride.

All in all he'd seen them only a few times after Josh was born, and again at his own mother's funeral. In fact, the last time he'd seen April and Josh was eight months ago, at yet another funeral. That time he'd mourned the loss of his only brother, Lane.

He'd been shocked that day to see how fast his nephew had grown. In spite of his grief, he couldn't help noticing how April had blossomed into a full-blown woman.

She had been barely nineteen the night he told her he was leaving to join the rodeo. She'd looked so young and innocent, standing there in the shadows of the barn behind her house with the moonlight silvering her light-brown hair.

He could tell she was doing her best not to cry. He'd felt like crying himself. But grown men didn't cry, and right then, even though he was just twenty-two, he'd felt like a hundred years old. That was all of ten years ago, and he still felt the ache of that night whenever he looked at April.

Which was why he'd stayed out of her way as much as possible. Now Josh was here, larger than life, bringing with him more problems than the boy could ever imagine.

"Things must be real bad for Josh to run away from home," Denver muttered, thinking out loud. "Don't know why the heck he came to me. Can't figure out what the boy was thinking of."

"You're the only kin left besides his mom. Who else would he go to?"

Denver shrugged. "I dunno. April must have plenty of friends who know Josh better than I do."

"None that ride rodeo, I reckon." Cord stuck out his feet and examined his scuffed boots. "He says he wants to join the team."

"Thank God he's too young for that. I just hope Jed can keep him out of the way until I've had a chance to talk to his mom. Maybe I can calm her down a bit."

"Jed's good with kids. Kids and animals both. Often

think he'd be better off taking care of a wife and kids than riding broncs.''

Denver shook his head. ''Jed? He'd never settle down with a family. He's got his mind too set on other things.''

''Yeah, I know. He wants the all-around championship.'' Cord yawned and stretched out his arms above his head. ''Don't we all?''

Denver studied his friend for a moment before answering. ''Not as bad as he wants it, I reckon. You and me, we want the championship to prove something to ourselves. Jed wants it to prove something to a whole town.''

''Yeah, well, maybe he'll do it this year.'' Cord surged to his feet and ambled over to the door. ''I think I'm gonna get me a beer. Wish you luck when the kid's mom gets here.''

''Yeah.'' Denver leaned back again as the door closed with a thud. It would take April about another ten minutes or so to drive down to the rodeo grounds, he figured. He'd offered to take Josh to her, but she'd insisted on coming out to him.

If he'd had any idea the kid would pull a stunt like this, he would never have come back this close to Portland. Both Cord and Jed had talked him into it, reminding him of the prize money and how the winnings would add to their score. They all needed every ride they could get to keep their place in the standings.

He glanced around the comfortable camper, which not only served as the group's transportation but had also been their home for seven years. He'd hooked up with Jed and Cord at the Barstow Stampede in California. He'd liked their setup, shared a few beers with them, and ended up accepting their offer to buy into their partnership with the rig. They'd been traveling together ever since.

Their friendship was solid, based on trust and shared experiences. They didn't talk about the past, and no one asked questions. It was a sort of understanding they had. They each lived for the moment, for the next ride…sticking by one another in the rough times and celebrating in the good.

Rodeo was a tough life but a good one, Denver mused, and probably more than he deserved. This year looked as if it would be the best yet. All three of them were doing well enough to make the finals, and all of them had a good chance at the championship.

He'd be happy just to make world champ for bull riding again, Denver assured himself. Though the all-around would be real nice. The best there was. What self-respecting rodeo cowboy wouldn't want that?

The sound of a car door slamming scattered his thoughts. He gave another cursory glance around, this time wondering what April would think of his home. Remembering the fancy house she'd shared with Lane, he pulled a face. This probably would look like one step away from poverty to her.

He pulled his shoulders back and braced himself. He was not going to let her get under his skin again. He'd explain what happened, hand Josh over to her when Jed brought him back, say goodbye and that would be the end of it. After that he'd make darn sure that he put some distance between them. The farther he stayed away from his sister-in-law, the better for both of them.

Outside the camper, April shut off the engine and sat for a moment to gather her composure. Her hand shook as she dropped the keys into her purse. The anguish of the past hour or so had shattered her nerves, and it didn't help to know that she was about to face Denver again.

She'd been frantic when Josh hadn't returned home from Little League practice. Her call to the coach had confirmed her worst fears. He hadn't seen Josh all afternoon. Her calls to the homes of her son's friends had intensified her terror.

No one had seen him. She'd been at the point of phoning the police, when Denver had called to say Josh was with him.

She hadn't waited to ask questions. She'd told him she was on her way and more or less hung up on him. Now she would have to deal with the problem...all by herself. It was times like this that she really missed her husband.

Lane had always been the buffer between her and Denver. Until the funeral, her husband had been a comforting wall, separating her from the past. But now Lane was gone, and April was very much afraid the past was about to catch up with her.

Drawing in a long breath, she opened the door and climbed out. The heat was almost overwhelming. Accustomed to milder temperatures, she wished she'd worn something lighter than the yellow T-shirt and jeans she'd pulled on that morning.

She'd tied her newly lightened hair back into a ponytail and hadn't bothered with makeup. The urge to run a lipstick over her mouth was strong. She resisted the temptation, refusing to acknowledge her vulnerability where Denver was concerned.

Her hand was still shaky when she rapped on the door of the camper. It opened at once, and she knew he'd been waiting on the other side for her.

As always, her first sight of him robbed her of speech. He was taller than his brother, and although they'd both had the same black hair and husky build, Lane had accumulated a layer of fat over the years. Denver's rugged body, on the other hand, was corded with muscle and his lean, weathered features were in direct contrast to Lane's pallid, fleshy cheeks.

It was the eyes, though, where April saw the biggest difference. Though similar in color, Denver's steel-blue gaze seemed to penetrate her soul like a diamond slicing through glass. There were times when she felt she could never hide anything from that penetrating stare.

She gave him a tight nod and stepped past him into the shadowy interior of the huge vehicle. Her gaze swept around the empty benches, and her stomach contracted. She turned to face Denver, who stood by the door, watching her with an unusually wary expression on his face.

"Where is he?" she demanded huskily. "Don't tell me he's gone again?"

"No, of course not. He's fine." Denver moved away from the door and took a step toward her.

Without thinking, she backed off, and saw a wry look flick across his granite features.

"He's with Jed," he added, motioning for her to sit down. "He'll be back soon. They went for ice cream."

"Jed?" She sat on the edge of the bench, her fingers clenching the edge of the seat.

"He's one of the guys I travel with. I must have mentioned him and Cord before. They own part of this rig."

She vaguely remembered him talking about his travel partners to Lane. She looked at her surroundings again, really seeing them this time. She'd never visited Denver in his own environment.

Flowered curtains hung at the small windows, and cushions with the same pattern sat on each end of the benches. For some reason the sight of them reassured her and she relaxed her fingers.

A couple of swivel armchairs were riveted to the floor in front of the rear window, and she noticed a small TV set mounted on the wall above her head.

A tiny kitchen divided the room from the rest of vehicle, where she assumed the bedrooms were. The place looked cozy and comfortable, and much roomier than she would have imagined.

"This is very nice," she said quietly.

"It works for us."

She looked at him solemnly, and he cleared his throat. She had the distinct feeling that he would rather be anywhere but sitting with her in that silent room.

She needn't have worried, she thought wryly. The wall was still there. If anything, it seemed even more formidable now that Lane wasn't around to act as a buffer. It wasn't exactly hostility she sensed behind Denver's wary gaze; it was closer to indifference. As if he suffered her presence because he felt responsible, for some reason.

She lifted her chin slightly. Well, he didn't have to feel responsible for her just because she'd married his brother. She was perfectly capable of managing her own life, or she would be if she didn't have this problem with Josh.

"Believe me, I had nothing to do with this," Denver said, as if reading her thoughts. "He'd taken a bus as far as he could go, then one of the guys spotted him walking along the road a couple of miles out of town and brought him in. Josh told me you said it was okay, but I figured you wouldn't have let him come all this way on his own, so that's when I called you. He got pretty steamed up about that."

"I imagine he did," April said wryly.

"I've no idea why he came looking for me."

"I know why he came to you." She let out a long sigh. "I told you on the phone that I've been having trouble with him ever since Lane died. He's always looked up to you. He's fascinated by—" she waved a hand in the air "—all this. You are his hero. He came because he needed you."

Denver frowned. "Are you saying he sees me as some kind of replacement for Lane?"

April shrugged, trying to still the urgent flutter in her stomach. "I don't know. I'm only guessing. He's been talking about you for the past few weeks, asking all kinds of questions about what you do and where you live. I think he has some wild fantasy in his mind about coming to live with you, since he's so unhappy with me.''

Denver looked even more uncomfortable. ''He's bound to miss his dad. We all do, but it must be tougher on a kid to lose his father like that. He'll come around in time.''

April nodded without much conviction. ''I certainly hope so. He's been getting into trouble at school—talking back to the teachers, skipping classes, not doing his home-work....''

''Some kids go through phases like that.''

Something in his tone warned her, and with a sickening thud of her heart she remembered. In her anxiety over Josh she had forgotten for the moment.

Denver's father had walked out on the family when Denver was just a little younger than Josh. Lane had been four-teen at the time and had handled it well, taking over as the man of the house. Denver, on the other hand, turned into a rebellious, disobedient hell-raiser, always in trouble and defiant in the face of anyone who tried to control him.

How could she not remember how he was? Or how many nights she had fantasized that it was Denver, the tormented loner, kissing her good-night, instead of his elder, sensible brother?

She'd been dating Lane on and off for several months before he'd taken her home to meet his mother. Denver had been there that night, though he hadn't stayed for dinner. April had gotten one look at his attractive, brooding face and had known in that charged, unforgettable moment that she was dating the wrong brother.

Unable to control her yearning, she'd done everything she could think of to get Denver's attention whenever he was around, which wasn't often. She might just as well have been trying to capture a moonbeam.

Denver acted as if she were part of the furniture. He barely spoke to her, and when he did, he rarely looked her straight in the eyes. Even so, the thrill of seeing him walk into the room could make her heart leap and her chest ache with wanting his arms around her.

Once in a rare while she'd catch him looking at her with such a fire burning in his piercing blue eyes she'd lose her breath. But always when that happened he'd turn away and leave the room.

Although Lane had never mentioned it, she knew he was aware of how she felt about Denver. Still, she enjoyed Lane's company and she continued to date him now and again, though her feelings for him were far from what she felt for Denver.

Then there was the fatal night she'd driven over to see Lane, not knowing he'd had to work late. His mother had gone to the movies, leaving Denver alone in the house. At first Denver wouldn't let her in, until she told him that she would sit on the doorstep and wait for Lane.

She could never remember afterward who had made the first move. She recalled only that she was alone with Denver, listening to the slow, seductive throbbing beat of a country song, while she talked about losing her own parents when she was four years old. She'd wanted him to know that she understood his pain, and she must have succeeded, because somehow she'd ended up in his arms.

He blew her mind that night. He changed the world for her forever, stealing her heart and breaking it all at the same time. Then, days later, while she was still glowing with the passion they'd shared, floating on a golden cloud of sheer, indescribable pleasure, he'd told her they must never see each other again. He was going away, and he wouldn't be back.

She'd argued with him, accused him of being afraid of his brother. Nothing she said made any difference. She'd finally had to accept the fact that he'd taken advantage of her feelings for him, and that it had meant nothing more to him than a night's entertainment. Hurt, she'd vowed never to see either brother again.

"Try not to worry so much. Josh is a good kid. He'll come out of it."

Startled out of her thoughts by Denver's gruff voice, April took a moment to answer. "I hope so," she said at last. "I just hope he pulls it together before he gets into some real trouble. He was caught stealing from one of his classmate's lockers just before school was out last month. His principal warned me that if Josh gives him any more trouble he'll suspend him."

"I guess there's no use talking to him?"

"I tried." She pressed her fingers to her forehead to relieve the growing pressure there. "He won't listen to me or to anyone else. I've talked to his counselor, his doctor, his teachers.... They all say the same thing. Time will help. I'm not so sure we have time."

Denver's eyes narrowed as he looked at her. "So what do you want me to do about it?"

Up until that moment she hadn't thought about him doing anything. But now that he'd mentioned it, she began to wonder if perhaps this was where the answer lay.

Josh and Lane had enjoyed such a close relationship, sometimes to the point of excluding her. She knew that deep down Josh resented the fact that his father had died while she had lived. The pain of that was always with her.

She'd tried getting closer to her son. He'd just rebelled all the more. She was at the end of her rope. No amount of talking or pleading seemed to help. Punishment just seemed to make things worse, and she was really worried that Josh might do something that would result in a stigma against him for the rest of his life.

Maybe this was the answer. Maybe Denver could provide the father figure that Josh needed so desperately right now. Maybe he would have the influence that she appeared to have lost since the night Lane had flown his small plane into the side of a mountain and left her alone to cope with her grieving son.

In the next breath she knew that was impossible. It would be too dangerous. She had far too much to lose. Though her lips felt cold and stiff, she managed to force a smile. "That's real nice of you to offer, Denver, but this is my problem. I'll take care of it."

He started to answer, but just then a clattering sounded on the steps outside and the door burst open.

The man who came through ducked his head to clear the frame, then straightened. His direct gaze, sent from glinting gold eyes, rested on her face.

Denver got lazily to his feet. "April, meet Jed Cullen. Most folks around here call him 'J.C.'"

"Pleased to meet you," April murmured, extending her hand. "Do I call you 'Jed' or 'J.C.'?"

"'Jed' will do just fine, ma'am."

Her fingers disappeared briefly in the tall man's palm, then he let her go. She suddenly felt overwhelmed by all this potent masculinity in such a small space.

"Where's Josh?" Denver asked, echoing April's thoughts.

Jed swung around toward the door. "He's right here...or he was," he finished lamely. "Dang it, where'd the boy go?"

April edged by him and stepped outside. Josh stood several yards away, watching a group of wranglers herding horses onto a trailer. His head was tilted, and for a fleeting moment he looked so much like his father her breath caught in her throat. The older the boy grew, the more the resemblance was there.

Denver's voice directly behind her made her jump.

"You want to talk to him alone?"

She shook her head. Raising her voice, she called out, "Josh! Come here. Uncle Denver wants to speak to you."

"I don't know what to say to him," Denver muttered from behind her.

She glanced at him over her shoulder. "Just answer his questions about the rodeo. That should satisfy him for a while."

"I'm gonna look for Cord," Jed said, squeezing past Denver's broad shoulders. "I reckon we should leave here in about an hour if we're going to make Flagstaff on time."

April couldn't help the little stab of disappointment. "You're going to Arizona?"

"Yes, ma'am." Denver's gaze fastened on Josh, who approached at a snail's pace, scuffling his sneakers in the dust. "Can't afford to miss a ride."

April looked down at her son when he paused a couple of feet away. "Josh? Why did you do this? Don't you know how worried I was?"

Josh shrugged his thin shoulders. "I wanted to stay with Uncle Denver. He doesn't want me, though."

Denver cleared his throat, then moved forward to squat in front of the boy. "It's not that I don't want you, Josh. There's just no room in that little ol' camper for another cowboy. Besides we're leaving tonight to go to Arizona. You'd miss your mom."

Josh sent a defiant look up at April. "No, I wouldn't."

"I think you would," Denver said firmly. "And I know your mom would miss you."

"But I want to ride in the rodeo," Josh mumbled, looking as if he were about to cry.

"I'm afraid you're a little too young, cowboy." Denver paused, as if turning something over in his mind. "Tell you what, when I get back from Arizona, I'll send you a souvenir from the rodeo. How about that?"

Josh's eyes filled with tears. "I want to go with you.

Why won't you let me go with you? I always went everywhere with Dad—why can't I go with you?''

Denver glanced up at April for help.

''Because you can't,'' April said gently. She reached for
Josh's hand, but he snatched it away. ''Uncle Denver has
a job to do,'' she went on evenly, ''and he doesn't have
time to take care of a little boy.''

''I'm not a little boy,'' Josh shouted, backing away from
them. ''I'm almost grown up. And if he won't take me I'll
run away and join the rodeo by myself.''

''Josh—'' April started forward, but Josh twisted around
and raced off across the parking lot.

''I'll go after him,'' Denver said grimly, and sprinted
after the flying boy.

April felt the familiar sense of helplessness sweep over
her. She had never felt quite so lonely in her entire life.
She was at a loss as to the best way to handle her son, and
she had no one to turn to for help.

If only her mother were still alive, she thought with a
growing ache in her heart, or the kind, elderly aunt who
had brought her up. If only she had someone who understood and could advise her.

But there was no one. She was alone in the world with
Josh…except for Denver.

She watched them walking back to her, her son and the
big man by his side. Denver was looking down at Josh, his
hand on the boy's shoulder. He was talking earnestly to
him, and Josh appeared to be listening, though resentment
still glowered on his tear-streaked face.

If anyone could get through to Josh, it would be Denver,
April reluctantly admitted to herself. She hadn't exaggerated when she'd called him Josh's hero. If there was one
man who came close to his father in her son's estimation,
it was his larger-than-life uncle…a rodeo champion who

made his living risking his neck on the back of snorting, stomping, killer bulls.

In Josh's eyes, Denver was the knight fighting the dragon, the ghost buster banishing monsters, the spacecraft captain battling alien invaders. In Josh's eyes, Denver was invincible. If anyone could save her son from himself, it would be Denver Briggs.

Panic welled in her when she realized what she was contemplating. How could she take the risk? How could she balance the desperate need of her son for a male figure in his life against the consequences if either he or Denver ever found out the truth?

How could she throw these two together, knowing that the longer Denver was around her son, the greater the danger of him realizing what she had hidden from him all these years? She had kept the promise she had made to Lane then, and she had every intention of keeping it forever.

But if Denver became suspicious enough to ask questions, would she be able to lie? Would she be able to look him in the eyes and deny him what was his right to know?

He would be shattered, of course. Not to mention furious—as he'd have every right to be, knowing that she'd kept the truth from him. It could be enough to wreck her relationship with him forever.

Most of all, how would Josh feel if he knew that the man who walked by his side at this very moment was, in actual fact, his biological father?

It would be enough to destroy them all, April thought, forcing a smile as the two remaining members of her family approached. She couldn't take the risk after all.

"I reckon we got things straightened out," Denver said as they reached her. "Me and Josh have made an agreement."

"You have?" April looked hopefully at her son, but he refused to return her smile. "What kind of agreement?"

"Well, Josh here has promised to behave, on condition that I spend some time with him. I reckon I can do some of the things he used to do with his dad, and if he's real good, I might even teach him to ride."

Josh's eyes lit up for an instant at that, but April's heart started thudding. "We can't expect you to do that. How are you going to find time? You're always on the road."

Denver shrugged and squeezed the thin shoulder under his hand. "I'll fit it in between rides, whenever I can. The boy needs me right now. It isn't very often someone needs Denver Briggs."

And Denver needed to be needed, April realized suddenly. It looked as if the decision had been taken out of her hands. Under the circumstances she could hardly refuse such a generous offer without explanations she couldn't afford to make.

Now her heart thudded for a different reason. There was a further complication that she hadn't considered until now. All the time Lane was alive she hadn't let herself remember the way it was with Denver.

When Lane had discovered she was pregnant, he'd begged her to marry him. By then Denver had left town to join the rodeo, and she'd had too much pride to let him know the result of that stolen night. He might do the right thing by standing by her, but she didn't want him that way, realizing she and the baby would be nothing but a burden to him.

So she'd married Lane, promising to keep their secret forever. Lane had been good to her and Josh, and although she could never love him with the wild, untamed passion she'd felt for Denver, she had found peace and security and a measure of contentment in her life with him.

Now it was different. Now Lane was gone, and there was nothing standing between her and Denver, except for the secret she held in her heart. And as much as she tried to deny it, the passion was still there, a glowing ember of the past just waiting to be fanned into the fire that had once consumed her.

And that could never happen again, April warned herself fiercely as she stared down at her son. Denver had made it clear long ago how he felt about her. It was obvious his feelings hadn't changed over the years. He wasn't doing this for her; he was doing it for his dead brother's son.

She must never let herself forget that, for now he had the power to hurt her even worse than he had before. He must never find out the truth about Josh, for that could bring disaster down on all their heads, and she would have to live with the regrets the rest of her life.

"I'll walk you back to the car," Denver said, breaking into her thoughts.

His mind was already on the next ride, she noted, with a flash of irritation. It was obvious he couldn't wait to get rid of them. She just hoped he wouldn't disappoint Josh, or he'd make things worse than they already were.

She barely glanced at him as she climbed into the car and waited for Josh to scramble in beside her.

"I'll see you when I get back, cowboy," Denver said, reaching through the window to pat her son's shoulder.

"Okay," Josh mumbled, then leaned forward to turn on the radio.

Denver touched the brim of his hat as he glanced at her, then straightened, his face disappearing from view.

April caught the glint of sunlight on the large silver belt buckle he wore, then he stepped back, and she switched on the engine. A minute or two later she pulled out of the parking lot, resisting the urge to look in the rearview mirror for a last glimpse of her unsettling brother-in-law.

Denver watched until the powder-blue T-bird had disappeared around the bend; then, thrusting his thumbs into the pockets of his jeans, he walked slowly back to the camper.

Now that he'd had a few moments to think about his decision to spend time with Josh, he wasn't at all sure he'd done the right thing. At first he'd been thinking of Lane, what his brother would have wanted him to do.

He could see the path that Josh was taking. He'd taken it himself all those years ago, and for the same reason. The circumstances might be different, but the result was the same. A fatherless boy, lost, alone and confused... struggling with a desperate need to be understood.

Denver paused in the shade of the firs, needing a few moments alone before returning to his partners. Not that Cord or Jed would pester him with questions. Still, it was hard to concentrate while his friends did their best to take his mind off his troubles.

He leaned his back against a sturdy trunk and shoved his hat back with his thumb. Already the vehicles were leaving the parking lot in a steady stream, most of them probably heading for Flagstaff.

Denver watched a camper bounce over the curb as it took the corner too close. It wasn't as if April wasn't doing her best, he silently acknowledged. After all, no one knew her son better than she did. She certainly loved him enough.

But sometimes that wasn't enough. Sometimes a boy needed a man's hand to guide him. Maybe if he'd had that, Denver thought, as he watched the camper roar by him in a cloud of dust, things might have been different for him.

He shut down immediately as a vision of April rose in his mind. That was a path he'd stopped going down a long time ago. He'd known right from the start that he and April weren't meant to be. He was too much like his father, whose footsteps he'd followed almost all the way.

The one good thing he'd done in his life was letting her go. She'd deserved better. She'd deserved Lane, the hard-working, upright, sensible one. Most of the time he could live with that. Most of the time he concentrated on his goal—the all-around championship—as a way to forget the past and keep his mind fixed on the future.

It was only when he saw her that the ache in his gut reminded him of what might have been.

Now he'd promised to try to help a small boy avoid the mistakes he'd made. But at what cost to himself? He didn't want to think about it.

In fact, he told himself, as he propelled his body away from the tree, it was time he pushed it all out of his mind and got back to what was important right now. The next town. The next ride. One step closer to the championship. One more chance to forget.

Chapter 2

As the days passed without a word from Denver, Josh once more became sullen and difficult. His tension communicated itself to April, who jumped every time she heard a car door slam near the house in the quiet cul-de-sac.

Although she hadn't allowed herself to depend on Denver's promise, she felt a crushing sense of disappointment as each day ended without her hearing from him.

Josh spent most of the day alone in his room, refusing her offers to take him to the movies or even to the arcade, one of his favorite treats.

Each morning April's anxiety intensified as she tore off another page of her desk calendar. Soon summer vacation would be over. She'd given up her part-time job as a dentist's receptionist to be with Josh after Lane died. Sooner or later she would have to find another job, and she'd promised herself to start looking just as soon as Josh went back to school in September.

It wouldn't be easy to juggle a full-time job with the

responsibility of her son, especially if he couldn't struggle out of the depression that had such a cruel grip on him. How she hated to see him wasting the beautiful summer days shut up in his room, instead of enjoying the fresh air and warm sun that were so essential to a healthy body.

When she woke up to yet another morning of bright sunlight, she decided to take matters firmly in hand. Today she would drive Josh somewhere fun if she had to carry him to the car and force him inside.

She waited until after their silent breakfast before broaching the subject. Josh pushed his chair away from the table and she caught hold of his hand.

He snatched it away immediately but remained where he was, his gaze aimed at his feet.

"It's such a lovely day," April said, her voice brittle with the effort to sound upbeat. "Why don't we go down to the beach for the day. We can go in the arcade on the seafront, have lunch at that restaurant overlooking the ocean and find some seashells to bring back with us. Doesn't that sound like fun?"

Josh shrugged but to her relief didn't give her his usual negative response.

Determined not to waste a moment in case he changed his mind, she jumped to her feet. "Go get your jacket, and I'll be ready to leave by the time you get back."

She rushed around, grabbed up her purse, a sweatshirt and jacket and a couple of beach towels and threw them into the car. She was backing the car out of the garage when Josh returned a few minutes later.

"I'll just lock up and then we can go," she told him, beginning to feel more lighthearted than she had in weeks. Maybe she was finally breaking through that awful barrier he'd put up around him.

"I don't want to go."

Her hopes died. April stared at her son's mutinous face

and fought down her irritation. It wouldn't do any good to get mad at him, she warned herself. "Why not?" she asked quietly.

"It won't be any fun without Dad."

"I know how you feel, Josh. I feel the same way. We could try to make it fun for just the two of us. Your father would want us to at least try to do that."

Josh thudded the back of his heel on the paving stone without answering.

Behind her April heard a car door slam, but her gaze was intent on her son and she barely registered it. "Josh," she said gently, "I really wish you would come with me to the beach. I'd be real lonely all by myself."

Josh lifted his head, and her heart filled with dismay to see tears glistening on his dark lashes.

"I don't want to go," he shouted. "My dad always went with us to the beach. I don't want to go if he's not there."

"How about me?" a deep voice inquired behind April. "I'd love to go to the beach. How about taking me, instead?"

Josh's eyes widened, and April swung around, her heart leaping at the sight of the tall, sunburned man who stood smiling down at her, his keen blue eyes shaded by the brim of his Stetson.

Her voice shook slightly when she said, "Josh has been looking forward to seeing you again. I'm sure he'd love to have you go with us to the beach."

Denver's gaze rested on her face for a brief second or two, his expression unreadable, then he looked at Josh. "How about it, cowboy? You reckon I can come along?"

Josh shrugged, though the frown had disappeared from his face. "I don't care," he mumbled.

"Fine." Denver took off his hat and set it on Josh's head. "In that case, you can wear my hat, just until we get to the beach, okay? Take good care of it, mind. I don't usually let anyone wear it 'cept me.''

Josh's eyes widened, and he raised his hand to touch the brim.

"Go get your jacket, then," April said, smiling at him. She watched her son hurry back into the house. He looked almost swamped by the wide sweep of the Stetson. "That was real nice of you," she said unsteadily. "Especially the hat. It means a lot to Josh."

Denver looked self-conscious as he combed his dark hair back with his fingers. "I reckon I had some making up to do on account of me taking a while to get back to him."

She pursed her lips, determined not to let him know how anxious she'd been. "You're under no obligation," she said stiffly.

He studied her for a moment, his face serious. "I gave my promise to the boy," he said at last.

"No one expects you to keep it."

She regretted the words the minute she saw the hard expression in his eyes.

"I expect me to keep it," he said quietly.

To April's relief, the awkward moment was broken by Josh's return. His jacket swung from one hand, and April's pulse skipped when she spotted the camera his father had given him hanging around his neck. It was the first time since the accident that she'd seen him touch anything Lane had given him.

"I'll drive," Denver said firmly, as April opened the door on the driver's side. "Josh can sit up front with me and give you some room in the back."

Not sure she cared for the way he'd taken over, April nevertheless relinquished the wheel. Relegated to the rear seat, she leaned back as they drove out of the street and did her best to relax her tightly wound nerves.

Even though she'd half expected him for days, it had

been a shock to see Denver standing there. She was still unnerved by the thrill that had chased down her body at the sight of him. She couldn't even look at the back of his dark head now without feeling a little shiver of excitement.

He wore a blue T-shirt with his jeans, and she could see the muscles in his back and shoulders contract beneath the stretched fabric as he controlled the wheel. Above the prominent tip of his backbone his neck looked smooth and tanned. She felt an almost irresistible urge to touch the enticing spot with her fingertips.

She had to look away in an effort to control the sudden surge of heat she felt at the thought. Buildings flashed by her confused gaze as she struggled with her turbulent feelings. She had to stop this, right now. Josh needed this man, and she couldn't let her adolescent fantasies jeopardize that relationship.

Whatever had been between them happened long ago and was probably forgotten as far as Denver was concerned. Which was just as well, considering the circumstances. She had to put the past to rest and concentrate on the future—hers and Josh's—and it didn't include Denver. At least not permanently. She had no illusions about that.

Denver was a drifter, unable to settle down anywhere with anyone. His father had been the same way and had ridden rodeo until the final accident that had taken his life. He'd abandoned his family for the life of a roaming cowboy, leaving his wife to bring up his small sons.

From the pictures she'd seen, Denver was the image of his father. Lane had told her how his mother was always reminding Denver of that, telling him he was just like his father and would end up the same way.

It was no wonder Denver had had problems when he was growing up, April thought, gazing moodily out of the window at the new subdivisions springing up on the once wooded hills. With that kind of legacy it was a miracle he hadn't been in worse trouble. At least he hadn't made the mistake of marrying someone, the way his father had.

"Isn't that right, April?"

Denver's deep voice from the front seat made her jump. "Sorry," she said, a little too loudly. "I didn't quite catch that."

"Yeah, I figured you were off on some other planet." Denver's shrewd gaze met hers in the rearview mirror, making her squirm a little. "I was just explaining to Josh here how the rodeo clowns keep the bull's attention so's we don't get hooked by the horns."

A shudder quivered down April's back. "So I've heard. I've never actually seen a rodeo, so I don't know too much about it."

"Well, we'll have to take care of that, won't we, cowboy?" Denver drawled, winking at Josh. "How would you like to come see me ride?"

Josh's thin shoulders rose in the inevitable shrug. "I don't care."

Detecting an underlying curiosity in his voice, however, April said carefully, "I think that might be fun. Don't you, Josh?"

Josh didn't answer.

"Well, I reckon that's settled, then." Denver's strong hands swung the wheel as they turned onto the state highway that would take them to the beach. "We've got a ride coming up in a couple of weeks…July fourth weekend. Not too far from here. How about I get you grandstand seats? Maybe Josh would like to ride with me in the parade."

Josh turned his head to look up at his uncle. "The parade?"

"Yep. There's a flag ceremony at the start of the rodeo. I don't reckon anyone would mind if I took you around with me."

Josh's voice sounded cautious when he said, "You mean ride on your horse?"

"Sure."

"But I can't ride a horse."

"Well, I guess you won't have to worry about that none, seeing as how we'll just be walking the horse." Once more Denver's gaze sought April's in the mirror. "'Course, we have to get permission from your mom first."

Josh turned to look at April, and her throat closed at the carefully controlled expression on his face. "So can I?"

"If Uncle Denver says it's all right, then I guess you can."

"I guess it's okay, then," Josh said, sinking back in his seat.

April blinked hard. There would have been a time when Josh would have been ecstatic over such an exciting prospect. His lack of interest was a clear indication of the depth of his depression. She was beginning to think he'd never snap out of it.

Aware of Denver's efforts to make conversation with her son, April joined in, filling in for Josh's silences as best she could. The journey was a strain, however, and she was relieved when the car finally turned onto the coast road.

The sweeping view of miles of golden sand edged with froth-tipped Pacific rollers helped relax her tension. She and Lane had spent many a weekend at the beach, but this was the first time she'd been back since his death.

She felt strange, being there with Denver. It was as if she were sharing some kind of intimacy with him, allowing him into a special part of her personal life.

Josh's silence seemed to grow deeper as Denver parked the car a block from the beach. April prayed her son wouldn't be difficult, after they'd driven all the way down there.

"So, what do we do first?" Denver asked, without making any attempt to get out of the car.

Once more Josh shrugged.

Denver reached over to take his hat from Josh's head and cram it down on his own. "Well, I don't know about you, cowboy, but my fingers are itching for those machines down in the arcade. Trouble is, I don't know how to play all these newfangled games they got now. I need someone to show me how. You know someone who could do that?"

April held her breath through the long pause that followed.

"I guess I could do that," Josh finally mumbled.

"Really? Well, what are we waiting for, then?"

April smiled at the excitement in Denver's voice. If she didn't know better, she thought, she'd swear he *was* thrilled at the prospect of playing the games.

Josh scrambled out of the car as if he, too, were anxious to get to the arcade now. Silently blessing Denver, April followed them down the street toward the sound of rock music blaring out a welcome to the young patrons milling around the machines.

After buying them each a bag of buttered popcorn, Denver led the way into the noisy, jostling crowd of youths. April did her best to ignore the smell of sweaty sneakers and bubblegum and pushed her way through behind Josh.

Two young boys were climbing out of what looked like the front half of a car inside a cubbyhole. Two gangly teenagers headed for the vacated machine, but Denver beat them to it.

April watched in apprehension as he fitted his long body into the narrow seat behind one of the steering wheels, his knees raised under his chin. "Come on, cowboy," he ordered, with a wave of his hand at Josh, "let's see how well you can drive a car."

Josh shot a look at April, hesitated for just a minute, then hopped in the empty seat beside him. The next minute the two of them swayed from side to side, clinging to the wheel for all the world as if they were driving a real car.

A grin tugged at April's mouth as she watched the two of them, both faces set in grim determination while they peered at the screen in front of them.

Seeing them together like this, she realized, the resemblance was startling. Her grin faded, and she felt a stab of apprehension. How long before Denver noticed it, too?

In the next instant she chided herself for being so paranoid. Even if Denver did see a resemblance, it could be easily explained. After all, he and Lane had been brothers. They shared genes. True, Lane had looked like his mother, while Denver was a carbon copy of his father, but even so, it was quite feasible that Josh would have inherited some of his grandfather's looks.

After an hour in the arcade, Denver announced that he was hungry, much to April's relief. She had reached the point where one more clanging bell or shrieking whistle threatened to give her a massive headache.

Josh had pushed buttons, pulled levers and twisted handles with all the intensity of a normal ten-year-old boy, but his expression had remained aloof throughout the entire morning.

To give Denver his due, April thought, as she followed them out into the fresh air, he didn't seem to notice Josh's sullen mood. He chatted constantly, telling Josh about the rodeo and his life on the road with Jed and Cord.

They were seated by the window for lunch, with an expansive view of the ocean. With only half an ear on Denver's one-sided conversation with her son, April gazed out the window, enjoying the relaxing vista of water, sunlight and sand.

Two or three kids braved the cold temperature of the water and jumped in and out of the foamy waves racing into shore. Farther out, a lone surfer in a black wet suit coasted along the top of a heaving swell, then swooped to disappear in a frothy cloud of spray.

April watched a young couple pause at the water's edge, their arms about each other. The woman stooped to pick up something from the sand and showed it to her companion. Their heads drew together while they examined the object, then the woman gazed into the face of the man. Oblivious of onlookers, he pulled her into his arms and kissed her, while she clung to him as if she would never let him go.

April turned away and reached for her glass of water. The ache under her ribs was familiar enough. She'd dealt with the pain many times over the years. Seeing a couple so obviously in love reminded her of how she had once felt, so long ago. She'd given up any chance of finding that kind of love again, for the sake of the baby growing inside her.

Lane had been good to her and Josh. He'd never given her cause to regret her decision. Yet there had been many a night in the dark heat of summer when she'd lain awake, her body craving the excitement that Lane couldn't give her.

Those were the times she cursed Denver for that one night of passion, when he'd awakened her body to the tumultuous sensations she had never dreamed were possible. If she hadn't discovered what she was capable of feeling, she wouldn't be lying there aching with emptiness.

But then she only had to see Josh the next morning to know that she could never regret that stolen night or the consequences. Her only regret was that Denver hadn't shared her feelings and had brushed them aside as easily as he would sweep a cobweb from his face.

"You're looking awful serious over there," he commented.

Once more, his deep voice startled her from her thoughts. She glanced up, her heart turning over at the question in his intent eyes. "I was just wondering if it would be warm enough to dabble our toes in the sea," she lied, gazing at Josh to see how he would take this suggestion.

Josh simply looked bored.

"Great idea," Denver said with enthusiasm. "I haven't dabbled since I was a kid. How about it, cowboy? Want to dabble with me and your mom?"

Josh's shoulder lifted in the predictable shrug. "Okay."

"We could hunt for some more shells," April suggested hopefully.

Josh gave her a scornful look. "I don't need any more."

"Well, I do." Denver folded his arms across his chest. "I need some seashells to decorate the shelf next to my bunk bed. I could use help in finding good ones."

Josh fiddled with his water glass, then mumbled, "Okay."

April flashed Denver a grateful look, and he winked back at her, unsettling her once more. Just then the waitress arrived to take their order, and she made herself relax. No matter how much of an ordeal this arrangement was for her, she would have to put up with it for Josh's sake.

If it hadn't been for Denver, her son would have spent yet another day shut away in his room. Already Josh was looking better, with color creeping into his cheeks and his eyes brighter and more alert. She could put up with a lot just to see a little improvement, she assured herself.

Denver relaxed his relentless efforts to keep Josh entertained long enough to enjoy his lunch. The boy seemed content to munch on his hamburger while he watched the antics of a huge, furry, lolloping dog playing with his master along the water's edge.

Denver glanced at April from under the brim of his hat. She seemed absorbed in her thoughts, and he would have given a great deal to know what she was thinking right then.

He'd put off coming to see Josh for as long as he could, knowing it wouldn't be easy to be around April. He'd planned on taking the boy out on his own, figuring things would go better if he wasn't distracted by the sexy way she walked or the vulnerable expression in her beautiful green eyes. Only things hadn't worked out that way.

He couldn't look at her without remembering that night. He still went hot and cold when he thought about her lithe body urgently rocking with him until the world exploded into a million tiny pieces.

He still hurt with the agony of walking away from all that pleasure and the sweet promises life with April had offered. It had been sheer torture to see her with Lane, to see them so contented together.

All his life he'd walked a step behind his elder brother, always aware that Lane was the good one, the successful one, the reliable one, while he had inherited the devil genes of his dad.

He'd tried to be happy for them all—April, Lane and little Josh. He might have succeeded if his need for her, his potent longing to hold her in his arms again, hadn't burned in his gut every time he saw her.

Looking at her now across the table, seeing her so pensive and fragile, made the craving to take her into his bed and once more smother her urgent cries with the hungry demands of his mouth almost overwhelming.

In fact, he was getting pretty uncomfortable just thinking about it. With an abrupt movement he shoved his chair back and stood. "Be right back," he said, giving Josh's shoulder a reassuring squeeze. Before April could answer he left the table and headed for the bathroom.

April watched his tall figure stride rapidly across the room. She wondered if he was regretting his offer to spend more time with Josh. He'd barely said a word while they were eating, and now he'd rushed off as if he were anxious to escape for a while.

She glanced at Josh, who still seemed absorbed in watching the people on the beach. She longed to ask him if he was enjoying his uncle's visit. It was hard to tell from his reactions.

She'd made up her mind not to pressure her son about it, however. It was enough that Josh had accepted Denver's presence and was at least looking less miserable than he had lately. Now, if only Denver didn't let him down and continued to see Josh until he was through this awful phase, things might work out after all.

April sighed, then reached for her water glass again. That was the trouble with Denver. He was so unreliable. So many times he'd promised to visit them over the years and then had canceled at the last minute.

She'd learned not to expect too much from him. The rodeo was his life, and that took first place—always. She understood that. It had just taken her a long time to accept it.

"What would you like to do this afternoon?" she asked Josh, in an effort to put her depressing thoughts out of her mind.

Josh shrugged. "I don't care."

"Would you like to help Uncle Denver find some shells?"

"Okay." In the instant before he turned away she saw the pain in his eyes, and her heart went out to him. His collection of shells had been gathered with the help of his father. They had spent hours poring over them, examining each one to make sure it was a perfect specimen. It wouldn't be easy for Josh to share that with Denver.

"You don't have to if you don't want to," she said, reaching out to touch her son's hand.

He moved it away, but his face had lost the hostile expression when he looked at her. "It's okay."

"All right." She smiled at him, longing to see the ready smile that had once lit up his face so often.

For a moment he seemed to be battling with his emotions, then he turned away to stare out the window again.

"Well, if you guys are ready, how about we go find those shells?"

April looked up into Denver's piercing gaze. "Sure. Lead the way." She turned to her son. "Josh? Are we ready?"

Josh got up without a word and headed for the exit.

"Is he okay?" Denver asked quietly, as they followed a short distance behind him.

April nodded. "I think so. I think he's actually enjoying this very much but doesn't want to admit it to himself."

Denver looked puzzled. "How come?"

"I think he feels guilty for enjoying himself without his dad."

Denver shook his head. "Poor kid. Maybe this wasn't such a good idea."

April paused in the doorway and glanced across the parking lot to where Josh waited by the car. "No, it's a good idea," she said, feeling suddenly reassured. "You might not notice the difference, but I do. It's very small, but it's there. In time I think you'll get through to him."

"Well, that's good to know." Denver pulled off his hat, smoothed his hair back with his hand and settled the hat back on his head. "To tell the truth, I was feeling a little nervous about it. I've never had dealings with kids before. I wasn't sure how well I could handle something like this."

April smiled up at him. "You're doing just fine. Just keep up what you're doing. Josh will respond in time—I know he will. I'm really grateful for you taking the time to be with him. It can't be easy for you."

Denver raised his shoulders in a close imitation of Josh's careless shrug. "Well, I got some good advice from a friend of mine. When I told Cord I was worried about how to treat the kid, he told me that kids are just like adults, only shorter. I got the message, and talked to Josh the same way I would an adult. I guess it worked."

April laughed and started walking toward her son. "You have a very wise friend. Is he married?"

"Cord? Married?" Denver made a small sound of contempt in his throat. "That guy would trust a rattlesnake more'n any woman. We figure someone did a real good number on him some time ago, and he won't have nothing to do with women…unless one's willing to add a little comfort to his bed for an hour or two."

That sounded familiar, April thought wryly. "How does he know so much about kids, then?"

"I guess he just has a knack for it. Same as horses. I never saw anyone handle a spooked horse better'n Cord McVane."

"Does he ride bulls, too?"

"Nope. Cord rides horses—bareback. And Jed's a saddle bronc rider."

She glanced up at him. "I suppose he's not married, either."

"Jed's too busy chasing after the championship to think about settling down." Denver reached the car and unlocked the rear door. "Jed's got something he's gotta do… something he's gotta prove. He has a whole town down on him, including his folks. He's out to show 'em all he's better than what they think of him."

Her curiosity aroused, April stared at him. "It sounds as if he needs that championship pretty badly."

Denver nodded. "About as bad as anyone could need it, I reckon."

"What did he do to put a whole town against him?"

"Well, it was a pretty small town from what I hear," Denver said, holding the door open for her, "but whatever it was he did, Jed isn't saying. And we don't ask."

"Maybe that's just as well," April murmured, as she climbed into the back seat. "You might be shocked by what you hear."

"I don't think so. Whatever it was, I'd be willing to bet a year's winnings that it wasn't Jed's fault. I'd trust both him and Cord with my life. There isn't anyone I'd rather have in my corner when the chips are down than those two guys."

April watched Josh clamber into the seat in front of her. It seemed strange to hear Denver talk about his partners that way. She would have said that Denver was too much of a loner to form any kind of relationship.

She was happy to hear that he wasn't entirely on his own, but oh, how she wished she could share that kind of trust and loyalty with him.

Dark clouds had begun to form on the horizon by the time they parked the car again and walked down to a firm stretch of sand left moist by the receding waves.

Preoccupied with her thoughts, April was only vaguely aware of Denver and Josh talking to each other. It wasn't until she saw their heads close together that she realized Josh was explaining to Denver what made one particular sand dollar better than all the rest.

He was repeating what his father had taught him, apparently without conscious thought of where he had gained the knowledge. April felt a small stirring of hope.

The last thing she wanted was for Josh to forget his father and everything they had shared. At the same time, she knew it was imperative that the boy not shut himself up in those memories, refusing to let go. This sharing with Denver was the first indication that Josh might be ready to do that.

He'd left the camera in the car, however. Apparently, he wasn't ready to take pictures yet. Time, April thought, watching her son stoop to pick up yet another shell. All Josh really needed was time. She prayed that Denver would be able to give it to him.

Once more Denver did all the talking on the way home, while Josh answered in monosyllables and the occasional grunt. Rain spattered the windshield when they turned the corner of the cul-de-sac.

"Would you like to stay for dinner?" April asked tentatively.

Denver parked the car in the driveway and shut off the engine before answering. "I have to catch a plane back to Colorado tonight. We're set to hit the road again in the morning."

She stared at him, ignoring Josh, who had climbed out of the car and was waiting impatiently for her to open the front door. "You came in from Colorado today?"

"Yes, ma'am." He turned to look at her, his face shadowed by his hat. "We're heading into Montana in the morning."

"I hadn't realized… I thought…"

"You thought I'd dropped in while I was passing through."

"Something like that." Knowing that he'd come so far out of his way to see Josh made it hard to find the words to thank him. "I don't know what to say," she said at last. "That was so good of you to come all that way."

"I figured I owed that much to Lane, to help out with his son now and again."

She felt a pang of resentment and just as quickly stifled it. Denver had made it clear from the start he was doing this only for Josh. She had no right to feel hurt just because he'd reminded her of that.

"I'm sure Josh will appreciate it," she said stiffly. "As I do. The least I can do is drive you to the airport."

"No need. I'll call for a cab." He eased himself out of the car and opened the door for her. "That's if you don't mind me using your phone?"

"Of course not." She thought she detected a slight note of sarcasm, then chided herself for over-reacting. "I'll get you a beer while we're waiting."

"Sounds like a good plan." Denver clapped a hand on Josh's shoulder. "Thanks for helping me sort out those shells, cowboy. That's a real nice collection you picked out for me."

"Sure." Josh darted through the door the minute it opened and a second later clattered up the stairs to his room.

Denver paused inside the door and watched the boy with an odd expression on his face. April held her breath, afraid for a moment that somehow his suspicions had been aroused. She relaxed again when he glanced around the living room.

"Where do you keep your phone book?"

"In the kitchen on the counter by the phone." She waved a hand in the direction of the kitchen, then followed him in there. While he looked up the number she took a beer out of the fridge and handed it to him.

He thanked her without looking up. "I guess this one will do," he murmured, and dialed the number.

After he'd ordered the cab and hung up, she said a little defensively, "I could have taken you to the airport. Josh would have enjoyed going out there."

The look he gave her was carefully devoid of expression. "I didn't want to wear out my welcome. I don't want Josh to think I'm pressuring him in any way."

"No, of course not."

Searching for something to say to break the sudden tension, April said brightly, "So when do you think you'll be back?"

He avoided her gaze and lifted the beer can to his lips. "I don't know. Depends on how the rides go. If I get lucky next week I can afford to miss a ride or two. If not, I'll have to stay until I catch up again."

She nodded, not really understanding. "I see."

He took a long swig of the beer, then set down the can. "If I want to compete in the finals at the end of the year I have to keep my place in the standings. Only the top-fifteen moneymakers in each event get to the NFR."

"What's that?"

"National Finals Rodeo in Las Vegas. That's where we compete for the world titles. The more money you earn in the regular season, the better chance you have of getting one of those titles."

"Didn't you already win a bull-riding championship?"

"Yep, I did. A few years back." He picked up the can and took another swig of the beer. "And I lost the title the next year. This year I'm aiming to get not only the bull-riding championship but the all-around, as well. That's the cowboy who wins the most money in all the events. The best of the best."

"What about your travel partners? Are they competing, too?"

"Yes, ma'am. As a matter of fact, we've had a personal bet for the past six years on which one of us makes the all-around first."

She could see it in his eyes...the thrill of competition. He thrived on it. He had turned his back on so much for so little. What she couldn't figure out was why. Unable to contain the words any longer, she burst out, "Why do you do it?"

He narrowed his eyes. "It's a way of life. My way of

life. If you ride professional rodeo, the rodeo *is* your life. It has to be. There just isn't time or space for anything else."

She couldn't accept that; it was too easy. "I don't understand how people can live that kind of life, risking their necks to travel from town to town, never putting down roots, never having anywhere to call home. It must be incredibly lonely."

He looked at her for a long moment, holding the beer can poised in midair. "I guess," he said slowly, "we do it because there isn't anything else out there for us. All those empty highways, depressing taverns, broken bones...that's all part of it. I guess it is lonely, but in the end it all comes down to that moment when you're in the chute hanging over a two-thousand-pound bull who's going to move heaven and earth to buck you off his back. That's what counts. It's me against him."

"But you risk so much...for what? The glory? Or the money?"

He shook his head. "Most of us rarely get either. I reckon we do it for the challenge. In a way, I guess we're trying to hold on to a dying American dream. Most every kid wants to be a cowboy at some time in his life."

"Most kids grow up," April said evenly.

Very slowly, he put down the can. "Well, I guess we can't all be company executives with nice homes and private planes."

But you could have been, she cried silently. *You should have been.*

The doorbell rang then, and immediately she was ashamed for causing a disagreement. "Thank you again for coming," she said quickly, as she followed him across the living room to the door. "Josh enjoyed it immensely, even if he didn't show it."

Denver paused at the door and looked at her. "I'll get back when I can. Say goodbye to him for me."

"I'll do that." She was ridiculously close to tears and shut the door behind him with a sense of relief. The day had been every bit as much an ordeal as she had anticipated. She had the distinct feeling that the tension could get worse the longer Denver was around.

If it meant getting back her son's sunny disposition, it would be worth it. She just hoped she had the strength to keep her emotions out of it. It wouldn't do to let Denver know how bitter she was about the past…he might just put two and two together.

It sure wouldn't help, either, to let him know that he could still make her heart race and her body heat up whenever she was around him. Keep things uncomplicated, she urged herself, as she climbed the stairs to say good-night to Josh. It was the only way to safeguard her secret.

Chapter 3

Jed and Cord were both snoring by the time Denver got back to the camper late that night. When he woke up the next morning, they had already gone to get breakfast at the restaurant across the street. Denver read the note they'd left him with a wry grimace: "Didn't expect you back last night," Jed had written.

He'd more or less figured on his traveling partners giving him a hard time about his side trip. He'd have to step on that one hard, he told himself, as he crossed the busy street at the light. Usually he could take a ribbing, but not this time. Not where April was concerned.

He found Jed and Cord seated in a corner of the crowded room, halfway through a plate of pancakes and eggs. The enticing aroma of bacon and maple syrup made him hungry, and he looked around for the waitress as he took a seat at the table.

"Well, if it isn't lover boy," Jed said, winking at Cord. "Must have struck out last night, huh?"

Denver caught the eye of the waitress and signaled to her. She nodded back and disappeared into the kitchen. "First of all," he said, directing a dark look at Jed, "I never strike out. Second of all, that's my sister-in-law you're talking about, and I don't like what you're suggesting. Third of all, I'd like it real well if you'd just mind your own damn business."

Jed laughed good-naturedly and held up his hands. "Sorry, pardner. Subject closed. But I have to tell you, Cannon, you missed a darn good rodeo yesterday."

Denver winced at the use of his nickname. He'd been given it some time ago when Jed remarked that he'd exploded out of the chute like a bullet from a gun. A group of riders had overheard, and from then Denver had been known as Cannon. Try as he might, he hadn't been able to lose the name.

"Who won the bull riding?" he asked, reaching for a piece of toast off the stack in front of Cord. "Rooster again?"

"Yep." Jed closed his hand around a mug of steaming coffee. "Wiggy came in right behind him, though."

Denver shook his head. "Got some catching up to do, I reckon."

"Better not let yourself get sidetracked too often," Cord murmured, his gaze fixed on his plate. "It won't take long for those greenhorns to catch up with you in the standings."

Denver nodded, only too aware of Cord's concern. "Don't worry," he assured him. "I won't miss more'n I can afford. I'm going to beat the pants off both of you in the finals—I promise you that."

"Humph!" Jed slapped the coffee mug down so hard the hot liquid slopped over the edge and spread a dark puddle around his plate. "You're gonna lose that bet, both of you. This is the year I'm gonna take that gold belt buckle back to my hometown and shove it in everyone's faces. I've been waiting for this for a long time. All those folks in that rodeo-loving town are gonna know that Jed Cullen beat out everyone else. The best there is.''

Cord uttered a low, mocking laugh. ''You're gonna need more'n that gold belt buckle if you want them to sit up and take notice.''

''They'll notice me,'' Jed said grimly. ''It's a small town.''

Cord nodded slowly. ''Well, in that case, I'd find me a real nice fancy car and drive it right down main street.''

Jed's gold eyes gleamed with anticipation. ''Now you're talking.''

''Reckon you'll need more than that,'' Denver said, joining in the game. ''What you really need sitting next to you is a wife. Give you an air of respectability.''

Cord's black eyes flashed with humor. ''Ain't no woman ever gonna settle for ol' Jed here. He's too ornery.''

''Is that right? Well, I reckon I could find me a woman if I wanted one.''

Cord looked alarmed. ''Hell, Jed, you're surely not gonna sacrifice yourself to some woman just for the sake of getting back at a few townsfolk, are you?''

Jed shrugged. ''I'll do whatever it takes.''

''Won't make no difference anyhow,'' Denver said dryly. '''Cause Jed will have to put me out of action first if he wants to win that buckle.'' He leaned forward and helped himself to a slice of toast.

''I'll put you out of action right now if you don't stop stealing my toast,'' Cord growled. ''That's if that sister-in-law of yours doesn't do it first.''

Denver's amusement vanished. ''What the hell does that mean?''

Cord shrugged. ''Just a friendly warning, that's all. Doesn't do to get tangled up with a woman, specially when she's got a kid. Kids aren't that easy to turn your back on. Women know that.''

Denver swallowed his resentment. It wasn't like Cord to mess in other people's business. Not unless he was really worried about them. "You don't have to worry yourself on that score," he said quietly. "I'm just keeping an eye on my brother's kid until he gets himself straightened out, that's all."

Cord's dark gaze met his for an instant. "Reckon you do know what you're doing at that," he murmured.

Jed changed the subject just then, much to Denver's relief. But Cord's words echoed in his mind long after the pancakes and eggs were forgotten. He could only hope that Cord was right. And that he really did know what he was doing.

"Where have you been?" April demanded, her voice arresting the small figure creeping up the stairs.

"Playing," Josh muttered, without turning around.

"You know you're not supposed to go anywhere without telling me, and you know very well you're supposed to be home for dinner...that was over two hours ago." Anxiety made her voice sharp and she tried to soften it. "Josh, please turn around and look at me when I'm talking to you."

He hesitated for a moment longer, then slowly faced her.

April stared grimly at his right eye, which was swollen almost shut. "You've been fighting again."

Josh kicked his heel back into the steps behind him but didn't answer.

April curbed the urge to yell at him. "Who was it this time?"

Josh shrugged.

"Answer me, Josh."

"Matt." Josh looked up, his good eye blazing with suppressed fury. "He started it," he shouted. "He said my dad was stupid for crashing his plane."

A cold shiver touched April's spine. "Oh, Josh... I'm so sorry..."

"I don't care!" Josh yelled. "He *was* stupid. He couldn't even miss something as big as a mountain—"

"Josh!" April started up the stairs, intent on trying to comfort her son. Before she reached him, however, Josh spun around and sprinted up the rest of the steps. A second later his bedroom door slammed shut.

April followed him, her heart heavy with grief for her son's agony. "Josh?" She tapped on the door. "You might feel better if you talk about it."

Josh's answer was to turn the TV set up so loud he couldn't possibly hear her voice. Frustrated, she left him to work out his anger as best he could. There was no point in trying to reach him when he was like this.

She made herself a cup of coffee, hoping to dispel the lead weight that seemed to have settled in her stomach. She should eat something, she thought, staring at the fridge without enthusiasm. So should Josh for that matter. As far as she knew, he hadn't eaten since lunch.

She sank onto her favorite armchair and stared moodily out the window. Through the branches of the pines she could see the rosy haze of the sun dipping below the smudged line of the coastal range.

It had been almost two weeks since she'd last seen Denver. That was what had triggered this latest episode with Josh. For the third time that day he'd asked her when they would see his uncle again. Nerves already stretched taut by the growing certainty that Denver had forgotten about his promise, April had snapped at Josh.

"Forget about Uncle Denver," she'd told him. "I doubt very much if he'll be back...not for a long time, anyway."

"It's all your fault," Josh had yelled back. "You were mean to him the last time he was here."

Realizing Josh must have overheard her conversation

with Denver had only irritated her more. "Your uncle is well-known for breaking his promises," she'd said bitterly. "If I were you, I'd quit relying on him for anything."

Josh had flung himself out of the house, ignoring her demands to know where he was going. She'd paced the house, afraid that he'd run away again. Her relief when he'd finally turned up had flared into anger, and now he'd locked himself in his room once more.

April leaned back and closed her eyes. She should have known it would be a mistake to trust Denver to keep his promise. Not only was she back where she started with Josh, but Denver's betrayal could set her son back even further.

"Damn you, Denver," she whispered. She had learned to accept his indifference as far as she was concerned, but she could not forgive him if he ignored her son when he needed him so much.

The shrill ring of the phone snapped her eyes open. For an instant hope leaped in her heart, then she quickly suppressed it. More likely it was a sales call, she thought wearily as she reached for the receiver.

In spite of her brief moment of anticipation, Denver's deep voice was such a shock that she took a moment or two to catch her breath.

"Everything okay there?" Denver asked, while she struggled to recover her composure.

Irritated by the spasm of excitement she'd felt at the sound of his voice, she answered coolly, "As well as things usually go. Josh is locked in his room, not speaking to me and nursing a black eye, but that's pretty normal nowadays."

There was a short pause, then Denver said warily, "I'm sorry. I was hoping the trip to the beach had helped some."

"It's going to take more than one trip to the beach."

April pulled in a deep breath, determined not to give in to her bitterness. "But that's not your problem."

Again the pause, this time a longer one. "Then how come I feel that it is?" Denver asked at last. "You sound about ready to take a shotgun to my head."

She relented immediately, acknowledging that once more she was overreacting. "I'm sorry. I'm just really tired. And worried about Josh. I didn't mean to take it out on you."

"No offense taken." He hesitated, then added, "I was calling to see if you and Josh wanted to come to the rodeo day after tomorrow. I've arranged for Josh to ride in the parade with me...if he still wants to, that is."

Again she felt that ridiculous jump of her pulse. "I'm sure he'd love to," she said evenly. "Why don't you ask him yourself. I'll go get him."

She put down the receiver and hurried up the stairs to pound on the door of Josh's room. "Josh? Uncle Denver's on the phone. He has something he wants to ask you."

Fortunately Josh had turned down the TV. After a second or two the door opened and he stood framed in the doorway. "What's he want?"

"You'd better go down and find out." April stood back as Josh slipped by her and clattered down the stairs.

She could hear his voice as she followed more slowly, and was pleased at the raised note of anticipation. She walked into the living room just in time to hear Josh say, "I'll tell her. Thanks, Uncle Denver."

He put the phone down and looked at her with his one good eye. "He wants me to ride in the parade at the rodeo," he said, his voice hushed with disbelief. "He remembered."

"I guess he did." April felt the smile creeping over her entire face. "In that case, you'd better let me take a look at that eye. You'll want to see out of both of them when you circle that arena."

Josh nodded, his face flushed with suppressed excitement. For once he didn't complain when April dabbed antiseptic on the cut above his eye, and she silently blessed Denver. He had come through for her after all. For Josh, she quickly amended. She'd be a fool not to remember that.

Denver saw April and Josh approaching as he leaned against the wall of the ticket office, oblivious of the admiring stares from the customers lining up for tickets.

Josh saw him almost at the same time and broke away from April to race over to him. "We're not late, are we?" he asked breathlessly.

Denver shook his head, wincing at the sight of the boy's bruised eye. "You're right on time, cowboy. Ready for your ride?"

"I guess so."

"Don't worry," Denver said, noting the uncertainty in the young voice. "I won't let you fall off."

"I'm not worried," Josh said scornfully. "But Mom is."

Denver glanced up as April reached them, and felt a tug low in his belly. Sunlight glinted in her dark-blond hair, and a touch of red accented her full lips. Her white jeans clung to her hips, and the red T-shirt she wore stretched taut across her ample breasts. His hands itched to touch her.

"Hello, Denver."

Her voice still had that sultry sound that had turned his insides to mush all those years ago. He managed to mutter an answer, then dragged his gaze away and looked determinedly down at Josh. "Okay, pardner, I guess I'd better take you backstage in the arena."

"Cool!" Josh glanced around. "Where do we go?"

"Over there." Denver nodded at the side entrance, where a couple of cowboys stood guard at the door.

Josh headed over to them, while Denver fished a pair of

tickets out of his jeans pocket. "Here—the best seats in the house."

She took them from his hand and examined them. "Thanks, Denver. This is very nice of you."

She sounded aloof, as if he were a stranger. He felt the distance between them as if they were standing on opposite sides of the Grand Canyon. No one would ever think that they had shared a night of unforgettable, mind-blowing passion…the kind of loving that had spoiled other women for him forever.

"You're welcome to come back with us," Denver offered, hoping she'd refuse. He didn't need this kind of distraction right now. He'd drawn a mean bull in the ride today, and he was going to need all his concentration.

April glanced over to where Josh waited impatiently for Denver to join him. "I'd like to see what it's like behind the scenes. I've never been to a rodeo before."

Denver pulled his hat down to shade his eyes. "Well, in that case, I'd better show you both around."

"Do you have time?" She glanced at her watch, then back at Josh.

"I've got time." Time to reassure her that Josh would be safe with him, he thought wryly, which he guessed was her main reason for wanting to go back there.

He led the way over to the entrance, where Josh was talking to the two cowboys.

"Can I meet the clowns?" Josh asked, as Denver ushered him through the door.

"Sure you can." Denver lifted a hand in reply to a cowboy's greeting. "But first I want you to talk to Cord. He's the best bareback rider on the circuit."

Josh looked impressed. "Is he going to ride today?"

"You bet he is. So's Jed. You remember him, don't you?"

"Oh, yeah." Josh nodded. "He bought me ice cream. Does he ride bareback, as well?"

"Nope, he rides saddle bronc."

"But none of them ride bulls, do they?"

Denver smiled. "Not anymore."

"Those men out there told me that bull riding is the most dangerous part of the rodeo. They said that you could get killed by the bull if he gets his horns into you."

"Well, I have no intention of letting the bull get his horns into me, so quit worrying, okay?"

"They said you had a real mean bull to ride today," Josh went on, looking up anxiously into Denver's face. "They said you wouldn't stay on his back longer than a second."

"Did they?" Denver clasped a hand over Josh's shoulder. "Well, we'll just have to prove them wrong, won't we?"

"Is it really that dangerous?" April asked.

He glanced at her, his stomach tightening at the concern in her face. "Bulls are always dangerous, and I'd be a fool to think otherwise. You've gotta have respect for them or you could end up getting real hurt. As long you keep your concentration, though, bulls are not that tough to handle."

"But what if they're real mean?" Josh asked, his eyes glowing with excitement.

Denver patted his shoulder. "The meaner they are, the better for me. Half the points go to the bull...the more bucking and twisting he does, the higher my score."

"I wonder what it is about the Briggs family," April said quietly, "that makes them so anxious to take risks with their lives."

The comment stung, but he kept his features smooth. "Reckon we were just born wild," he said easily.

The sound of shouts and a deafening crash and banging brought them all up short.

"What's that?" Josh twisted his head around toward the source of the noise. A large trailer had been backed up against a holding pen and the pounding seemed to be coming from that.

Denver gave him a wry smile. "That, I reckon, is my ride. His name is Thunderball, and he doesn't sound in too good a mood."

April's look of dismay was almost comical. "He sounds as if he's out of control."

"Guess I'll just have to show him who's boss, then." Denver winked at Josh, who appeared impressed.

"Is he really mean?" he asked, eyeing the rocking trailer with awe on his face.

"Not as mean as some." Denver tipped his hat back with his thumb. "There's this one bull named Balderdash that's near impossible to ride. I remember—"

"Hey, Cannon!"

Denver swung around to face the newcomer. "Hey, Cord. You remember my nephew, Josh. He's gonna ride in the parade with me. This is his mom, April."

"Ma'am." Cord's cool black gaze swept over April briefly before resting on Josh's face. "Howdy, pardner. Gonna show us how to ride old Thunderball?"

Josh shook his head in alarm. "No way."

Cord nodded. "Guess you're smart at that. Best way to break your bones is riding bulls. Just ask Cannon here."

Denver shrugged. "Bones mend."

Cord gave him a straight look. "Some do," he said quietly.

Denver read the warning clearly in his friend's eyes. "I'll be okay. I've got to win this one if I'm gonna win that all-around buckle."

"Yeah, well, forget that. I already got that one sewed up." Cord tipped his hat, glanced briefly at April and slapped Josh lightly on the shoulder. "Nice to meet you, April. See you in the parade, pardner."

He ambled off, waving at a couple of wranglers on his way.

"Strange man," April murmured, watching him go. "Does he ever smile?"

"Now and again." Denver caught sight of one of the clowns and beckoned him over. "This is Sam," he told Josh, who was staring wide-eyed at the bright-red wig and garish paint on the young cowboy's face. "He's the one with the most dangerous job. He gets the bulls mad at him so's they chase him. More often than not he has to jump the fence to get away from them."

Sam grinned, bent low from the waist and shook Josh's hand. "Cannon's jealous 'cause I can run faster'n he can. He's getting too old to outrun a bull."

"I'm not too old to teach you a thing or two," Denver retorted good-naturedly. "I'd stake my life on experience more than speed any day."

Sam winked at Josh. "He's right, you know. I wouldn't sit on the back of one of those bulls for a million bucks. That's too close to those killer horns for my liking."

He straightened and grinned at April. "And who's this pretty lady?"

"I'm Josh's mom," she said, before Denver could answer. "It's nice to meet you, Sam."

"Pleasure's all mine, ma'am." Sam swept her an exaggerated bow. "Hope you enjoy the show."

"I'm looking forward to it." She flicked a glance at Denver, her expression clearly revealing her doubts about that.

"Speaking of which," Denver said, as Sam rushed off, "I'd better get this young man suited up for the parade."

Josh looked apprehensive. "I have to wear a suit?"

"You'll like it," Denver promised.

"I guess I'd better get back to my seat, then," April said, looking as if that were the last thing she wanted to do.

"Just go through that gate over there," Denver said, nodding in that direction. "Someone will show you where your seat is."

"Okay." She gave Josh a nervous smile. "You be careful, okay?"

"He'll be fine."

She looked at him, and again his gut twisted at the vulnerable expression in her eyes. He wanted to crush her in his arms, capture her mouth and hold it until she begged for mercy. He wanted to feel her smooth skin against his naked belly, her legs wrapped around his hips, her soft, full breasts thrusting into his bare chest—

"I'm trusting you to take care of him," April said quietly. "Remember, he's all I've got."

Her words shattered his rampant thoughts. He was sweating, and it wasn't from the warmth of the sun. He lifted his hat and smoothed his hair back with his hand before settling the Stetson once more on his head. "I'll see that he gets back to you safe and sound after the parade."

She gave him a half smile, then turned away and hurried through the main entrance. He watched her go, his eyes on her swaying hips, his mind on a hot summer night and the panting heat of desire.

Inside the arena, April edged her way past the drawn-up knees of three young women to reach the empty seats in the middle of the row. Denver was right; she and Josh would be in a perfect position to see everything from there.

Music blared from the speakers, while a man in a fringed jacket and wide-brimmed hat stood in front of the chutes, singing a country song into a mike.

The farmyard smell of dried hay and horses mingled with the pungent aroma of hotdogs, held in the hands of two small boys seated behind April. The overhang shaded her from the sun, which was just as well, she thought ruefully, since she'd forgotten her suntan lotion.

She glanced around, surprised to see such a large crowd.

The seats were crammed with eager onlookers, most of the men sporting western hats and shirts. Kids scrambled over the seats to get to the aisle where a young man sold cotton candy and popcorn from a tray hung around his neck. In another aisle someone yelled at the top of his lungs while waving programs in the air.

The whole scene reminded April of the circus she'd been taken to as a child. She'd never cared much for the circus. She'd spent most of the time worrying that the animals were suffering. She suspected she was going to feel the same about a rodeo.

The music shut off abruptly, and a restless silence settled over the arena. All faces turned expectantly toward the ring, as people scrambled to get to their seats. The announcer's voice thundered out from the speakers, welcoming everyone to the rodeo.

The strains of a patriotic song echoed across the arena while the announcer read a poem, then asked the hushed audience to rise for Old Glory.

In spite of the heat rising from the stands, April felt shivers along her arms as two cowgirls in red-and-gold costumes rode out into the ring carrying the American flag.

Behind them followed a parade of men and women on horseback, and right in the middle of them she saw Josh astride a horse led by Denver. Someone had given her son a hat, which totally hid his face, but April could tell by the set of his shoulders that he was scared.

He wore a red adult-sized shirt emblazoned with huge white stars, the sleeves rolled up over his wrists. She felt sudden tears prick her eyes and dashed them away. He looked older in the shirt. Josh was growing up.

The horses paraded around the ring in front of the cheer-

ing crowd, then slowed to a halt. Again silence fell in the
arena as the opening strains of the national anthem echoed
above the heads of the onlookers.

Carried on the summer breeze, the voices rang out across
the crowded stands. Led by the country singer, they
drowned out the screams from the carnival outside. Then
the notes died away, and the horses and their colorful riders
filed out and disappeared behind the chutes.

Minutes later, as the first ride was announced, April saw
Denver leading Josh down the steps to her seat in the front
row. The young women nudged one another and giggled
when Denver asked them to excuse Josh, who squeezed by
them with a self-conscious look on his face.

Denver touched the brim of his hat in thanks, which drew
more sighs and giggles, then with a wave of his hand at
April, he bounded back up the steps.

April felt the young women's curious stares on her as
she greeted her son. She ignored them and moved over to
let Josh sit beside them.

"You looked great," she said, smiling at his flushed
face. "How did you like riding a horse?"

Josh shrugged. "I wasn't really riding him. I was just
sitting on him. I want to learn to ride like that." He pointed
to the chutes, where a cowboy was about to lower himself
onto the back of a horse.

Seconds later the gate opened, and the horse and rider
shot out together in a blur of thrashing legs, flailing arm
and twisting bodies. April held her breath as the horse
bucked and writhed in a desperate attempt to get the an-
noying weight off its bare back.

Left arm pumping, the cowboy grimly hung on until the
buzzer sounded the end of eight seconds. The rider swung
his legs over the side of the rearing horse to land neatly on
his feet without the help of the pickup man riding along-
side.

"Jed Cullen, ladies and gentleman," the announcer intoned above the cheers from the crowd.

"That was Jed!" Josh exclaimed, his rapt gaze on the lanky cowboy climbing the fence.

The announcer informed the crowd that Jed had earned eighty-one points, then announced the name of the next rider. A roar from the appreciative audience greeted his words.

Josh sat for the next hour obviously enthralled by the wild activity in the ring. April could hardly bear to watch as cowboys thudded to the ground, wrestled with frightened steers and roped the legs of struggling calves.

She preferred to watch the women race around the barrels, though she winced when the horses skidded in the dirt at each turn. She was relieved when the intermission was announced and she could relax her tense muscles.

Josh devoured a hotdog and drank thirstily from a huge carton of soda, then settled down in his seat, prepared to enjoy the second half.

April's nerves tightened again when she heard Denver's name over the speakers. She saw the rearing head of the bull that was being led into the chute and sucked in her breath. The animal looked enormous, his murderous horns butting furiously at the gate in front of him.

"There's Uncle Denver!" Josh pointed to the man climbing up on the chute next to the snorting, pawing bull.

April clenched her hands into fists. She didn't want to watch this. She couldn't bear to see this man risk his life on the back of a killer bull. She closed her eyes, then opened them again when Josh nudged her arm.

"Look, Mom, he's getting on the bull."

April peered reluctantly across the ring to where Denver was lowering himself onto the heaving back of Thunderball. She watched Denver take the end of the rope and wrap it around his hand. She held her breath while he settled his hat more firmly on his head, raised his left hand, then gave a sharp nod.

The gate flew open, and April slid forward on her seat, her hands pressed between her knees. Now she had to watch; she had to know he was going to make it.

The crowd roared as the bull leaped, spun and twisted his massive body in a red heat of rage. Denver's body soared with the bull, jerked from side to side, leaned back and then forward, always anticipating the next sudden, violent move of the animal beneath him.

It seemed like an eternity as the eight seconds ticked by, but as April watched, her anxiety faded in the sheer thrill of seeing Denver's control of the huge animal. It was almost like watching a ballet, the movements and counter-movements carefully choreographed in a magnificent exchange between man and beast.

At last the buzzer sounded, and with a final twist of his agile body, Denver dropped to his knees beside the thrashing bull. Sam rushed in to distract the snorting animal, and Denver scrambled to his feet. He paused for a second to wave to the cheering crowd, then sprinted for the fence and clambered over it.

"Oh, man," Josh breathed, "that was awesome."

"It certainly was," April unsteadily agreed.

The crowd roared their approval when the announcer declared that Denver had scored eighty-four points for his ride, putting him into first place.

"Can we go see him?" Josh pleaded, when the show finally came to an end.

"I don't think he'll have time to spend with us right now." April stepped out into the aisle and let Josh go ahead of her.

"Why not?" Josh stomped up the steps to proclaim his disappointment.

"Because he's probably busy." The truth was, she didn't

feel like facing Denver. Her reaction while watching him duel with the bull had shaken her. The performance had seemed highly erotic to her, though she couldn't explain why. She knew only that she had been reminded of that sultry summer night when he had goaded her into a frenzy of passion, expertly controlling her until she thought she would lose her mind.

She didn't want to remember that night. She didn't need any reminders that Denver Briggs could arouse her just by looking at her—that the sound of his voice could make her weak and the touch of his hand could destroy her willpower.

She just wanted to go home and try to forget the vision of Denver astride the bull, dominating the animal with his powerful legs and iron will.

"Hey! There's Uncle Denver." Josh darted away from her up the steps.

All the blood in her body seemed to rush to her head when she saw him. He waited for them at the top of the steps, exchanging nods with admiring fans who congratulated him on his win. Dressed in his jeans and long-sleeved striped shirt, his tan hat pulled low on his forehead, he looked every inch the conquering cowboy.

Her insides turned over when he saw her and lazily grinned. "So how were the seats?"

"Awesome!" Josh exclaimed, before she could answer. "I want to be a rodeo rider when I grow up. I want to ride the bulls. Will you teach me how to ride a bull, Uncle Denver?"

"Whoa!" Denver laughed and held up a hand. "Wait there a minute, cowboy. You've got a ways to grow before you can ride a bull."

"But I rode a horse today," Josh said, showing signs of turning sulky.

"So you did," Denver said, squatting in front of the boy.

"But that was just a gentle ride. You've got to learn how to control the horse, or he'll control you."

April felt a tiny shiver slide down her spine. She turned away, pretending to watch the crowd dispersing into the grounds below her.

"Well, you can teach me, can't you?"

"I reckon I can. But we have to ask your mom if it's okay first."

There was a long pause, then Josh said impatiently, "Mom?"

April twisted her head to look at him and met Denver's piercing gaze, instead. She saw a flicker of recognition in his eyes, as if he'd read her thoughts and could see her racing pulse. She swallowed and looked at Josh. "We'll talk about it," she said huskily.

"She always says that," Josh said, kicking the toe of his sneaker against the nearest seat. "She won't let me do anything."

Denver straightened. "I guess Mom knows best."

"No, she doesn't," Josh muttered. "She doesn't know anything. Dad used to let me do all kinds of things."

"Josh," April warned sharply. She'd had just about all she could handle that day, and now she just wanted to go home.

"Maybe we could all talk about it," Denver suggested. "I'm free until the final round day after tomorrow. How about I come over in the morning?"

It was on the tip of her tongue to make some excuse to put him off. She needed a breathing space, time to collect her thoughts, time to remind herself of all the reasons she had to stop thinking about the past, and how Denver Briggs could still make thrills chase down her spine.

But one look at Josh's eager face and she knew she had to put her son first. This was the first time since Lane had died that she'd seen Josh interested in anything, much less excited about something.

He was obviously responding to the attention he was getting from Denver, and that was what this was all about anyway. Josh's problems. She would just have to lock her own problems away in her mind and concentrate on what was good for Josh.

"I think Josh would like that," she said carefully, "though I'm not making any promises about the riding lessons."

Josh seemed satisfied with that, and Denver nodded his approval. She wondered what he would say if he knew what she was thinking. That she couldn't afford to commit to any long-term arrangements between her son and his elusive uncle.

For one thing, she couldn't rely on Denver to stick to his proposals. It would be better to disappoint Josh now than have him totally involved in riding lessons, only to be forced into giving them up when Denver got too busy or too distracted to keep them up.

But there were other considerations at stake, far more important than lost riding lessons. There was always the chance that somehow Denver would find out the truth about Josh…a careless word…anything that could trigger doubts in Denver's mind.

She was not a good liar, and Denver was shrewd. She hated to think what would happen if he confronted her head-on.

Most of all there was her weakness as far as Denver was concerned. He had hurt her so badly in the past. She could not go through that kind of pain again. She had accepted the fact that Denver would never settle for one woman. He had made that very clear in the past.

That had been easier to forget when Lane was alive and she hadn't seen much of Denver. But now she was beginning to rediscover all the sensations she'd long forgotten. The thrill of his pensive gaze on her face, the memory of the strength of his body and the knowledge of how incredible it was to see that power unleashed.

To be around Denver spelled danger, yet the sheer excitement of it made her feel more vibrant, more daring, more alive, than she'd felt since those days when she'd first fallen in love with Denver Briggs.

But she wasn't in love with him any longer, she reminded herself. That was a different April. And if she wanted to get out of this with her heart intact, she had better remember that.

Chapter 4

Denver drove the truck slowly through the city streets, doubts plaguing his mind once more. He could be making matters worse by hanging around Josh. He didn't want the boy depending on him too much.

He swung the wheel to turn the corner that would lead him to the suburbs and April's house. A truck roared by him, sending diesel fumes into his open window. He scowled, and squinted against the dazzling sunlight.

He just hoped he was doing the right thing. He had no experience with kids. He was a pretty poor substitute for his brother. Lane knew all about being a good husband and father. But then, Lane had always been good at everything. He'd taken after their mother, who'd given them a good home even though her no-good husband had gone off and left her to raise her boys alone.

Denver glanced in the rearview mirror, frowning at his image. It was like looking at his father...or the pictures of him, anyway. His mother had never let him forget whom he took after. Every time he'd screwed up, she'd told him he'd never be any good to anyone, just like his old man.

Not that he could blame her, Denver thought gloomily. She was right. He'd screwed up pretty badly at times. Always in trouble at school, always fighting…just like Josh. Not too good a role model for the boy.

He turned the wheel once more, braking as he rounded the corner into the subdivision. Still, April seemed to think he was doing some good. If he could just let Josh know that he wasn't alone out there, that someone understood his pain, someone was there he could talk to when he couldn't talk to his mother. Sometimes a boy just needed a man to confide in.

He only hoped he wouldn't let the boy down—that if Josh did decide to confide in him, he'd know the right thing to say and do.

This business of the riding lessons, for instance. He thought it might be good for the boy to have an interest in something like that. He wasn't sure April agreed with him. He wasn't sure why not, but it wasn't up to him to argue with her if she felt strongly about it. But then that would put him in a bad light with Josh if he didn't stand up for him.

Denver sighed as he pulled up in front of April's house. This whole mess was so damn complicated. How was he supposed to know what was right, when he'd never had to deal with family problems? If only things had been different. If only he'd turned out like Lane—

But he hadn't, he reminded himself as he climbed down from the truck. He and Lane were as different as a cougar from a kitten, and no amount of wishing was going to make any difference. He was on his own, and would just have to muddle through as best he could.

As he walked up the path, he spotted a curtain twitching in Josh's bedroom window. He smiled to himself. The boy had been waiting for him. He must be doing something right.

April opened the door, looking so appealing his breath caught in his throat. She wore a striped pink cotton sweater over a pair of white shorts, and her feet were thrust into a pair of leather thongs.

She'd left her hair loose, and he itched to run his fingers through the silky strands. She avoided his gaze and glanced over her shoulder, instead, to where Josh was clattering down the stairs.

"Uncle Denver's here," she announced unnecessarily.

She stepped back to let him in, and he breathed in a whiff of an exotic, sultry perfume as he passed her. Damn her, he thought irritably. Why did she always have to look and smell so good? Why couldn't she look baggy eyed, or wear sloppy clothes and smell of cigarette smoke, like a lot of the women he met on the circuit?

There had never been a time when he'd set eyes on her without wanting in the worst way to haul her into his arms. It had been easier in the past. She'd chosen his brother. He'd only had to think of Lane to remind himself of the reasons he had to stay away from her.

Now Lane was gone, but it was too late to turn back the clock. He couldn't change who he was, or the life he'd built for himself. It was just too late.

"When are you going to teach me to ride?" Josh demanded, as soon as Denver had sat himself down in the living room.

"We haven't decided that you can have lessons," April reminded him. She glanced at Denver, and just as quickly looked away. "Can I get you something to drink? A soda, iced tea or a beer?"

Denver shook his head. "Thanks, but I thought we could all go down to the carnival on the waterfront. I don't know if this broken-down old body can handle some of those hair-raising rides, but I reckon I can take Josh on the tamer ones.''

Josh's face lit up and he turned eagerly to his mom. ''Can we?''

She smiled at him. ''I don't see why not. Put your good sneakers on—you'll need them if you're going to run around the carnival all day.''

Josh rushed off, and Denver eyed April warily. ''I hope this is okay.''

She nodded but once more refused to look him in the eye. ''He'll enjoy it,'' she said simply. ''I'll get my purse.''

She left the living room and Denver frowned. Was it his imagination, or had she cooled toward him since the day at the beach? Even yesterday he'd noticed she didn't have much to say to him. He wondered what it was he'd done wrong.

Determined to ask her at the first opportunity, he got up and went out into the sunlight to wait for her and Josh. He never spent any more time than he had to inside a building. It was as if he needed the fresh air and the open sky in order to breathe properly.

It was just as well he hadn't tried to settle down, he thought wryly. He'd have driven a woman crazy spending all his time outside the house.

''I brought the truck with me,'' he said, when April and Josh joined him on the doorstep. ''It's a little beat-up, but it'll get us there.''

''We could take my car,'' April offered, shading her eyes to look at the truck parked outside.

''How'd you get it off the camper?'' Josh wanted to know.

Denver tried to ignore the impression that April felt his truck wasn't good enough to ride in. ''I unhooked it,'' he said, answering Josh. ''Come on, I'll show you.''

Josh followed him down the path, and he pointed out the

hitch on the back of the truck and explained how they jacked up the camper to unhook it.

"I want to ride in the truck," Josh said, when April reached them.

Denver braced himself for an argument, but after a moment's hesitation, she said, "Okay."

Josh cheered and tried to open the handle of the door.

"Here," Denver said, stepping over to open it for him, "hop right in. You can sit in the middle, since you're such a skinny little thing."

Josh leaped up into the seat, and Denver moved back to let April climb in. Her bare legs looked smooth and tanned, and when she sat down the shorts rode up to uncover even more tanned skin.

He shut down on the question that tantalized his brain. It was none of his darn business how high the tan went. He slammed the door and strode around to his side of the truck. It was going to be a long day.

April kept her gaze firmly on the road ahead as they rode down the highway. She heard Josh's eager voice asking questions and Denver's deep tones answering him, but she couldn't have said what they were talking about. She was thinking about Lane, and what he would have said if he could have envisioned the situation as it was now.

He was so adamant about her keeping their secret—so determined that no one would ever know, least of all Denver. She couldn't help wondering how he would feel if he could see Denver with Josh now.

He would probably worry, as she did, that Denver would guess the truth. Lane had always been jealous of Denver. Jealous of the feelings she'd had for him, jealous of the night she'd shared with him and jealous of his brother for producing the son Lane had called his own.

From the day she'd married Lane, she'd buried her feelings for Denver. Yet she knew that Lane had never forgotten, for one minute, that if she'd had the choice, she would have chosen his wild, adventurous brother.

When they reached the fairground, Josh insisted on riding the bumper cars first. April passed on Denver's invitation to join them and stood at the rails, instead, to watch her son and his uncle chase each other around the ring.

It made her day to see Josh laughing and whooping as the cars jolted him nearly out of his seat. This was the Josh she knew, the happy little boy full of the enjoyment of life.

When he came off the cars she couldn't resist giving his thin little body a hug, much to Josh's disgust.

He wriggled out of her grasp with a muttered, "Aw, Mom," but the hostility that had hurt her so much had faded from his eyes when he looked up at her.

"Can we get some cotton candy?" he pleaded, and darted ahead of her and Denver to where a crowd of people hung around a stall.

"I'll get it." Denver quickened his stride to get there ahead of her.

When she reached him he'd already ordered one for her.

"Can you imagine what this does to your teeth?" she said, as she took the pink, frothy cloud of sugar from him.

He grinned down at her. "You can't come to a fairground and not eat cotton candy. It's an American tradition."

"So is duck hunting, but I manage to live without that." She took an experimental bite. The tangy taste dissolved in her mouth, bringing back memories of her childhood. Had it really been that long since she'd eaten cotton candy?

She glanced up at Denver and found him watching her with an odd intensity in his steel-blue eyes that sent a shiver all the way down to her knees.

"Here," he said quietly. "You've got a dab on your face." Before she could move he reached out and gently brushed her cheek at the corner of her mouth.

The touch was as light as a butterfly's wing, and just as fleeting. Yet the impact of it shuddered throughout her entire body. In that brief moment, with Denver's fingers on her skin, his eyes penetrating her soul, the blare of raucous rock music and ear-piercing shrieks faded to an insignificant hum.

In that brief moment, there were no hustling people, no balloons popping, no babies crying, no kids darting through the crowd with tickets stuffed in their sweaty hands.

There wasn't even Josh. There was just Denver—tall, rugged, powerful Denver, and in that moment April understood why Josh adored him.

Her son had loved his father, but his uncle was special, a fantasy figure and a hero, someone to brag about at school, someone who commanded not only the respect of thousands of people, but also the powerful animals he rode.

Every boy needed a hero, especially when he'd lost his father. Just as every woman needed someone to lean on, especially when she was all alone.

Something must have revealed itself in her expression. For an instant she saw heat flame in Denver's eyes, and then it died. He let his hand drop onto Josh's shoulder and said casually, "I bet you'd be too scared to go on the Rocket Train with me."

Josh glanced at his mother. "I'm not scared at all. It's fun."

April bit back the warning. Denver knew what he was doing. He'd take care of Josh. "Have a good time," she said lightly. "I'll wait for you outside."

Denver gave her an approving nod, then grabbed Josh's hand and led him over to where the gleaming silver chain of cars waited to plunge its riders into a maze of twisting tunnels.

It seemed ages until the two of them emerged again, Josh looking a little paler than when he'd climbed aboard the train. "That was awesome!" he exclaimed, when April reached them. "You should have tried it, Mom. It was really cool. Dad never took me on anything like that."

April felt a stab of surprise. That was the first time Josh had mentioned his father except in anger. Feeling compelled, however, to defend Lane, she said lightly, "Dad took you lots of places, though, didn't he?"

Josh nodded, "Sure! Mostly ball games."

"Ball games?" Denver rubbed his hands together. "Now you're talking. Your dad and I used to go to ball games all the time when we were kids."

Josh looked at him in surprise. "You went to ball games with my dad?"

Denver chuckled. "We were brothers, remember? We grew up together."

"Oh, yeah." Josh's face fell. "I wish he was here now," he mumbled.

April's heart ached for him. She was about to say something comforting, when Denver put an arm around his shoulders.

"So do I, cowboy. I really miss him, too. And I know your mom misses him just as much as you do."

Josh looked as if he were about to cry, and April's heart sank. It was a mistake to talk about Lane now.

"Tell you what," Denver said, bending over to make himself heard above the renewed shrieks from the Rocket Train. "How would you like to go to a ball game tomorrow night? I hear the Portland Rockies are playing at home."

"Don't you have to ride tomorrow?" April reminded him.

Denver shrugged. "In the afternoon. I can make it back in time for a ball game."

"All right!" Josh pointed to a ride that resembled two giant boats swinging precariously. "Can I go on that?"

Denver looked over at it and winced. "Maybe I should

have left the cotton candy alone.'' He grabbed Josh's hand, however, and marched over to where a line of passengers waited in eager anticipation for the ride.

Denver was really trying, April thought, as she followed more slowly. And as long as Denver was around, Josh seemed to forget his misery over his father's death. But Denver couldn't be around forever. Already he was talking about leaving for Canada. She could only hope that Josh wouldn't feel as if he were being abandoned.

Watching her son devour a hotdog later, she pushed her worries aside. Josh was enjoying this day at least, and he had the ball game to look forward to tomorrow. She'd worry about the rest of the week later.

Denver felt pretty satisfied with his efforts as he drove Josh and his mom home later that afternoon. It had been a good day, and Josh seemed to have had a good time. Worn out by the effect of warm sun, exhausting rides and his fill of junk food, the boy dozed in the front seat, his head lolling against his mother's shoulder.

Denver glanced at them out of the corner of his eye. The warm gorge wind had mussed April's hair, and the sun had flushed her cheeks. She seemed a little sleepy herself and sat with her chin resting on her son's head.

Denver felt a warm tug of tenderness. How good they looked together. Lane had been lucky to have that, at least for a few good years.

A sigh whispered up from his chest. It wasn't often he allowed himself to dwell on what might have been. He'd known from the start that he was doing the right thing by turning his back on April and all that life with her promised.

It had been better to make the break then than to make them both miserable later. How could he face up to the responsibilities of a family, knowing that sooner or later he was bound to screw up again?

Right now it was fun to take Josh out and show him a good time. As long as the boy understood that it was only temporary. He just couldn't be the man Lane was, and he shouldn't even try. He'd only let them down.

It was just as well he'd never had kids of his own. Denver gripped the wheel as the inevitable pang of remorse hit him. It would always be his biggest regret that he'd never have a child to carry on his genes.

In the next instant he shook off the melancholy. That was all the world needed, he reminded himself wryly, another Denver Briggs to complicate someone else's life.

"It was a nice day," April said suddenly, jolting him out of his meditation. "Thank you. We had a good time."

He flicked a glance at her, but her gaze was on the road ahead. "So did I." He checked Josh's face and reassured himself that the boy was asleep. "I could be wrong," he added casually, "but I had the impression this morning that you were kind of upset with me."

That got her attention. He could almost feel her tense up.

"I don't know why you should think that."

Her cool tone warned him he could be treading on dangerous ground. Well, he was used to walking through minefields, he thought, as he pulled up at a light. He looked straight at her, and this time, she didn't turn away. There was a question in her eyes, and something else. Something he didn't want to think about.

He'd seen that little flicker of awareness a couple of times already. He wasn't sure what it meant. He didn't want to know what it meant. If he thought for one moment that she would welcome a move from him, he'd oblige her so fast it would make her head spin. And that, without any doubt at all, would be a big mistake.

He couldn't afford that kind of mistake. Not with April. She wasn't like all the others. He'd walked away from her once. He wasn't at all sure he could do it again. And everything he'd sacrificed, everything he'd thrown away would be for nothing.

It was easier to be strong now, with only a faded memory between them. Once he refreshed that memory of how good it was to make love to her, it would be near impossible to leave again. And he would have to leave again.

He looked back at the road as the traffic in front of him moved forward. "I just wondered if I said or did something to upset you."

"No, nothing. You've been very kind to Josh, and I appreciate it."

Her voice was brittle, as if she were afraid of something. He couldn't imagine what it could be. "I had a good time, too," he said gently. "I think the little guy enjoyed it, as well. Even if we didn't talk about riding lessons."

"I'm sure he did. The riding lessons can wait." She hesitated, then to his surprise added, "Would you like to stay for supper? I don't suppose you get too many home-cooked meals."

"That'd be real nice." The warm glow inside him spread up to his chest.

"Josh would like that," she said deliberately.

He nodded. He got the message. She was asking him for Josh's sake. It didn't take the pleasure away from the prospect. He'd enjoyed the rare times he'd tasted her cooking. And that was why he was looking forward to it so much, he told himself. No other reason.

Josh woke up enough to pick his way through the chicken his mother cooked for dinner, then reluctantly took a shower before falling into bed. April tucked him in, her heart glowing with pleasure when he suffered a good-night kiss on his forehead. It was the first time he'd tolerated any show of affection from her since Lane's death.

Denver had earned his dinner, she thought, as she slowly descended the stairs again. Which was the only reason she'd invited him. She just hoped he'd leave now, and not make things awkward. The last thing she wanted was to be alone with him.

The quivery feeling she always got when she was around him seemed to intensify when she walked into the living room and saw him seated in an armchair with the day's newspaper spread out before him.

"Just checking the scores," he said, as she began clearing the dishes from the table. "Don't mind, do you?"

"Not at all." Her hand shook, and a knife clattered off the plate she was holding onto the one below. She snatched it up and fled into the kitchen with the dishes.

She turned on the hot faucet and watched the water gush from it in a cloud of steam. She had to stop letting him get to her this way. For Josh's sake. For her own sake. For everybody's sake. She lifted one of the plates and rinsed it under the tap.

"Can I help?"

His voice, coming from right behind her shoulder, startled her so much she almost dropped the plate. "Thanks," she muttered, "but I can manage."

"I reckon you can, but I'd feel better if I did something." He reached over her arm and took the plate from her nerveless fingers. "Why don't you finish clearing the table out there and I'll put these in the dishwasher."

Standing that close to him, she was in no position to argue. "Thank you," she said meekly.

"You're more than welcome."

She backed away from the sink, and bumped right into him. She might just as well have backed into an electrified fence. Shock waves sparked up her body as she jumped away from him. "Sorry."

She expected him to sidestep out of her way, but he

remained where he was, unmoving in the suddenly charged silence. Her lungs ached with the effort to breathe normally. She dared not look at him, dared not move, dared not make a sound.

"April."

She forced herself to face him, unnerved by the husky sound of her name.

"What are you so damn scared about?"

She went hot and cold, wondering what he meant. Had she said something to arouse his suspicions about Josh? She searched her mind, frantically going over everything that was spoken that day.

She managed to make her voice sound natural when she said, "Scared? I don't know what you mean."

With a slow, deliberate movement that made her stomach squirm he put down the plate. "Look," he said quietly, "I know we haven't talked about this, but maybe we should. Maybe it would help to clear the air between us."

She could hear the thumping of her heartbeat echoing in her head as she met his gaze. "Talk about what?" She would have to lie, she told herself frantically. She couldn't deal with this right now.

"What...happened between us all those years ago."

She saw a pulse beating at his temple and knew he was as unsettled as she was. The knowledge helped to calm her a little. "I don't think there's anything to talk about," she said evenly.

"Well, I do." He stared down at her, then looked away with a little shake of his head. "I didn't say anything about it all the time Lane was alive. I thought it was best buried in the past, where it belonged. But now that Lane's gone, things seem to have changed between us."

Her hand strayed to her throat, while she fought to cool the heat suffusing her body. "Changed?"

"Yeah." His gaze returned to her face, and there was

such agony in his eyes she cringed. "I just lost my only brother. I don't want to lose his family, too. What we did back then was a mistake, and I really wish it hadn't happened. I can't take it back, but I want you to know I'm real sorry. I just hope you won't let it cause any bad feelings between us now."

Pain knifed through her, so sharp she almost cried out. He made it seem so easy. Just forget it ever happened. Well, she couldn't do that, but she sure didn't have to let him know that.

"I had forgotten all about it," she said stiffly. "It was so long ago I hardly remember it at all."

His eyes appeared to lose their warmth, and he reached for the plate again. "Okay," he said quietly. "I just wanted to get that straight."

She gave him a tight nod, then hurried out of the kitchen before something in her face gave away her thoughts. If he only knew, she thought, as she gathered up the rest of the dishes. If he only knew what he was doing to her body every time he came near to her.

If he only knew how many nights she had lain awake next to her sleeping husband, wishing she could feel again the hot, vibrant fury of the passion she'd felt that night with Denver. If he only knew that even now, her body ached to recapture what she had given up for the sake of her son. Even though she realized what it would cost. Even though she realized the risks.

One more day, she told herself. Just one more day of this ordeal, then it would be over. Denver would be on his way to Canada and she wouldn't have to watch every word she uttered, every move she made. All she could hope for was that Josh wouldn't revert to his moods once Denver left.

"I'm not sure I'll have the truck tomorrow," Denver

said, as he got ready to leave. "It might be better to meet you at the ballpark, if that's okay with you."

She nodded, relieved that he wouldn't be coming to the house after all. "Sure, that'll be fine."

"I'll meet you in front of the main ticket office." Denver picked up his hat and jammed it on his head. "About seven-thirty?"

"We'll be there." She smiled awkwardly at him. "And thanks again, Denver."

"Sure." He stood in the doorway, looking down at her with that odd, intense expression in his eyes she saw so often. "And thank you and Josh," he added quietly. "I can't remember when I had such a good time."

She held the smile, even though her heart thudded loud enough to be heard. She wanted so much to feel his arms about her. The longing to taste his mouth on hers was so acute she ached with it.

She couldn't go on like this, she thought frantically. She had to put Denver Briggs out of her heart and out of her mind, and she couldn't do that all the time she was standing so close to him, feeling the warmth of his body and the thrill of his smile.

"I guess I'll be getting along." He stepped outside and touched the brim of his hat. "I'll see you both tomorrow."

She nodded. "Tomorrow."

She watched him stride down the path to his truck, then quietly closed the door. She let her head rest against the cool wood for a moment, trying to erase the heat of her turbulent thoughts. Then, with a long sigh, she turned off all the lights and prepared herself for the long night ahead.

Denver's thoughts whirled in confusion as he drove back to the rodeo grounds. There was something on April's mind, that was for sure. Maybe she didn't approve of his spending so much time with her son. Not that he could blame her. He was the last person in the world who should be trying to fill in for Josh's father.

Yet if that was the case, why hadn't she said so? Why did she act as though she was happy that he and Josh were having such a good time together? It didn't make sense. Nothing made sense.

He shook his head. Women were tough to figure out anyway. Just when he thought he had one pegged, she turned out to be the opposite of what he'd figured. No wonder he had trouble with them.

The camper was empty when he got back, which meant that Jed and Cord were probably at the tavern across the street. He decided to join them for a nightcap. Maybe then he could forget April's impassive expression when he'd mentioned the night they'd spent together. Maybe he'd stop thinking about her casual words, and the fact that her lips said one thing while her eyes said something else. Something that made his heart beat faster and his hands itch.

He found Jed at the bar, talking to Kristi, the young daughter of the stock contractor who supplied most of the animals for the rodeo in the area. At least, Kristi was doing all the talking. Jed was doing his best to ignore her, as usual.

Everyone in the place with half an eye could see that the pretty blonde had the hots for Jed. Everybody but Jed, that was. As far as J.C. was concerned, women didn't belong in the rodeo. They slowed things up, according to Jed.

"Cord in here?" Denver looked around the crowded tables. It was hard to distinguish one man from another when their faces were hidden by the sea of hats. Laughter burst from a group in one table, while nearby two cowboys argued with each other, gesturing with their free hand as they grasped a foaming mug of beer in the other.

A bored-looking woman with flaming red hair slouched in a chair, listening to them, while a waitress in a skirt that barely skimmed her thighs did her best to edge between the tables with a loaded tray.

Smoke curled around the plastic Tiffany-style lamps hanging low over the tables, infusing the air with its noxious smell. Denver felt the compelling urge to get out into the fresh air again.

"Over there, on his fifth beer," Jed muttered, nodding to where a man lounged in his chair, his black hat pulled low over his eyes.

A woman sat opposite him, leaning across the table in an obvious attempt to get him to notice her generous cleavage.

"We'd better get him out of there." Denver put down the beer he'd ordered. "You know how he gets when he drinks."

"Too late. He's already there."

Denver pulled a face. "Well, the way I look at it, we've all got a big ride tomorrow. If we don't get him out of here now he'll be spending an hour or two in some cheap motel. Then he'll head home in the middle of the night, crashing and cursing around while he finds his way to his bunk." Denver shook his head. "And you know how I hate to lose my sleep."

Jed nodded. "Okay, let's get him."

"I thought you were going to buy me a drink." Kristi pouted and thrust her hand back to flick her blond hair from her shoulder.

"Not tonight, darling," Jed murmured. "Me and Cannon here's got some business to take care of."

Leaving the disappointed woman at the bar, Jed and Denver sauntered over to the table, where Cord was leering at the middle-aged groupie opposite him. Denver flicked his glance over her in disgust. He'd seen too many like her in places like this. Too much makeup and not enough clothes, and old enough to know better.

"We're going home, pardner," Jed muttered, taking the beer mug out of Cord's fist.

"Hey," Cord mumbled. "No one steals my beer and lives to talk about it."

"Leave him alone," the woman said, with an ugly look on her face.

Jed leaned down until his nose was inches from hers. "Make me," he said, smiling pleasantly.

The woman's expression changed to alarm. She backed off, and Jed took one of Cord's arms, while Denver grabbed the other. Between the two of them they got the staggering, swearing cowboy out of the bar and across the road.

They had to wrestle him into his bunk, dodging his flailing arms and ignoring his belligerent threats. But the minute his head touched the pillow, he was out like a felled ox.

"Mission accomplished," Denver said, grinning as he held up his palm.

"Sure thing, pardner." Jed high-fived him, then sank onto his bunk with a yawn. "I don't know where he gets the energy from. I'm bushed."

He looked up at Denver. "How'd things go at the fair?"

Denver avoided his gaze. "Pretty good. Josh seemed to be having a good time."

"How about his mother?" Jed asked slyly.

Denver gave him a biting look. "What about her?"

Jed held up his hands. "Okay, okay. One fight on my hands is enough for one night. Let's get some shut-eye."

"Good idea," Denver muttered, knowing full well that he was going to have trouble falling asleep with the image of April firm in his mind and his imagination filling in everything that Jed had just implied.

April slept better than she'd anticipated that night and woke up the next morning filled with renewed optimism. It was going to be all right after all, she told herself as she prepared breakfast for her and Josh.

All her fears were apparently unfounded. Denver didn't seem to notice his resemblance to his nephew, or if he did he'd accepted it as a normal function of family genes.

What was most important was that Josh was definitely responding to his uncle's visits. He sat at the table chattering on about the day at the fair and all the questions he was going to ask Denver about the rodeo when he saw him that night.

"You'd better not ask too many questions," April said, smiling. "You'll miss the game if you do."

"I'll ask him between the innings," Josh said, his face lighting up at the prospect. "I hope the Rockies win tonight. Can we have hotdogs? I want to put all that neat stuff on them myself. Does Uncle Denver like hotdogs?"

April sighed. After all the junk food her son had eaten yesterday and would no doubt eat today, it was just as well Denver was leaving town tomorrow. "I guess so," she said in resignation. "After all, what's a ball game without hotdogs?"

"Yay!" Josh waved his toast in the air. "It'll be just like it was when Dad was here...." His voice trailed off. "Almost," he added, sounding subdued.

April's throat ached. "I know you miss Dad," she said softly. "You will for a long while. But he wouldn't want you to always be sad. He'd be real happy to know you were having a good time with your uncle."

Josh looked at her, and her fingers curled when she saw

tears glistening on his dark lashes. "You don't think he'd mind?"

Impulsively, April put her arm around her son's slender shoulders. "Oh, honey, of course he wouldn't mind. He loved your uncle as much as you do. He'd be happy to know you were getting along so well together."

She hadn't realized until now that Josh was feeling guilty for enjoying himself with a man other than his father. It was a measure of how much loyalty her son felt for Lane. And how shattered Josh would be to learn that Lane wasn't his real father.

He must never know, she told herself fiercely. Lane was right. This was one secret that had to be kept at all costs.

Throughout the day Josh asked a torrent of questions about Denver. He seemed most interested in the dangers of riding the bulls. April played down that part of it, wary of scaring her son and spoiling his enjoyment of his uncle's somewhat glamorous profession. At least in Josh's eyes.

At last it was time to leave for the ball game. Josh sat in the front seat of the T-bird with her, squirming around and asking the inevitable questions.

April answered as best she could, her nerves already tightening as she thought of seeing Denver again. She was being ridiculous, she told herself. She was a grown woman with a son, and had no right to be feeling so excited and nervous about someone who was so obviously indifferent toward her. At least in that way.

Not that she wanted him to be any different, she hastily assured herself. It was better this way; then there could be no misunderstandings. They both knew where they stood...as much as anyone could with Denver. At least this way she wouldn't run the risk of being hurt again.

As they drew closer to the stadium, cars lined the streets bumper to bumper. The big drawback to the city stadium was its lack of parking. April had to park several streets away and then join the crowds on the long trek back to the stadium.

Josh skipped along impatiently by her side, trying to make her go faster. "Uncle Denver will be waiting for us," he complained, when she paused to get her breath at the top of the hill. "He'll be wondering where we are."

She grabbed his hand to prevent him from darting across the road against the light. "Don't worry, he's not going anywhere. He'll wait."

"But the game will be starting without us."

April glanced at her watch. "We have ten minutes, and we're almost there."

Still hanging on to Josh's hand, she turned the last corner. "There," she said with relief. "The ticket offices are right there."

"I can't see Uncle Denver," Josh said, as they drew closer.

"He's probably waiting behind one of the booths." April scanned the crowds streaming through the gates. "Over there."

Josh broke away from her and sprinted across to the booths. "He's not here," he said, looking accusingly at her. "I told you we'd be late."

"Josh, he'll be here. He wouldn't go in without us. He'd realize we wouldn't know where to find him. Besides, the game hasn't begun yet."

Josh looked at her, his eyes filling with tears. "He didn't wait for us, and it's all your fault."

"He'll be here," April repeated, trying to ignore the anxious fluttering in her stomach. "He probably just got held up at the rodeo. We'll just wait here until he comes. You watch out for him and you'll see him coming."

Josh stared across the street, his face set in the stubborn

scowl she'd hoped she wouldn't see again. A dreadful, cold, heavy feeling settled in her stomach as she watched the latecomers dwindle to a scattering of people.

Music blared from the stadium, and the crowd roared. The game had started. Something told her that Denver was not going to be there after all. Once more, he'd let her down. Looking into her son's face, she was afraid that this time Denver's broken promises could be disastrous.

Chapter 5

"I guess Uncle Denver got held up somewhere," April said, when another ten minutes had passed without any sign of her errant brother-in-law. "I think we should go in to see the game anyway, now that we're here."

If she'd hoped to cheer Josh up with that suggestion, she was doomed to disappointment.

"I don't want to see the game," Josh said, kicking his heel in the dirt. "I want to wait here for Uncle Denver."

"I don't think he's coming." A surge of anger at Denver almost took her breath away. "But if he does, I'll leave a message at the box office window, so he'll know how to find us."

Josh took one last hopeful look down the road, then shrugged. "Okay," he mumbled. "But it won't be any fun without him."

Seething with anger, April did her best to cheer up her son throughout the long evening. Josh halfheartedly ate a hotdog and finished half his soda before managing to spill the rest of it all over the feet of the man sitting next to him.

April's red-faced apology was met with a stiff nod, and a minute or two later the man moved back a couple of rows. Josh seemed bored with the game and didn't even cheer when the Rockies won by two runs.

He barely spoke on the way home, and April's mood sank lower as she parked the car in the driveway. A small spark of hope remained that Denver might have left her a message, but there was no welcoming signal light on the answering machine, and nothing on the recorder when she checked to make sure.

Josh was unusually quiet when he went to bed, and refused to answer April's worried questions. She finally left him to sleep, hoping that by the morning he'd regain some of his good spirits.

As a rule, Josh had always managed to bounce back from a disappointment without too much trouble. But these weren't normal times, and she worried that Denver's irresponsible behavior could cause a serious setback in Josh's recovery.

How could he do this? she stormed inwardly, as she trudged down the stairs again. He knew how vulnerable the child was, how easily he could be crushed. Josh already felt that the father he'd adored had let him down by not taking better care of himself.

Now the man who was supposed to help him deal with that had broken his promise, and the disappointment he'd caused was far more crushing than anything Denver could possibly imagine.

She paused at the bottom of the stairs, aware that her own disappointment was adding fuel to her anger. She had to calm down. There had to be a reasonable explanation. Even Denver couldn't be so cruel as to deliberately disappoint a child. But why hadn't he called and explained? Or at the very least apologized?

She should have a glass of wine, she decided, to calm

her resentment. If he did decide to call before she went to bed, which was unlikely at this late hour, the last thing she needed was to lose her temper. She just might say a few things she'd regret.

She carried the wine to her favorite armchair and settled herself in front of the TV. After idly surfing the channels, she decided on the late-night news. That way she wouldn't be tempted to stay up half the night to watch the end of a movie. Maybe seeing the problems of the world would make her own problems seem insignificant, she told herself with a wry smile.

Her eyelids felt heavy after a while, and she dozed off in the middle of an account of the latest efforts to save the salmon run in the Columbia. Forcing her eyes open, she picked up her glass to finish the last of her wine.

The sports news was on and she reached for the remote. She'd just sat through a baseball game. She'd had enough of sports for one night.

Her thumb hovered over the button, then froze, as she stared at the images on the screen. The reporter stood with his back to the rodeo arena. Behind him a rider fought valiantly to stay on the back of a rampaging bull, which bucked so furiously all four feet left the ground at once.

At first she thought it was Denver but soon realized it wasn't. It was the reporter, however, who held her attention. In a voice remarkably devoid of emotion, he was talking about something that had happened in the arena.

"And is reported in critical condition after being badly gored by an enraged bull. The tragedy took place late this afternoon during the bull-riding competition. This is the most dangerous contest in the rodeo, and in the past a number of men have lost their lives...."

April uttered a cry and jumped to her feet, ignoring the wine spilling down her arm. The reporter went on talking about the men who had died in the ring over the years.

"No," she muttered, "not now. Tell me who got hurt today." Her voice rose. "Tell me, you idiot. Who was it?"

The picture faded and the camera went back to the newsroom. "In other news," the sportscaster said brightly, "the Rockies won their seventh game at home with a three-one win over—"

April whirled around and snapped off the TV with the remote. Who could she call? She had to call someone. The newsroom. They would know.

She felt sick, and her head swam as if she'd swallowed a half-dozen glasses of wine instead of the half a glass she hadn't even finished. She clung to the back of the chair for a moment, trying to clear her head.

It could have been anyone. Denver wasn't the only one riding a bull today.

But he'd stood up Josh, without a word of explanation. He should have been at the ball game tonight and he wasn't there. *He wasn't there.*

"Oh, God." She gulped, closed her eyes and fought to keep her panic under control. All she could think about was that other night, a few short months ago, when a strange voice had told her on the phone that her husband's plane had disappeared and there was a possibility it had crashed in the mountains.

She hadn't believed that Lane was dead. Not even after they told her they had sighted his plane. Not even when they told her it was doubtful anyone could have survived the crash. She hadn't believed it until they had brought his broken, battered body back to town and had taken her in to identify him.

Even then, looking at the still, white face that was amazingly untouched, she'd wanted to shake his shoulder and beg him not to play such morbid games. It was days before she finally convinced herself that he wasn't going to walk in through the door with his cheerful greeting anymore.

"No," she whispered. "Not again. I can't do that again."

She had to call and find out, she thought, making a desperate effort to pull herself together. She couldn't go to bed not knowing, forced to wait until she could read about it in the morning paper. She had to know now. She had to prepare herself so that she could be strong for Josh…again.

She caught back the sob rising in her throat and made herself go to the phone. The number of the TV station was in the White Pages, and it took her another agonizing moment or two to find it.

Finally she punched out the number, slowly, carefully, knowing that she had to get it right the first time, because she didn't think she could dial it again.

The ringing on the other end went on and on…until she thought she would scream. At last the line clicked, and a bored voice answered.

"The man who was gored at the rodeo this afternoon," April said, trying to keep the tremors out of her voice. "Can you tell me if it was Denver Briggs?"

"Just a minute." The minute stretched into two while she waited, her fingers clenched around the receiver. Finally the voice said dispassionately, "The report says Denver Briggs was injured this afternoon. Is that what you wanted to know?"

She heard the echo on the line as if it were coming from a long way off. She tried to speak but couldn't, her lips too stiff to move. Two words kept drumming through her head, over and over. *Not again.*

"Hello?"

There was no hiding the trembling of her voice when she answered. "Can you tell me which hospital he's in?"

"Sorry." A note of sympathy crept into the voice. "I can try to find out."

"No," April whispered. "Never mind. I'll call them myself.'' She replaced the receiver as though she were afraid it would blow up if she put it down too hard. Not Denver. It had been hard enough to lose Lane. The thought of losing Denver as well was too terrible even to contemplate.

She had to call the hospitals. She had to find out where he was, how he was. She thumbed through the Yellow Pages until she came to the listings, then started going through them one by one. Her voice sounded mechanical as she asked the same question over and over. ''Did you admit a man by the name of Denver Briggs this afternoon?''

Half an hour later she still hadn't located the hospital. She was down to the last two. He had to be at one of them. Wearily she stabbed out the number.

Her doorbell rang suddenly, a shrill sound that seemed to pierce her eardrums. Startled, she glanced at the clock. It was way past midnight. She couldn't imagine who would be calling, unless it was someone…one of Denver's traveling partners, perhaps…come to tell her that Denver was…

She swallowed, fighting back the nausea that welled in her throat. The floor felt uneven as she made herself walk to the door. She saw her hand trembling as she turned the locks, twisted the handle and pulled.

At first, all she registered was a tall man wearing a cowboy hat. Then he stepped into the light spilling from the doorway, and her world spun crazily into a mass of spinning stars.

She grasped the door frame as the strength slipped away from her knees. ''I thought you…'' She gulped and tried again. ''They told me… I thought you…''

Denver swore softly. In one short stride he was inside the house, his arms closing around her as she collapsed against him.

She clung to him, just filling her mind with his presence.

He rocked her, murmuring her name, his hand stroking her hair. She breathed in the male fragrance of him, the faint, earthy cologne and the tangy smell of soap.

He pulled off his hat and dropped it on the nearest chair, then tugged her closer to his strong body. Her cheek lay against his firm chest, and she could hear the steady thud of his heart keeping time with her own. The comfort of his arms was overwhelming, and she fought to stem the rush of tears that drifted down her cheeks.

"I'm sorry, honey," he whispered against her hair. "Jed was supposed to meet you at the ball game to explain. But he went to the wrong place and couldn't find you. I was at the hospital with Sam and didn't find out until an hour ago that Jed hadn't contacted you. I tried to phone you, but the line was busy—"

"I was calling the hospitals." A shudder shook her body, and she drew back to look up into his face. The strong, craggy, beautiful face that she thought she'd never see again.

She studied him hungrily—the dark, uneven eyebrows, the steel-blue eyes so like her son's, the jutting nose, the mouth that could look so hard and so tender at the same time…and a sigh trembled on her lips.

"I heard it on the news," she said unsteadily. "But they didn't say who had been hurt. I called the newsroom and they said… " She swallowed. "They said it was—"

She didn't get any further. His mouth came down hard on hers, shutting off the rest of her words. Her whimper was lost in her throat as fire leaped along her veins.

She lifted her hands and threaded her fingers through his soft hair, losing herself in the demanding pressure of his mouth. She couldn't get close enough to him. She pressed her body against the length of him, and felt his hard response against her belly.

Time was roaring backward in her head, back to that

unforgettable night when she'd first learned the excruciating excitement of his touch. She wanted that again...needed it again with an intense yearning that was almost a physical pain deep inside her.

His hands roamed her back, and she felt weak with longing. She needed this man, wanted this man....

Dimly she became aware of a niggling anxiety that wouldn't let her abandon her thoughts entirely. *What about the risks?*

She stiffened as alarms sounded inside her head. What was she doing? She couldn't do this. It was wrong; it was stupid. She'd get hurt. Josh could get hurt.

Almost immediately, as if sensing her resistance, Denver let her go. "I'm sorry," he said thickly. "I didn't mean—"

"No!" She shook her head fiercely at him. "It was my fault. I was just so relieved you were all right that I didn't think."

His gaze bore into hers, still smoldering with the embers of passion.

She swallowed. "After Lane...well, you know..."

At the mention of his brother's name, the fire in Denver's eyes died. "I understand," he said brusquely. "We were both a little upset, that's all. Let's just forget it happened." He reached for his hat, his face an impassive mask.

Regret tugged at her heart so badly she was afraid she might cry again. "They said you were injured. Are you all right? Did you say it was Sam who was hurt?"

"Yeah." He turned to the door without looking at her. "He was trying to protect me. I just got a little bruised up, that's probably why the newsroom got my name in the report. I tripped as I came off Rasputin, the bull I was riding, and landed right in front of him in the dust. Sam came in to get the bull's attention and slipped in the dirt. The bull got him in the thigh."

April felt sick, remembering the fresh-faced young man with the engaging grin. "Is he going to be all right?"

Denver gave her a brief nod, his gaze sliding off her. "It was touch and go for a while. The horn hooked an artery. They were still pumping blood in him when I left, but the doctors say he'll be okay. I went back to the camper and took a shower, then Jed came in and told me he couldn't find you. I figured you might be a little upset with me, so when I couldn't get through on the phone I decided to come over."

"I'm glad you did." She smiled up at him. "Thank you."

Again he gave her a tight nod. This time his gaze lingered on her mouth just long enough to make her nervous again, then he said gruffly, "I'd better get off and let you grab some shut-eye."

She nodded, feeling the ache of loneliness creeping over her already. "You're leaving for Canada in the morning?"

"Yep, the Calgary Stampede."

"When will you be back?"

He stepped through the doorway, then paused just outside the patch of light, so that she couldn't see his face. "Tough to say," he answered casually. "Tell Josh I'm sorry I missed the game."

"I will. He'll be happy to know you didn't just forget about it."

"I wouldn't forget."

She nodded. "I know."

"But you thought I'd forgotten."

She was glad she couldn't see his face. "Something like that."

He seemed to go very still, then he said dryly, "Yeah, well, I guess I can't blame you. I'll be in touch."

She had to be content with that. She managed to smile as she bade him good-night, but her heart felt as if it were shriveling up inside her as she closed the door. She fervently hoped she was wrong, but something told her that it would be some time before she set eyes on Denver again.

Josh seemed to brighten at the news that Denver had been delayed at the hospital and had come over to say he was sorry. But as the days slipped by without a word from his uncle, his spirits plummeted and his questions became more persistent.

Every morning it was the same. April would call him down for breakfast; he'd arrive a minute or two later, demanding, "When is Uncle Denver coming back?"

Having answered the question a dozen times the same way, April was beginning to feel a little irritated. "I've told you, I don't know," she said sharply one morning after a sleepless night. "I expect we'll hear from him when he has time to come back and see us. Right now he's busy with the rodeo."

"Well, why can't we go and see him?"

"I've told you that, also. It's too far away. I don't know where he is."

Josh pouted and spread too much jelly on his toast. "You said he was in Canada."

"He was, but that rodeo is over. He must be at another one by now."

"Why hasn't he called us?"

Why, indeed, April thought grimly. Maybe he was getting tired of spending time with his brother's widow and son. Maybe he didn't want her getting the wrong idea about the night he'd kissed her. Maybe it was just as well he wasn't around, since she hadn't been able to get that night out of her mind.

His kiss was the last thing she remembered before falling asleep at night, and the first thing to drift into her mind upon waking.

"I expect he's busy," she murmured automatically. "He'll call when he has time."

"Well, I wish he'd hurry up and come back. I'm getting tired of sitting around here waiting for him."

He looked so forlorn she forgot about her own anxieties. "Why don't you go and visit one of your friends, then," she suggested. Josh hadn't been out of the house since the ball game, which was unusual for him.

"I don't want to." Josh picked idly at the tablecloth. "I want to be here in case Uncle Denver calls."

A pang of guilt hit her so hard she lost her breath. For the first time it occurred to her to wonder if she was doing the right thing by keeping her secret. Josh needed a father. He was beginning to get over Lane's death now, but he was becoming too attached to Denver.

Knowing Denver as she did, Josh was in for a good many disappointments. Denver could easily break her son's heart without even realizing it. Maybe if he knew that Josh was really his son, he'd be more inclined to spend what time he could with him. And with her.

In the next breath she knew that was impossible. Even if Denver could forgive her for not having told him before, she couldn't tie him to her that way.

Pride had kept her from telling him in the first place, and she would not use Josh as a means to force Denver into a relationship he didn't want. In any case, she had given Lane her promise, and she owed it to his memory to keep that vow.

"I think we should go to the movies this afternoon," she announced, watching Josh slouch in his chair.

"Don't want to."

"I'll put the recorder on. If Uncle Denver calls, he'll leave a message and we can call him back." There was no guarantee of that, of course, but Josh didn't have to know.

"What are we going to see?" Josh asked, without too much enthusiasm.

"You choose. Anything you want to see."

She was taking a chance, and felt relieved when Josh picked an adventure movie that sounded fairly innocuous.

For the first time in a long time, she and Josh had found common ground. Maybe they'd be all right, even if Denver decided he'd had enough of family life.

A thousand miles away, Denver sat on the fence, watching the wranglers put the horses through their paces. The men were patient, coaxing the horses to obey the pressure of knees against their flanks and the sharp tug on the bridle.

The communication between a roper and his horse was essential. Knowing horses as well as he did, Denver had a tremendous respect for the roper's ability to train his horse.

It was against the horse's nature to walk backward, yet every roper had his horse so well trained it would back up the minute the rope snagged a calf, then pull back hard enough to keep the rope taut without dragging the animal. It was some feat, and Denver never tired of watching the ropers work with their animals.

The wind blew dust across the hard Montana ground, and Denver turned his head to shelter his face. Out of the corner of his eye he saw Jed striding toward him, and lifted a hand in welcome.

"I wondered where you were at," Jed said, climbing up onto the fence next to him. "Thought you might have taken off for Oregon again."

Denver kept an impassive face. "Now, what would make you think that?"

"Oh, I don't know. It's just that you've seemed to have something on your mind ever since you got back from seeing that pretty sister-in-law of yours."

"If I've got something on my mind," Denver said easily, "it's worrying about how Sam is doing."

"Oh, yeah." Jed tilted back his head and narrowed his eyes against the sun. "I hear he's already on the circuit again."

Denver nodded. "A little too soon if you ask me."

"So when are you planning on going back to Oregon?"

"Why do you want to know?"

"I was just wondering, that's all. We were both wondering… Cord and me."

Jed looked uncomfortable, and Denver guessed they'd been talking about him. "Why don't you just let me do the wondering and worrying," he said, with a hint of warning in his voice.

"We don't want you to get hurt, that's all," Jed mumbled.

Denver sighed. "I reckon I can take care of myself. How about you? Found that wife yet?"

Jed shook his head. "I'm not looking for a wife. Wives cause a man too much trouble from what I've heard."

"Well, you can't believe everything you hear." Denver climbed down from the fence. "I guess I'll go get something to eat before we sign on this afternoon."

He took off across the stockyard, intent on putting some space between himself and his friend. Jed and Cord meant well, but they were beginning to frazzle his nerves with their fussing over him like a couple of grandmothers.

The camper was parked across the street from a fast-food restaurant. Normally he would have picked up a couple of hamburgers and taken them back to the camper to eat, but he wasn't in the mood for company right then. He took the hamburgers out to the field in back and sat on the fence to eat them, instead.

The problem was, Jed and Cord were right. He did have something on his mind. Something he wished he could forget. Try as he might, he could not rid himself of the memory of April's mouth under his. Every time he closed his eyes, he could feel her body crushed against him, driving him crazy.

He was all set that night to pick her up and carry her to her bedroom. Thank the Lord April had enough sense to call a halt, because he was certain he couldn't have stopped what was happening.

One thing he did know, it sure as heck couldn't happen again. He couldn't start something he didn't have a hope in hell of finishing.

April and Josh needed someone stable in their lives, someone who could support them and be there for them whenever they needed him, someone they could rely on. Someone like Lane.

April knew that. She knew that he was nothing like Lane. She missed having Lane around; that was why she'd reacted the way she had the other night. He couldn't let himself think otherwise.

If it wasn't for Josh, he'd get out now before he totally lost his reason and messed things up for good. But no matter how much he told himself it would be for the best, he couldn't turn his back on that boy until he knew Josh was going to be all right.

He owed Lane that much, at least.

Denver swallowed the last of his hamburger and rolled the wrapper into a tight ball before stuffing it in a pocket of his jeans. He opened the other burger and bit into it without much enthusiasm.

He hadn't had much appetite lately. He could blame no one but himself. He'd dug his way into this hole and it was up to him to climb out of it.

Somehow he had to keep his promise to Josh and teach him to ride. He'd let enough people down in his life. He wasn't going to do that to a young boy who had just lost his father.

At the same time he had to try to forget how it felt to hold April in his arms and feel her heart pound against his chest. He had to stop watching her, wanting her, and try to ignore the ache that wouldn't let him rest.

Somehow, while he was around her, he must remember who he was and why he had walked out of her life the first time. Above all, he must never let himself get that close to her again.

And if the thought of that gave him more pain than he'd ever imagined, it was no more than he deserved.

It was late one afternoon when April opened the door to find Denver standing there. At first she was speechless, shocked at the leap of joy she felt at the sight of him. By the time she finally found her voice, he was beginning to look a little concerned.

"I can come back later if this is a bad time," he said, sounding more awkward than she ever remembered hearing him sound.

"Of course not," she said quickly, standing back to let him pass. "I was just surprised to see you, that's all."

"Yeah," Denver said dryly. "I guess I do have a habit of turning up like a bad penny." He walked into the living room, filling the house with his presence, the way he always did.

"That's not what I meant." Aware that she sounded defensive, she forced her tangled nerves to calm down. "Usually you call before you come."

He crinkled his eyes at her. "Sorry. I just got back from Montana and came straight here from the airport."

"There's no need to apologize." She felt ridiculously close to tears. They were being so horribly formal with each other. Obviously Denver regretted the kiss of a few nights ago. A move that she had initiated with her ridiculous display of emotion.

She had promised herself that when she saw him again—if she saw him again—she'd keep her emotions under better control. That promise had flown out the window the moment she'd set eyes on him. The knowledge that she was so susceptible to his magnetic presence unnerved her.

She watched him take off his hat and drop it on the armchair. The familiar gesture produced a tug of awareness that she quickly suppressed.

"Where's Josh?" Denver asked, looking around as if he expected his nephew to be hiding in the room somewhere.

Of course. Josh was the reason he'd come back. Why couldn't she remember that? Why did she have to go on being torn apart with shattered hope? "He's at a friend's house, next door. I'll call him." She walked across to the phone, trying not to let her dejection sound in her voice. "He'll be so thrilled to see you again."

"Don't drag him away on my account."

She heard the creak of the armchair as he lowered himself onto it. "He'll be mad at me if I don't." She dialed quickly and got Josh on the phone almost immediately. "Uncle Denver is here," she told him, and held the phone away from her ear when her son whooped with delight.

"He's on his way," she said, replacing the receiver. "Would you like a beer?"

"I'd like to talk to you about something first."

She felt her heart thump and kept her back to him until she had crossed the room and regained some measure of composure. She sat down on the edge of the chair and prayed that he wasn't going to hash over what had happened between them the last time they'd met. She wasn't at all sure she could pretend to be as indifferent about it as he seemed to be.

"It's about Josh's riding lessons," Denver said, after

studying her in silence for a few moments. "I have a ten-day stretch between rodeos, starting next week. I thought it might be a good time to start on those lessons."

She fought a silent battle, torn between indecision. Josh had talked about little else for the first few days after Denver had left. Then he'd stopped talking about it and was showing signs of slipping back into his destructive moods again. The lessons would go a long way toward improving his attitude.

On the other hand, it meant more exposure to Denver, more disappointments and maybe more damage in the long run. If Josh accepted right now that Denver couldn't be a permanent fixture in his life, she might be able to save him from that hurt.

"I'm not sure that the lessons would be such a good idea," she said at last. "In another month or so Josh will be back at school and won't have time to spare. He has a lot of catching up to do with his schoolwork."

"Well, maybe we can use the lessons as an incentive." Denver stretched his feet out in front of him and leaned back.

He looked so much at ease April felt a ridiculous surge of resentment that he wasn't sharing the turmoil raging inside her. "What do you mean?" she asked carefully.

"We could tell Josh that if he wants to learn to ride, he has to promise he'll catch up on his grades when he goes back to school."

"We could do that." April clasped her hands between her knees. "There's no guarantee he'll keep his promise."

She sensed the sudden change in Denver's attitude before he spoke. "And one Denver Briggs in the family is enough, is that it?"

She sat up, her raw nerves bristling. "That's not what I meant and you know it. I just don't want Josh to get passionate about something, then have to drop it when he goes back to school. He hates school as it is. To have to give up something he loves to go back would only make things worse.''

''Who says he has to drop it? I'll be happy to pay for riding lessons for him after he's back in school. He could take them on weekends. There are enough riding schools around here—''

She finally lost it. She surged to her feet, furious with him for not understanding and for not caring enough. ''It's not the riding lessons, Denver. It's the fact that *you* will be teaching Josh that makes it so special to him. He doesn't care about riding horses. He cares about being with you. He won't miss the lessons when he goes back to school nearly as much as he'll miss seeing you.''

He stared at her in silence, his face carved in ice. Then, so slowly he made her nervous, he got to his feet. ''In that case, I reckon the best thing I can do for both of you is to leave now. Seems that whatever I do, I mess up your lives.''

It was too late to call back the words. They'd been said, and they hovered there between them like ugly boulders of solid rock. ''You must do whatever you think is best,'' she said, fighting to keep her voice even.

''Best for you? Or best for Josh?''

He started across the room toward her, and she stood her ground, her heart thumping painfully against her ribs.

He stood close enough to her for her to feel the warmth radiating from his body, the faint fragrance of his cologne making her senses spin. Desperately she hung on to her composure, refusing to let him know by the merest flicker of emotion how much she longed to go into his arms and wipe away the pain from his eyes.

He made no move to touch her but stood towering over her, his gaze cold and hard on her face. ''Don't worry,'' he said quietly. ''I have no intention of touching you again.

The other night was a mistake. I know that. It won't happen again.''

Cold washed through her when she answered him. ''I'm sure of that.''

A flicker of pain crossed his face. ''I know you think I'm a no-good, unreliable bum, and I can't say I blame you. But I can promise you I won't let the boy down. It's important to me. I'll teach him to ride, and I'll explain when the time comes why I can't be around as often as I'd like. But I'll be there for him as long as he needs me. I can't promise more than that.''

She studied his hard expression, wondering how much more pain would she have to suffer before he left her forever.

''April, don't let your feelings about me deprive Josh of something he really wants to do. I know what he's going through. I want to help him.''

Her throat hurt with the effort not to cry. ''So do I,'' she whispered. ''It's all I've ever wanted.''

''Then what d'you say we bury our feelings for his sake? I'll try to stay out of your hair as much as possible.''

He would never know what it cost her to force the smile. ''You've got a deal,'' she said, lifting her chin. ''Josh can have the lessons. I'm trusting you not to disappoint him.''

Denver placed his hand over his heart, and his wry smile knifed through her soul. ''I give you my word, for what it's worth.''

''Yay!'' a voice whispered excitedly from the doorway.

April started, wondering how long Josh had been standing there.

''Hi there, cowboy.'' Denver strode over to him and wrapped an arm around the boy's shoulders. ''I've got ten days to make a real cowboy out of you. Think you're up to it?''

Josh looked up at him, his face tense with anticipation. He didn't say a word, but his slow nod spoke volumes.

Watching him, April felt her anxiety slipping away. Denver was right. Nothing mattered as much right now as Josh's chance to straighten out. Denver had given his word, and now it was up to him to keep it. She wanted to trust him. With all her heart she wanted to trust him.

Please, she begged silently, *please don't let me down again. Don't let Josh down.* For she knew without a doubt that if he didn't keep his word, neither Josh nor she would ever be able to forgive him.

Chapter 6

Denver arranged for Josh to take lessons at the Second Chance Ranch, owned by a local horse breeder who'd retired from rodeo. According to Denver, the owner was an old friend of his.

April drove slowly down the winding country lane early one morning, looking for the sign that Denver had described—a shamrock and two horseshoes.

Josh spotted the sign before she did, pointing it out as they drove around a bend in the road. "There it is! And there's Uncle Denver."

April's heart thudded in answer, and she eased her foot on the brake as they approached the double gates under the swinging sign.

Denver leaned against the fence, watching her, his face inscrutable. He tipped his hat back with his thumb when she came to a halt, and sauntered over to the car.

"You're right on time," he said, leaning down to look in the open window.

"I don't like to be late." She bit her lip, aware that the words sounded like an accusation.

But Denver appeared not to notice. He winked at Josh, then opened the door for him. "You ready, cowboy?"

Josh nodded but looked more than a little apprehensive as he climbed out of the car.

"Shall I just leave the car here?" April asked.

"No, wait there. I'll open the gates for you and you can drive up to the house. Me and Josh will walk up, stretch our legs a bit before we tackle the horse."

Josh seemed even more nervous and April gave him a dubious look. "Is that okay, Josh?"

He gave her a scornful look back that was sheer bravado. "Of course."

She watched him walk with Denver to the gates, then stand back by the fence while his uncle opened them wide. He appeared so small and defenseless next to the tall cowboy that she had a moment of misgivings. Then, as Denver waved her on, she dismissed them.

Denver knew what he was doing. Josh would be fine.

She drove past them and pulled up in front of an impressive-looking house. The driveway bordered a beautifully landscaped yard, and pink rambling roses climbing up the whitewashed walls of the house.

The front door opened as she shut off the engine, and an attractive dark-haired woman about her own age ran lightly down the steps to greet her.

"I'm Caroline Harding," she said, holding out her hand as April climbed out of the car. "You must be Denver's sister-in-law. April, isn't it? I just love that name."

Confused, April shook the proffered hand. Somehow, when Denver had mentioned the old acquaintance, she'd expected to see a crusty old cowboy. Certainly not this graceful woman smiling so pleasantly at her.

"I'm so sorry about your husband," Caroline said, her

beautiful brown eyes clouding over. "That must have been so terribly difficult for you and your son. I know it hit Denver pretty hard."

"Thank you," April murmured, wondering how much Denver had told this woman about her private life.

"Your son must be such a comfort to you. Oh, here they are now!" Caroline ran down the driveway to where Denver and Josh had appeared from around the bend.

April watched the other woman fling her arms around Denver's neck, and tried to ignore her spasm of resentment. She prepared a smile on her face as the three of them approached her, with Caroline happily chatting to Josh about the horse he was going to ride.

"I guess you two have met," Denver said, when he reached April's side.

"We introduced ourselves." Caroline looked down at Josh. "I just can't believe how much your nephew resembles you, Denver. It's startling."

April felt the blood draining from her face while she searched frantically in her mind for something to say. She didn't dare to meet Denver's eyes, for fear of seeing the look she had dreaded on his face...a look of recognition and accusation.

The silence seemed to go on far too long, then Denver broke the tension with a dry chuckle. "Poor kid. I kept thinking he reminded me of someone. I never realized it was me."

"You must have looked a lot like your brother," Caroline said, appearing absolutely fascinated.

"Not that I can recall." Denver settled his hat more firmly on his head.

"Well, people never can see the resemblance to themselves," Caroline said, smiling down at Josh.

April felt as if she were going to scream if they didn't stop talking about it. Across the lawn she spotted an empty paddock. "So where do you keep the horses?" she asked, hoping to change the subject.

"In the stables at the moment," Caroline said, laughing. "Would you like to come and see them? Or can I offer you some coffee and Danish first?"

"That sounds real good," Denver said, making the decision for all of them. He led the way up the steps, with Josh trailing behind him.

April didn't want to go into the house. She didn't want Josh and this woman together anywhere that Caroline could dwell on the resemblance between Josh and his uncle. She wished now she'd put her foot down about the lessons. It was a mistake, and one she could pay for dearly. Somehow she had to keep Josh and Caroline apart, or her whole world could come crashing in on her.

"We've already had breakfast," she said, as Caroline waited for her to follow Josh up the steps. "Perhaps it would be better if Josh started the lessons now. He's pretty nervous about it, and the more he thinks about it, the worse he's going to get."

"He'll be fine," Caroline said. She patted April's arm. "Once he gets on that horse he'll forget all about being nervous. Denver is a good trainer. He taught me a lot about controlling a horse. I don't think I would have survived as many years in rodeo as I did if it hadn't been for Denver's coaching."

She tightened her fingers and gently guided April up the steps. Helpless to argue any further, April had no choice but to go along with her.

The inside of the house was as elegant as the outside. Paneled oak walls gleamed in the hallway, and a rich gold carpet climbed up the sweeping staircase. A skylight poured sunlight onto a huge arrangement of asters and daisies balanced on top of a marble pedestal.

Caroline ushered them into a small sitting room, where

a low coffee table held a tray laden with Danish pastries and thin slices of nut bread. "I'll get the coffee," she said warmly. "Just go ahead and help yourselves."

Josh looked longingly at the Danish and April sighed. "Take a plate, Josh, and don't make a mess," she murmured automatically.

Josh eagerly grabbed a plate and dumped a large Danish on it.

"Are you okay?" Denver asked, sounding wary.

She glanced up and found him watching her with an intense look in his eyes that started her pulse fluttering. "I'm fine," she said quickly. "I got up with a headache this morning, that's all. I'm hoping the fresh air will help clear it."

The lie slipped out easily, covering, she hoped, her initial reluctance to come into the house.

Denver immediately appeared sympathetic. "I can ask Caroline if she's got aspirin—"

"No, I don't want to make a fuss." She made herself smile at him. "She seems very nice."

Denver picked up a plate from the coffee table and handed it to her. "She's a good friend. One of the few people I can trust."

April picked up a slice of the nut bread and put it on her plate. Josh had sat down on the end of a long, orange tweed couch, and she took the space next to him. "How did you meet her?" she asked, as Denver settled himself in a graceful green armchair opposite her.

"Caroline used to rodeo. Barrel racing." He took a bite out of his Danish and swallowed it before adding, "Her husband was a bull rider."

"Oh, so she's married?" She'd tried to keep the relief out of her voice, but there was a glint in Denver's eye that unsettled her.

"Was," he said, and took another bite of the pastry.

April was about to ask where Caroline's husband was now, when Denver added quietly, "Baron died a few years ago. That's when Caroline gave up racing."

"Oh." Remembering the sympathy in the other woman's eyes when she'd mentioned Lane, April felt a little sick. "I'm sorry."

Denver nodded. "It was a shock to all of us. Rodeo lost a good man when they lost Baron Harding. He was the best bull rider I ever saw. Made world champion three years in a row, and best all-around in two of them."

Slowly April lowered the slice of nut bread to her plate. She didn't want to ask, but something compelled her to know. "What happened to him?"

Denver shrugged, though his face had hardened. "Came off a bull. It got him in the belly. He never made it to the hospital."

She stared at her plate, fighting down the fear. She'd always known that riding the bulls was dangerous. She'd heard it a dozen times, whenever rodeo was mentioned on TV or in the papers. She'd heard it that awful night when she'd thought that Denver had been hurt. Bulls sometimes killed their riders. Even the best riders.

But it had never seemed real until now. Now she truly understood. Every time Denver climbed onto a bull, he was risking his life.

"You won't get hurt by a bull, Uncle Denver, will you?"

Josh had put her thoughts into words and she shivered.

Denver sounded confident when he said, "Not on your life, cowboy. I'm meaner than any bull they can put me on, except maybe Balderdash."

"Who's Balderdash?"

"He's the meanest, orneriest critter you ever did set eyes on, and only a handful of cowboys have ever stayed on him for the full eight seconds. There are more men wearing scars from Balderdash than all the other bulls put together."

Josh stared at Denver, wide-eyed with curiosity. "Have you ever ridden him?"

"Never had that pleasure. I'm not sure I care to meet up with that one. I've seen him in action and I know what he can do."

"Did he kill that lady's husband?"

Although Denver's face didn't change, his mouth hardened again. "Nope. That was a different bull. I reckon Baron's luck just ran out on him that day."

"Were you there? Did you see him get killed?"

"Josh!" April's blood ran cold. That was something she hadn't considered. She knew the answer to Josh's question, however, by the haunted look on Denver's face.

He gave her a quick shake of his head. "It's all right." He put his empty plate back on the table and leaned forward, his hands thrust between his knees. "As a matter of fact, Josh, I was there. I was the first one to get to him."

Thoroughly absorbed in the story now, Josh sat with his half-eaten pastry held in midair.

"Was he dead when you got there?"

"Pretty close to it."

"Was he all bloody?"

April decided she'd had enough. "I think you'd better finish that pastry," she said firmly, "if you want to have time for your lesson."

Denver nodded. "Your mom's right. Maybe I shouldn't wait for coffee."

"Don't tell me that now that I've made it," Caroline said cheerfully as she sailed into the room with a tray in her hands.

Denver stood up, beckoning to Josh. "I know April would enjoy a cup," he said, guiding Josh toward the door. "I'll just take my pardner here out to the stables and show him how to saddle up a horse. By the time you're through with your coffee he'll be ready to ride."

"Good idea. Then April and I can get to know each other." Caroline put the tray down on the low table and picked up the coffeepot. "I'm dying to know how an itinerant derelict like you ended up with such a charming, respectable sister-in-law."

Denver grinned. "Just lucky, I guess."

"You and your brother might have looked alike, Cannon, but I'm willing to bet your personalities were as different as winter and summer."

"That," Denver said dryly, "might be the truest words you've ever spoken."

He didn't look at April as he went out, but she got the strong impression that he was directing his words at her.

"Don't let Denver get to you," Caroline said, seemingly absorbed in pouring out the coffee. "His bark is a lot worse than his bite." She glanced up with a little smile. "But then, since he's your late husband's brother, you probably know that."

She didn't, April thought suddenly. It was odd to think that this woman probably knew a lot more about the man Denver had become than she did. The Denver she'd known, the volatile, restless, impulsive young man, no longer existed.

"I haven't seen much of Denver since...over the years. Not until recently, anyway."

Caroline nodded. "That was the impression I got. Denver's many things, but a family man he's not."

"I guess it's tough for a rodeo rider to be a family man."

Caroline handed her a steaming mug of fragrant coffee. "Some of them manage real well, but Denver is just like my husband. Baron could never settle down. If I hadn't been on the circuit with him, I wouldn't have seen him from one year's end to the next. Some men just don't have it in them to stay in one place."

April felt a cold, hard knot forming in her stomach. Was

this woman trying to warn her? If so, she needn't have worried. No one knew better than she did how little Denver cared about family life. He was happy doing what he did best. As he'd told her himself, rodeo was a way of life. His life. There would never be room for her or her son in that life. She knew that more than ever now.

"I suppose Denver told you that Baron died?"

"Yes, he did. I'm so sorry."

Caroline picked up her mug and sat down. "I miss him dreadfully, of course. My biggest regret is that we never had children. Baron didn't think it would be fair to a child, with us traveling on the road all the time."

She chatted on about the rodeo, talking about some of her adventures on the circuit. April was relieved that she didn't mention how her husband had died. She wasn't sure how she would have responded. She felt angry with Denver for risking his life for money, which was what it all amounted to, anyway.

She tried to tell herself that she was angry for Josh's sake. He'd already been deprived of a father who'd gambled with his life and lost. Maybe that was part of it. But deep down she knew that it was fear that made her angry. Fear for Denver. Fear for herself. She wasn't sure she could survive if she lost him, too.

Outside in the stables, Denver took his time showing Josh how to cinch the bridle on Salty, a patient chestnut with a reputation for being placid.

"You have to remember, Josh, that a horse is sensitive. Treat him well and he'll do anything for you." He held Salty's head still and took hold of Josh's hand. "Here, stroke his nose. That will tell him you're his friend."

Josh gingerly touched the tips of his fingers to the horse's nose. "It feels soft," he said, sounding surprised.

Salty lowered his head and nudged Josh's shoulder. Startled, the boy jumped backward, out of reach.

"It's all right," Denver said quietly. "Salty's just show-ing you that he likes you."

Josh appeared unimpressed. "Will he bite me? He has such big teeth."

"He won't bite you," Denver promised. "You have to trust him. Horses are a lot like people. They know who their friends are."

"He looks real big," Josh said doubtfully. "I hope I don't fall off him."

"You won't fall off him. Salty and I will make sure of that."

"What if he jumps up on his hind legs, like the horses you ride?"

Denver laughed. "I can promise you, Salty won't do that. He's been trained to be as gentle as a newborn lamb."

He led the horse out of stables, with Josh trailing behind, and crossed the yard. Pausing at the paddock gate, he smiled at the boy's solemn face. "Can you open the gate for us?"

"Okay." Josh darted to the gate and pulled it open, then latched it carefully behind them.

"Let's start by learning the right way to get up on his back," Denver said, turning Salty around to face the gate.

"You hoisted me up last time," Josh reminded him.

"So I did." Denver grinned. "But I reckon you're big enough to get yourself up there. Don't you?"

"I guess."

"Here." Denver reached down and lifted one of Josh's feet to place it in the stirrup. "Now, all you have to do is grab here with your hands and pull yourself up."

Josh grabbed, grunted and pulled while Salty stood per-fectly still, except for his twitching ears.

Feeling sorry for the boy, Denver grasped his foot and heaved him onto Salty's back. "Well, maybe that'll take some practice. But first I want you to get the feel of controlling the horse.''

He spent the next half hour teaching Josh how to use the reins and his knees and how to make clicking sounds with his tongue to control Salty. He was rewarded when Josh finally walked the horse around the paddock, turning him on command.

When the boy walked the horse up to him and brought him to a halt, Denver clapped him heartily on the shoulder. ''We'll make a regular cowboy of you yet, pardner.''

''When can I learn to go faster?'' Josh asked eagerly.

''When you're ready.'' Denver slipped Josh's feet out of the stirrups. ''But that's enough riding for one day, I reckon.''

''Aw, do I have to get off?'' Josh pouted. ''It's not even lunchtime yet.''

''Maybe not,'' Denver said cheerfully. ''But there's a lot more to riding a horse than just sitting on his back. We have to take him back to the stables and get all this tackle off him, then groom him and make sure he gets fed and watered.''

Josh looked even more disgusted. ''That's boring. I'd much rather ride him.''

Denver laughed. ''You're gonna find out as you grow up that life isn't all fun and games. Some of it's boring and some of it is downright hard work, and that's the way life is.'' He held out his hand. ''Come on, I'll show you how to get down.''

He ended up half lifting him down, and as he set him on his feet, Josh wound his thin arms around his neck. ''Thanks, Uncle Denver,'' he said shyly. ''That was fun.''

The hug took Denver by surprise. He clasped the small, wiry body in his arms for a moment, and felt a rush of tenderness that made his throat thicken. ''You're welcome, pardner,'' he said huskily.

Josh pulled back and waved his arm in the direction of the gate. "Hi, Mom! Did you see me ride?" He rushed over to where April stood by the fence, shading her eyes from the sun.

Denver watched Josh climb up beside her, talking and waving his arm about, while she laughingly listened. The ache in his heart seemed to spread throughout his body at the sight of them together. How much he had missed.

He'd never considered himself lonely. He had his travel partners and the people he met along the way. There were always new people, new towns, new adventures. Yet now, for the first time, he was beginning to realize that maybe it wasn't enough.

In the next breath, he reminded himself that it had to be enough. He just wasn't cut out to be anything else. He was only responsible for himself and no one else. That way, no one could get hurt. Except maybe him. Because right now it hurt to see his brother's wife and son together and know that he had no real part in their lives.

April turned and waved at him, and he packed up his melancholy thoughts and tucked them away. It wouldn't do to get morbid on her. She'd only worry about him. And he didn't need any woman worrying about him. He was doing just fine.

He tried to convince himself of that as he strode over to the gate. "Where's Caroline?" he asked, standing aside to let Josh open the gate.

He thought he saw a flash of wariness in April's eyes when she answered him. "She's got some errands to run. She said to tell you she'd see you later."

He nodded. "Well, I'll take Josh back to the stables and show him how to settle Salty down before you leave."

"All right. Can we give you a lift back to town? Or do you have transportation?"

"I'm going to stick around here for a while. Help Caroline out a little. She's a bit shorthanded right now."

"I see."

He wasn't sure he cared for the way she said that. Maybe he should set her straight about Caroline, he thought. But not right now. He had chores to do, and Josh had to learn there was a price to pay for fun. "You're welcome to come back to the stables with us if you want."

She shook her head. "Thanks, but I think I'll go back to the car and wait. How long will you be?"

"No more'n twenty minutes or so, I reckon."

She glanced at Josh, then back at him. "I guess I'll see you later, then." She wandered off, looking a little lost, and he almost chased after her. He couldn't help feeling she was upset with him for some reason, and he wanted to know why. But Josh was urging Salty toward the stables, and he shrugged off his doubts. Whatever it was, it could wait.

April sat in the car with the windows down, enjoying the sounds of nature drifting in on the summer breeze, until Josh's voice, chattering in the distance, alerted her that her son's lesson was over. She sat up, peering through the windshield to where Josh jogged along at Denver's side. Her heart turned over. They were so much alike in looks.

In temperament, too, she reluctantly admitted. Josh showed signs of being every bit as independent and restless as his true father, and just as stubborn. She only hoped the riding lessons wouldn't lead to Josh's eventually following in Denver's footsteps. And his grandfather's, for that matter. She wanted more for her son than a life in the rodeo.

"We fed Salty," Josh said, as soon as he was within hearing, "and brushed and combed him. Uncle Denver says I can ride him again tomorrow."

"If that's okay with you." Denver tipped his hat back to look down at her.

"I guess so." She opened the door for Josh to climb in the back. "You'd better let me know how much the lessons are."

Denver shook his head. "My treat. Caroline and I worked it out. I'll give her a hand around here in exchange for the lessons."

"How nice of her," April murmured, unable to keep the irony out of her voice.

Denver frowned. "April, about Caroline—"

"Well, I'm sure you must be in a hurry to get back to work, so don't let me detain you." She switched on the engine and slipped the gear lever into reverse. "I'll bring Josh back tomorrow. Same time?"

He put his hand on the window frame, and she waited, cursing herself for her immature reaction. "April," Denver said quietly, "I think we need to talk. I'll drive over tonight, after supper."

Trying to hide her sudden apprehension, she managed to smile up at him. "Why don't you come to dinner. I owe you for the lessons, and Josh would love to see you."

"Yeah," Josh said, bouncing in his seat. "I can show you my video games. I used to play them with Dad, but now I can play them with you."

Denver nodded, his eyes crinkling at the edges. "Sounds like fun," he said easily. "What time?"

"Six-thirty? I'll throw something on the barbecue."

"Why don't I bring some steaks, then."

Now her smile was genuine. "If you like. I'll provide the rest."

"It's a deal." He bent low to look across her at Josh. "So long, cowboy. See you tonight."

"All right!"

Josh's delight chased away the last of April's sour mood.

Her spirits lifted as she drove back to the house, her mind already working out the menu. Caesar salad, fresh fruit, garlic bread, baked potatoes…the day hadn't been so bad after all.

She refused to acknowledge the persistent knot of anxiety. Denver could want to talk about many things. It didn't mean he was having suspicions about Josh. She just had to stop worrying about that. She'd know if it was as serious as that. Wouldn't she?

When Josh opened the door to Denver, his face broke into a huge grin. Denver ruffled his hair as he stepped inside, resisting the impulse to give the boy a hug. He wasn't used to displaying affection, and Josh's embrace that morning had made him feel vulnerable.

"Mom's outside, lighting the barbecue," Josh informed him.

Denver took off his hat and laid it on the back of the armchair. "I guess I'd better get these steaks marinated then," he told Josh. "You want to grab a plate for me?"

"Sure." Josh darted into the kitchen, yelling, "Mom! Uncle Denver's here!"

Denver felt a strange sense of anticipation as he waited for her to come through the door. Something had changed between them. It was subtle, but it was there. Ever since he'd kissed her. They were on different ground than they'd been before, and he wasn't sure he liked it.

He couldn't relax with her the way he used to—he was on guard now, afraid of saying something that might be taken the wrong way. He had the feeling that April was being careful, too…they were stalking around each other like two hungry wolves, each waiting for the other to strike.

He could feel the tension in him, creeping up his spine, tingling in the back of his neck, pulsing at his temple. His lungs ached, as if he were coming down with something; his breathing was shallow, his throat dry.

He heard the back door open, Josh's voice telling her to hurry up, and his palms felt damp. He felt an almost irresistible urge to turn tail and leave, before the haunting sensations got the better of him.

He heard her light footsteps cross the kitchen floor, then saw her pause in the doorway. The sunlight played across her hair, turning it to gold. She wore shorts and a sleeveless denim shirt, and for a moment she looked exactly like the young woman of a decade ago. The woman who had so easily fired his blood and inflamed his senses.

He could feel the heat coursing through his veins at the memory of her smooth, pale body spread out beneath him on his bed. He closed his eyes for a brief moment, willing the vision out of his mind.

"Are you all right?"

Her soft voice, low and anxious, jerked him out of his stupor. He opened his eyes and managed a grin. "Sure. Where do you want me to put these steaks?"

"Here." She held out a slim, tanned hand. "I'll put them in marinade."

"I can do that if you show me where it is."

"In the fridge. I'll get it for you."

She disappeared and he took a long, slow breath. *Get control,* he told himself, before following her into the kitchen.

"I have the plate," Josh announced, dropping it on the table with a thud that made April wince. "You want to go see my video games?"

"Maybe I'd better help your mom first." Denver undid the wrapping on the steaks and laid them on the plate.

"I'll do that." April opened the fridge door and took out a bottle of marinade. "You go with Josh. I'll give you a shout when it's time to put the steaks on."

"Right." He felt a sense of relief as he followed Josh to his room. His unexpected reaction to April had shaken him, and he needed time to get himself together. He hadn't realized until now how much he wanted her. It was as if the past ten years had never been. He wanted her as much as, if not more than, that night all those years ago when the need had been impossible to ignore.

Even when he'd kissed her the other night, he hadn't felt this terrible yearning that now threatened to tear him apart. It was as if the craving had been buried all these years and was only now beginning to surface once more.

He had underestimated his hunger for her. There had never been anyone who had tormented his mind and his body the way she could. He should have remembered that, because now he would have to fight it with all his strength. And he wasn't at all sure that he had that much willpower.

Chapter 7

"That was the best steak I ever had." Josh dropped his fork on the plate with a clatter.

April smiled. "I agree. Your uncle knows his way around a barbecue, that's for sure."

Denver shrugged with false modesty. "We rodeo men can pick out a good piece of beef."

"That was even better than Dad used to make." Josh beamed at his uncle. "Wasn't it, Mom?"

She felt it again...that odd sense of being disloyal. "Well, Dad was a pretty good cook, too."

"He sure was," Denver said heartily. "He taught me how to cook."

Josh's eyes widened. "He did?"

"You bet he did." He gave April a wink that told her he'd fudged the truth.

She smiled back at him, grateful for his defense of his brother. "Would you like another beer?"

"Only if you'll join me."

"Well, I have to do the dishes, and Josh should get to bed. He has to be up early in the morning for his next lesson."

"Aw, Mom, do I have to?" Josh looked at Denver for help. "I'm not a bit tired."

"Maybe you're not tonight, cowboy, but I reckon you will be in the morning if you don't get a full night's shut-eye." Denver glanced at his watch. "It's almost my bed-time, too. Us cowboys need lots of sleep if we're going to be bright eyed and bushy tailed in the morning."

"I guess so." Josh looked pleadingly at his mother. "Can I play just one more game with Uncle Denver?"

April sighed. "Half an hour, no longer." She glanced at Denver. His gaze made her pulse leap with foreboding as she added, "That's if you don't mind."

"My pleasure, ma'am." He pushed his chair back and stood. "Can I help with the dishes?"

"Thanks, but I'll take care of them while you and Josh are playing."

"Share that beer with me when I get back?"

She nodded. "We can sit on the back porch. It'll be cooler out there."

Something flickered in his eyes, and again she felt the cold twinge of anxiety. She looked down at Josh, who was wriggling off his chair. "Half an hour, remember? I'll be in to say good-night."

"Okay." Josh darted over to the door. "Come on, Uncle Denver, we don't have that much time."

Denver gave her a resigned shrug. "I haven't beaten him at anything yet."

She managed a somewhat stilted laugh. "Don't feel bad. Neither could Lane."

"That makes me feel better." He ambled across the room after Josh and disappeared into the hallway.

She cleared the dishes quickly, then rinsed them under

the faucet before stacking them in the dishwasher. She'd enjoyed the evening far more than she'd expected. Denver had been entertaining at dinner, making them laugh with stories of his adventures on the road.

Josh had barely taken his eyes off his uncle throughout the entire meal. He'd interrupted Denver now and again with an eager question or comment, while she'd sat silent for the most part, enjoying the camaraderie between the two.

She'd managed to forget, for a little while, her fears. It was so wonderful to see Josh relaxed and happy, able to talk about his father without the agony that had been so evident just a few short weeks ago.

She refused to acknowledge the nagging reminder that sooner or later the piper would have to be paid. Right now her son was enjoying life again, and that was all that mattered. She could only hope that whatever Denver wanted to talk about, it wouldn't shatter this pleasant evening and spoil the memories.

"You're looking mighty solemn," Denver said a while later, as she finished wiping down the counter.

She jumped, unable to believe she hadn't heard him come in. For a man his size, he was incredibly light on his feet. "Josh beat you again?"

She smiled when he pulled a face. "Twice. But I'm beginning to get the hang of it. I have a return match scheduled for tomorrow night. If that's okay with you."

She dried her hands on a dish towel and turned to face him. "Don't let Josh monopolize your time," she said evenly. "He can be very demanding if he thinks he can have his way."

She felt the coolness in the pause that followed and immediately ached with regret.

"Are you telling me politely I've overstayed my welcome?"

How defensive they both were, she thought ruefully. If only they could go back to the days when Lane was alive, before things got so complicated. "Of course not." She looked directly into his steel-blue eyes. "I just don't want Josh to run you ragged, that's all."

He stared at her for a long time, while she willed herself to keep the smile on her face. Then, apparently satisfied, he nodded. "Don't worry, I'll see that he doesn't. I want to give him as much time as possible before I have to take off again."

There it was…the warning. She turned away, pretending to inspect her clean counter for stray crumbs. "That's real nice of you, Denver. I know Josh appreciates it as much as I do." It was on the tip of her tongue to ask him if he'd made it clear to Josh this visit was only temporary, but this didn't seem the right time. Maybe that was something she should do herself.

"He's waiting for you to say good-night," Denver said, opening the fridge door. "I'll pour the beers while you're gone."

"Thanks."

She hurried down the hallway to Josh's room, where he lay on his bed, shooting imaginary aliens with his ray gun. She tucked him in and kissed him good-night, and was about to leave when he said sleepily, "Does Uncle Denver really like me?"

She paused, wondering what he was leading up to. "Of course he does. What made you ask?"

Josh shrugged. "I dunno. He didn't give me a good-night hug like Dad used to."

"Oh, honey." April went back to the bed and sat down. "Your uncle isn't used to hugging people. It doesn't mean he doesn't love you."

"Why doesn't he like hugging?"

She refused to let her mind go back to the other night.

"I'm sure he does like hugging. Maybe he's not sure that you'd want him to hug you. After all, you told him you were almost grown up."

Josh opened his eyes to look at her, and something curled inside her. She'd seen that wounded look so often in Denver's eyes. "I don't want to be grown up," he whispered. "Not if I can't have hugs."

"I'll let him know that," April promised gently. "Now can I have a hug?"

She closed her eyes as his thin arms enveloped her in a warm, fragrant embrace. She loved this child of hers more than life itself, she thought. If she couldn't have Denver, she could at least have his son. It would have to be enough.

Denver had already settled himself on the porch when she returned to the kitchen. She felt nervous now, and tried to calm the fluttering feeling in her stomach. It seemed inevitable that Denver would seize this opportunity to tell her what was on his mind.

She wasn't at all sure she wanted to be alone with him again, yet she couldn't ignore the ripple of excitement that stirred her senses as she stepped out onto the darkened porch.

His face was in shadow, but his voice sounded reassuringly casual when he said, "Your beer's here on the table."

"Thank you." She sat down next to him, trying to still the rapid beating of her heart. The wind had freshened, and sighed through the branches of the tall firs bordering her yard. The breeze felt deliciously cool on her warm face, and she pulled in a deep breath, struggling to calm her jittery nerves.

Denver sat silently by her side, and she made the most of the respite to relax her tense nerves. The night fragrances of shrubs she'd never learned the name of permeated the air. Crickets chirped eagerly in the long grass down by the creek, joined in chorus by the bullfrogs.

"It's a lovely night," she said finally. She was anxious now to break the silence between them and get to whatever it was Denver wanted to say.

"It sure is." He heaved a long sigh. "Reminds me of when I was a boy. I used to sleep out in a tent in the backyard on nights like this. Stayed awake for hours just listening to all the sounds going on around me."

"It's amazing how noisy the sounds of the night can be."

"April..." He paused, as if pondering how to phrase his next words.

She felt her nerves tighten again and knew she wasn't ready to discuss anything emotional just yet. "Josh says he wants you to hug him," she blurted out.

In the surprised silence that followed, she cursed herself for not phrasing Josh's request better. She'd said the first thing in her head to ward off whatever it was he was going to say.

"Okay," Denver said carefully, just when she was about to apologize. "I'll remember that."

"I guess he needs to know you really like him," she said lamely, wondering what Denver must be thinking.

"Of course I like him. I wouldn't be spending this much time with him if I didn't."

She kept her gaze on the dark branches of the firs. "Sometimes a boy needs a little more reassurance."

"You're right. I guess I just didn't want to pressure the kid, that's all."

She nodded, searching for something else to say. "He cares for you a great deal, you know."

"I care about him, too. He's a good kid. Reminds me of myself when I was that age."

Aware that they were approaching dangerous ground, she changed the subject again. "What made you choose bulls to ride, instead of horses? You always loved horses when you were young.''

He was silent for so long she wondered if the question had upset him. Then he told her quietly, "Like I said, it's the challenge. The bull isn't like a horse. It's bigger and it's meaner, and it's out to get you.''

"And that's what it's all about?'' She'd heard the irony in her own voice, but when he answered, there was no echoing resentment in his.

"It's being able to forget about the fear. It's being able to forget about the crowd watching you and how much money you're gonna make. It's knowing how to relax, how to use your skills to control the animal. When the adrenaline gets going, that's when you know you're really alive.''

She shivered, trying not to think of Caroline's husband lying in the dirt.

"Now, you mind if I ask you something?''

She couldn't put it off any longer, she thought, and braced herself.

"Did Caroline say anything to upset you this morning?''

Relieved and a little surprised to know that was all that was on his mind, she said lightly, "Caroline? Of course not. I liked her.''

He didn't answer right away and she stole a look at him. She could see his rugged profile outlined against the night sky—the jutting nose and stubborn chin. He looked pensive, as if he were turning something over in his mind.

"What made you ask that?''

"I dunno. Something about the way you looked when you left, I guess.''

Remembering her resentment, she felt rather foolish now. "I told you,'' she lied, "I had a headache.''

"Better now?''

"Yes, thanks.'' She covered her embarrassment by picking up her glass and taking a drink of the refreshing liquid.

"I've known Caroline a long time," Denver said quietly. "Before she married Baron."

Again she wondered if there'd been anything between the two of them, then reminded herself for the hundredth time that it was none of her business.

"I was at their wedding," Denver went on, "and I was there the day Baron died."

She swallowed, her throat tight. "Yes, I know."

"I knelt beside him in the dirt."

She heard the harsh edge in his voice and knew how difficult it was for him to talk about it. "Denver—"

"Baron knew he was dying," he said, deliberately ignoring her attempt to halt what had to be painful for him. "He asked me with his last breath to watch out for Caroline. I gave him my word."

"I see." She wasn't quite sure what he was trying to tell her. She wasn't sure she wanted to know.

"That's why I offer to help her out whenever I have a few days to spare. Her spread may be small compared with the big ranches out East, but it's still a lot of work."

"I'm sure it is."

"Don't get me wrong. Caroline's a strong lady and runs that ranch with a firm hand. She's made a success of the place, and it hasn't been easy. She could use an extra hand now and again."

"Well, I know she must appreciate it."

"She's a real attractive woman," Denver continued, as if she hadn't spoken. "She's got an awful lot to offer a man. One day I reckon someone's gonna come along and realize what a great woman she is. The day that happens, I figure my part in it will be done. Until then, I'm kind of obligated to watch out for her."

April put the beer down with an unsteady hand. Was he talking about Caroline, or was this his way of letting her know that he felt obligated toward herself and Josh? That he was just watching out for both them for Lane's sake until 'the right man' came along?

"I hope she finds someone soon," she said carefully. "She must be very lonely."

"I reckon most people would feel lonely after they lost their partner."

Her mouth twisted wryly. "It's the loneliest feeling in the world. But I have Josh. Caroline doesn't have children to fill the emptiness."

"Yeah, that's sad. Maybe it's just as well, though. It's real tough on kids to lose their father."

"How well I know," April murmured.

"I guess I shouldn't be bringing all this up," Denver said, reaching for his beer. "I know it must still hurt a lot."

"I miss Lane," April said warily. "I know Josh does— dreadfully. But time really does help. There are days that go by now when I don't even think about it." She glanced at him, needing the reassurance of his approval. "Does that sound heartless?"

He gave her a surprised look. "Heartless? No, I don't think so. Lane wouldn't want you two grieving over him forever. I know he'd want you to get on with your lives." He drew a swig of beer and set down the mug. "What I still don't understand is why he took off in a small plane in the middle of a snowstorm. Didn't he know about the blizzard in the mountains?"

April nodded, the chill creeping over her again as she remembered. "He knew. I begged him not to go. He wouldn't listen to me."

"Must have been something real important for him to take off on a night like that."

She sighed and leaned back in her chair. She had told no one what had happened that night. She had tried so hard to forget, yet it kept coming back to haunt her. Maybe if she told Denver, she thought wearily, she could finally put it to rest.

"He left because we'd been fighting," she said, trying to keep the bitterness out of her voice. "He left because he didn't want to spend the night in the house with me."

The silence between them seemed to grow heavier, while the crickets and bullfrogs continued their harmony in sublime indifference.

"I didn't know you were having problems," Denver said gruffly, breaking the tension at last. "You two always seemed so happy together."

She shrugged, unwilling now to discuss it with him. "All married people have problems at some time in their marriage."

"Well, that's something I wouldn't know about." He didn't add, *Thank heavens,* but he might as well have done.

"I can't help feeling—" She stopped, unable to continue. His face was turned away from her. Drawing back into the shadows, she struggled to regain her composure.

"Can't help feeling what?"

When she didn't answer he turned his head to look at her. "April?"

Valiantly she fought to control her voice. "I blame myself for that night," she whispered brokenly. "If we hadn't been fighting, if I hadn't—"

"Damn it, April, you know better than that." He reached for her and it seemed the most natural thing in the world for her to go into his arms.

She was tired of resisting, she thought suddenly. She was tired of pretending she didn't care. Tired of standing on guard, terrified he'd know how she really felt about him. If only she could tell him about Josh, trust him to understand why she had kept the fact that he was the boy's father from him.

She leaned her head against his shoulder, drawing

strength from the masculine warmth of his body. It was enough right now to take comfort from him. Enough just to rest in his arms.

"April." He began stroking her hair, in a tender rhythm that soothed her. "Lane never let anyone tell him what to do, not even when we were kids. He was the man of the family after our father left, and he was always in charge. He made all the decisions. I reckon things didn't change when he got married. It was his decision to fly that night, not yours. He was an experienced pilot and should have known better. If anyone is to blame, it's my brother, for taking a risk with his life when he had so much to lose."

April stirred, dashing away the tears from her cheeks. "I think Josh will always blame me for what happened. He heard us arguing that night. I didn't realize he'd overheard until much later. By then it was too late to get through to him."

"He's young. In time he'll understand."

"I hope so." She sat up, embarrassed by her display of emotion. "Thank you for understanding."

It was too dark to see the expression in his eyes. She could hear the tension in his voice, however, when he said brusquely, "I guess I'd better get going."

She nodded and rose from her chair. A feeling of anti-climax swept over her as she walked back into the kitchen. She didn't know what she'd envisioned would happen. She had no right to feel disappointed, as if her expectations had been rudely shattered.

"Which hotel are you staying in?" she asked, as Denver picked up his hat and jammed it on his head.

"I'm not staying in a hotel. I'm bunking out at the Second Chance for the next few days."

"Oh." She'd meant it to come out casually, but the word dropped like lead off her tongue.

He looked at her, his gaze falling to her mouth. "You going to be okay?"

She nodded. The ache was back, and the uneven thumping of her heart. "I'm fine. I'll see you tomorrow."

His gaze still lingered on her face, almost as if he were trying to commit it to memory. "Sure," he said briefly. "Tomorrow."

She closed the door, then listened for the sounds of the van to fade into the night, before she walked back into the living room.

Signs of his presence were everywhere—the rumpled cushion on the couch, the empty beer cans on the kitchen counter, the chairs out of place on the porch. She could still feel the rough warmth of his shirt against her cheek, the strong fingers that could control a raging bull, yet stroke her hair with the gentleness of a baby's touch.

She felt like weeping again, and put it down to the long day. It wasn't like her to be so emotional. She had to be tired.

Yet she couldn't sleep, her broken dreams disturbed by a husky voice whispering her name, roughened fingers on her skin. She awoke with a start in the early hours of the morning and lay there, letting her thoughts drift until it was time to get up.

She would not think about Denver in the same house with Caroline, she told herself firmly. What he did with his private life was none of her business.

But as she stared at her pale image in the bathroom mirror, she knew that she'd made it her business. Because she was in love with Denver Briggs. She always had been and she always would be. And it was just as hopeless a love now as it had ever been.

Denver left the house early that morning, telling Caroline he wanted to saddle up Salty before Josh got there. What he really wanted was to be out in the fresh air, where his mind could flow freely and rid itself of the thoughts that had tormented him all night.

He couldn't mistake the signs any longer, he told himself, as he led the chestnut out into the pale morning sun. The longer he stayed around April, the deeper he was heading into trouble.

He didn't know if what he was reading in her eyes was for real, or if it was just wishful thinking on his part. He knew only that if he stayed around her much longer, he would not be able to control the hunger raging inside him.

He had promised he wouldn't touch her again. He had to keep that promise. The easiest way to do that was to stay away from her. The best thing he could do for all of them was to go back to the circuit, where he belonged. That way there was no chance he'd mess up their lives. That way he'd leave the field clear for the right man to come along.

He led Salty into the paddock and left him to graze, while he sat on the fence and tried to sort out the muddled mess inside his mind. Every instinct warned him to go now, before he got in any deeper and made it tougher to leave.

He would be doing both Josh and April a favor, he told himself. Sometimes you had to be tough on people for their own good.

He was still trying to convince himself when he saw the blue T-bird creeping up the driveway a few minutes later. His stomach felt as if he'd eaten a plate of rocks for breakfast instead of the pancakes Caroline had cooked for him.

He watched April and Josh climb out of the car, and at the sight of them his good intentions vanished in the wind. Josh spotted him perched on the fence and rushed over, waving his arm over his head. April followed more slowly, her bright-yellow shirt making a patch of sunshine against the backdrop of dark-green trees.

"Hi," Josh said breathlessly, as he reached him. "Are we late?"

Denver smiled down at him. "Nope. I'm early." He glanced up as April walked over. "Good morning, sunshine."

She laughed. "Good morning yourself."

Her eyes looked haunted and didn't reflect the smile on her face. He turned away, conscious of a sharp, intense need that almost took his breath away.

"Can I ride him now?" Josh asked, climbing up onto the fence beside him.

"Sure. We're gonna try a little trotting today."

"Is he ready for that?" April asked, sounding alarmed.

"Aw, Mom." Josh leaned over and opened the gate. "Stop worrying."

"He'll be fine." Denver jumped down and lifted the boy to the ground. "I won't let him go any faster than he can safely manage."

He let go of his chaotic thoughts and concentrated on teaching Josh how to nudge Salty into a slow trot. Within half an hour Josh showed every sign of handling the horse all by himself, and Denver felt a deep sense of satisfaction. The boy was a natural.

"I reckon you're all set to go for a short trip around the lake with me tomorrow," he announced, as Josh neatly brought Salty to a halt in front of him.

"Cool!" Josh looked over at his mom, who had perched on top of the gate to watch the lesson.

Interpreting the glance, Denver patted him on the back. "Don't worry, your mom will let you."

"I hope so." Josh chewed his lip. "She doesn't let me do much by myself since Dad died."

Denver felt a twinge of sympathy. "She's just worried that something could happen to you, too," he said, smoothing his hand down Salty's silky neck. "After all, you're all she's got now."

Josh looked at him in surprise. "She's got you, too."

Denver gave him a wry smile. "Well, it's not quite the same now, is it?"

"Why not?" Josh's lower lip jutted just a little. "You could come live with us and be like my dad."

Denver's throat tightened. "I don't think that's possible," he said slowly.

"Why not?" Josh's voice rose. "Why don't you want to live with us? Don't you like us?"

Denver glanced over at April, but she was watching one of Caroline's cats, which sat on the fence a few yards away, washing its face with a white, furry paw.

"Of course I like you, cowboy," Denver said huskily. "You and your mom are all the family I've got, too. But I'm a rodeo man, and rodeo men like me don't live in houses. We live in campers and travel all over the West, following the circuit. You know that."

Josh looked down at the reins in his hands. "You don't have to be a rodeo man," he mumbled. "Why can't you be an executive like my dad?"

"Because me and your dad are different kind of people, that's why. Come on now, cowboy, let me see you climb off that horse like a real wrangler."

To his relief, the boy obeyed, swinging his leg unerringly over Salty's back as if he'd been doing it all his life.

"Can I help groom him again?" Josh asked, as he trailed along at Denver's side to where his mom still sat on the gate.

Denver grinned. "I thought you figured that was boring."

Josh lifted his shoulders. "I like being with Salty. He's a neat horse. I wish he was mine and I could take him home."

"I think you might have a small problem fitting him into your bed."

That brought a smile to the boy's face.

April climbed down from the fence and greeted Josh with a hug. "I'm so proud of you. You ride just like a real cowboy."

Josh looked up at her, his eagerness glowing in his face. "Did you see me turn him into the corner? Uncle Denver says I can ride with him around the lake tomorrow."

Denver waited for April to express some concern at this announcement, but she surprised him by saying, if a little too heartily, "That's wonderful. That should be really exciting."

She turned to Denver for confirmation, and he said quietly, "He'll be fine. It's a real easy ride. I don't suppose I can talk you into coming with us."

She shook her head. "I don't ride. Besides, this is between you and Josh. You know, a man-to-man thing."

He knew it wasn't easy for her. It gave him a warmth he couldn't describe to know that she trusted him with her son. "I'll take good care of him," he promised.

"I'm sure you will."

He looked deep into her eyes and could feel it once more—that almost tangible vibration between them that seemed to hum with an energy and vitality too strong to ignore. His body tingled with it, as if touched by a thousand tiny pinpricks of electrical current.

He couldn't seem to tear his gaze away from her face, as he searched for a sign that she felt it, too. Part of him wanted to see it there, while another, more rational, part of him hoped she would never know how she affected him.

"Are you gonna come and play games with me again tonight?" Josh demanded.

Denver blinked, the moment splintered into tiny fragments of lost sensation. "Sure I am. But first I'm gonna take you and your mom out for spaghetti. A man needs to eat before he battles supersized aliens and man-eating dragons.''

"All right!" Josh looked up at April, who still wore a slightly bemused expression, as if she'd just woken up from a deep sleep.

Something curled in Denver's belly as he watched her.

"Can we go, Mom?"

She nodded and smiled down at her son. "Spaghetti sounds real good to me.''

"Cool!" Josh grabbed the horse's bridle. "I have to groom Salty now," he said, trying to open the gate with the other hand.

Denver reached over him and pushed it open. April stood back to let them by, and he paused at her side. "Pick you up around six?''

"We'll be ready.''

Her glance slid off him in that awkward, teasing way that always made him want to grab her chin and kiss her until she couldn't breathe anymore.

He was in deep trouble, he told himself, as he walked the horse back to the stables with Josh chatting at his side. The worst of it was, he would have to deal with it at least for a few more days.

He didn't want to think beyond that.

It seemed to April as if the week flew by, and by the end of it Josh was showing all the signs of becoming a proficient horseman. Even April could see the difference in him—the confident way he held himself, the relaxed grip on the reins and, above all, the joy in his face at the end of the day.

Denver had dinner with them every night, much to Josh's obvious delight and April's discomfort. She couldn't seem to look at him anymore without feeling as if she'd lost control of her hands and feet.

She dropped things and tripped over things, forgot what she wanted to say midsentence and more than once found herself standing helplessly in a room, trying to remember why she'd gone in there. It was almost a relief when Denver announced at dinner one night that he would be joining up with his travel companions for a rodeo in Washington that weekend. Jed and Cord had stayed with the camper in Idaho, catching up on their rides.

Josh looked so stricken to hear this that she felt compelled to say, "We could drive you there if you like. It's only a couple of hours away."

Josh still looked devastated. "What about my lessons?"

"I guess they'll have to wait for a while." Denver glanced across the table at April. "You sure you don't mind driving me? I could get a bus out there. It drops me real close to the rodeo grounds."

"We'd enjoy it, wouldn't we, Josh? Maybe we could even stay and see Uncle Denver ride."

Josh gazed at his plate and mumbled, "Okay."

"I have to go back to the rodeo, Josh," Denver said, reaching out to pat his shoulder. "But I'll be back real soon. Caroline says you can see Salty any time you want."

In answer, Josh pushed his chair back and rushed from the room.

"Maybe I should go after him," Denver said, getting to his feet.

"I think it would be better to leave him alone." April got up and began gathering the empty plates. "He has to face this disappointment sooner or later. He might as well get over it now."

"Maybe there's something that I can say—"

Her anger rose swiftly, fueled by her own frustration.

"There's nothing you can say, Denver. He's going to miss you—it's as simple as that."

Denver's expression hardened. "I explained to him at the beginning that I was going to be around only for a week or so."

April nodded, her lips compressed. "Well, sometimes small boys believe only what they want to believe."

She picked up the plates and carried them into the kitchen. As always, she didn't hear Denver until he spoke behind her.

"I'm sorry, April. I just wanted to help the boy, that's all."

She bit her lip, aware that was true. Denver had been more than generous with his time, and he had never promised her anything. She had known this time would come and she had to accept it. Denver would never change.

"I understand, and you have helped him. Josh has enjoyed this week so much." She placed the last plate in the dishwasher, added soap before closing it and turned it on. "We owe you a lot. Josh is a different child again, thanks to you." She made herself turn around and look at him. "Thank you, Denver, for caring about my son. It means a lot to me."

He stood inches away from her, his eyes troubled and wary. "He'll be all right?"

She nodded. "As long as he knows you haven't abandoned him. As long as you try to keep in touch as much as possible. Come and see us once in a while."

"You know I will. Every chance I get."

She noticed a tiny muscle twitch at the corner of his mouth. That small sign of vulnerability melted all her resentment. She stared up at him, thinking only of how much she wanted him to kiss her.

"I...guess I'd better go," he said, his voice dropping to a husky whisper.

She nodded, unable to drag her gaze away from his face.

He made no effort to move. It was as if the walls of the tiny kitchen faded away, leaving only a soft, misty cloud that closed out the outside world. She could hear the dishwasher busily swishing water over the dishes, yet it was part of that other world, where she and Denver no longer belonged.

"April."

Her name hovered on his lips, and something warm and fuzzy curled inside her. She wanted to touch him—had to touch him. Her hand seemed to drift up on its own to graze his face.

He flinched when she touched his coarse jaw, then he covered her hand with his, holding her palm flat against his cheek. Very slowly, he drew her fingers over to his mouth and pressed a gentle kiss into her palm.

She felt the effect of the sensuous pressure shimmy down her arm and settle deep in her belly. Voices in her head clamored to be heard—warning voices that told her she would regret this moment. She refused to listen, helpless to resist the demands of her yearning body.

He drew her slowly toward him, and she went without resistance, lifting her chin as his arms folded around her. "Damn you, April," he muttered thickly, then his mouth was hard on hers.

She gave herself up to it, the hot sensations pulsing through her veins. Eagerly she kissed him back, winding her arms around his neck to bring herself closer to him. Thrills chased through her as she felt the hard response of his body, felt his hands on her breasts, his mouth breathing fire along her neck and throat.

The world spun out of sight, out of hearing, out of mind. She tugged at the buttons on his shirt and shivered violently when he slid his hands under her sweater to find the clasp of her bra.

Somewhere outside a door snapped shut, jerking her rudely back into the real world. Instantly his hands fell away from her and she stepped back, tugging her sweater down over her jeans.

Her knees literally shook as she crossed the floor, leaving Denver to rebutton his shirt. Josh was just coming out of the bathroom when she reached the hallway.

"Are you going to say good-night to Uncle Denver, honey?" she asked, a little breathlessly. "He's just leaving."

"Okay." Josh's voice sounded odd, and he rushed out into the living room, where Denver waited, his hat in his hand.

April couldn't look at him but kept her gaze on her son as he went over to his uncle.

Denver jammed on his hat, then bent his knees and put his arms around the small boy. "I'll see you in the morning," he said, his voice sounding even deeper than usual.

"Okay." Josh gave him a brilliant smile.

"We'll take Salty for a long ride, enough to last you both until I get back and we can do it again, all right?"

Josh nodded.

"Okay, cowboy. You get a good night's sleep. I need you fresh in the morning."

April's throat tightened as her son wound his arms around Denver's neck. "I love you, Uncle Denver."

Denver briefly closed his eyes. "I love you, too, cowboy," he said softly. He dropped his arms and straightened, reaching immediately for the door handle. "'Night, April."

He didn't look at her as he left, and she closed the door behind him. Treacherous tears stung her eyes, and she dashed them away. Josh wasn't the only one going to miss him, she thought miserably. Somehow she would have to come to terms with her feelings. Somehow she would have to live with the fact that she could never have the only man she'd ever really loved. *Somehow.*

Chapter 8

Denver seemed ill at ease the next day when April dropped Josh off for his riding lesson. Although he greeted them both with his customary cheerfulness, April could sense an undercurrent of wariness that told her, more than any words could convey, how much he regretted what had passed between them the night before.

If he was concerned that she might want to talk about it, she thought irritably, he needn't be. She had no intention of bringing it up, or of allowing him that close to her again. If what had happened last night had taught her anything, it was that she couldn't trust her own willpower. Neither, it seemed, could she trust Denver not to take advantage of her weakness.

Not that she could blame him. She'd more or less made it pretty clear she'd wanted him to kiss her. If he'd followed up on that, she had only herself to blame. Which was why she couldn't allow herself to be alone with him again.

That night she suggested they go out to eat, and made

sure it was too late for him to come in when they returned to the house.

Josh was disappointed that he didn't get to play any video games, but, as she told herself, Josh would have to learn to deal with disappointment in his life. Especially where Denver was concerned.

"Will we get front-row seats again?" Josh asked the next day, as Denver led him and April across the parking lot to the arena.

"Best in the house." Denver grinned down at his nephew. "You're gonna have a grandstand view of the whole thing. Right next to the chutes."

Josh accepted this news with his usual boisterous whoop of delight. April felt a pang of apprehension. He was bound to feel the sting of saying goodbye to his uncle. She hoped he'd recovered enough from his father's death to deal with it.

Jed and Cord were waiting for Denver by the chutes. They both greeted April, though she had the disturbing impression that neither man approved of her being there.

Jed gave Josh a friendly slap on the back, while Cord merely nodded at him, his face masked in the usual deadpan expression.

"How'd the riding lessons go?" Jed asked, then listened patiently while Josh recited every detail of his lessons on Salty.

When he finally paused for breath, Jed nudged Cord in the ribs. "I reckon we'll have to keep an eye on this young buckaroo, or he'll be stealing that gold buckle right from under our noses."

"Uncle Denver says he's going to win the all-around championship this year," Josh announced with an air of supreme confidence.

"Did he, now?" Jed winked at Cord. "I wonder what gives him a fool idea like that."

"Reckon he figures on beating you and me to that buckle," Cord drawled. "He's gonna have to go some, after all the rides he's missed."

"I haven't missed that many," Denver said easily. "I reckon I can catch you both up in a couple of weeks."

Jed grinned. "Wouldn't like to bet on it, pardner, would you?"

"He *is* going to win the buckle," Josh said, rushing to Denver's defense. "He's going to beat both of you, and everyone else in the rodeo. You'll see."

Cord's black eyes gleamed as he settled his gaze on Josh's eager face. "Is he now? Well, I reckon with that kind of support he can't lose now, can he?"

A burst of raucous laughter from a group of wranglers nearby almost drowned out Josh's next words. Almost, but not quite. "And," Josh said defiantly, "he's going to be my new dad, so there."

April uttered a startled gasp. "Josh! That's not true."

"Yes, it is," Josh insisted in his young, clear voice. "I saw you kissing him so I know he's going to be my dad."

It seemed as if everyone in the arena had chosen that moment to be quiet. April could feel her face flame. She saw Jed and Cord exchange meaningful glances, while Denver looked at Josh as if he couldn't believe what he'd heard.

"Well," Jed said, finally breaking the silence, "seems you did a little more than give riding lessons, Cannon. No wonder you took off for so long."

Denver cleared his throat. "Drop it, J.C."

"Okay, okay." Jed held up his hands. "You don't have to be so all-fired touchy about it. You should have told us you and April—"

Denver took a threatening step toward his friend, as April watched in alarm. "I'm warning you...."

Cord shook his head and stepped in between the two of them. "We've got no time for arguing," he said tersely. "We should be in there registering right now."

Jed nodded. "He's right, Cannon. Sorry if I trod on your toes."

Relieved and embarrassed, April said quickly, "Why don't you tell us where our seats are, Denver, and I'll take Josh over there."

"I'll show you." With a last black look at his companions, Denver grabbed hold of April's arm with one hand and Josh's shoulder with the other. "Come on, this way."

April took one look at his grim face and decided not to protest at the fierce pressure of his fingers.

He said nothing to either of them until he reached the front row of the stands. "Go right to the end," he told April. "You'll have a good view of the chutes from there. I'll meet you out by the main doors when the competition is over."

He left before she could answer him, and she followed Josh past the row of knees, fighting down an unfathomable wave of misery.

Josh sat quietly in his seat, not even looking at the program Denver had given him earlier.

April put her arm around him. "Are you okay, honey?"

He didn't answer for a moment, then in a small voice he asked, "Why is Uncle Denver mad at me?"

"Oh, honey, he's not mad at you." April hugged him to her side.

"He looked mad at me."

"No, he was cross with his friends for making fun of him, that's all. No one likes people making fun of him. You don't like it when your friends make fun of you."

Josh appeared a little less worried. "Why were they

making fun of him? 'Cause I told them he was going to be my dad?''

The shocking sound of the words, so close to the truth, stabbed her with guilt. ''Josh, just because you saw your uncle kissing me last night doesn't mean—'' She broke off, unable to continue the thought. ''There has to be a lot more than that for two people to get married.''

Josh looked devastated. ''Like what?''

April fumbled for the right words, hoping she could make her son understand. ''Well, when a man gets married he usually does so because he wants to be with his family. Uncle Denver can't do that. He has to be away all the time, traveling to the rodeos.''

''He could stay with us and find a job.''

''He doesn't know how to do anything else, honey. He wouldn't be able to take care of us, the way your dad did.''

''We could take care of him,'' Josh said.

He looked at her with such pleading she felt a helpless anger against the man who couldn't love this little boy enough to stay.

''I'm sorry, Josh. I wish things could be different, but they can't. But just because Uncle Denver isn't going to live with us doesn't mean that he doesn't love you or that you won't be seeing him. He'll be coming back as often as he can to visit, and you'll still be able to ride Salty with him and play video games and go to ball games.''

Josh's face brightened just a little. ''Will he come back for Christmas?''

''I'm sure he will,'' April said, silently vowing to make sure Denver spent Christmas with them. ''And your birthday, and lots of times in between.''

Just then the announcer's voice informed them that the rodeo was about to begin. Watching Josh's eager face turn toward the chutes, April relaxed her tense shoulders. Maybe it was going to be all right after all.

It wasn't until late in the second half that the bull-riding round was announced. Denver was the second man to ride, and as he exploded out of the chute, April chewed on her nails, her eyes fixed on the whirling, stamping animal and the determined man on his back.

The crowd roared as the seconds ticked by. The bull arched and hunched his back, twisted violently, then kicked up his hind legs. Denver leaned back, then threw his weight forward as the bull bounced back and reared up.

"Mom, you're hurting me," Josh complained.

April released her unconscious grip on his arm. "I'm sorry, honey." She kept her eyes on the writhing animal, conscious once more of the stirring of excitement as she watched Denver's triumphant control. At long last the whistle blew, and a thunderous applause burst out as he swung himself off the bull and sprinted for the fence.

"Look at the clown," Josh shouted, as the brightly clothed man in a yellow wig tapped the bull on its rear. The irate animal charged at him, his horns aimed right at the clown's belly.

April felt sick, yet was compelled to watch until the clown danced and leaped out of harm's way. It was bad enough to watch Denver on the back of that monster. She would have died if he'd chosen to be a clown instead of a bull rider.

The name of the third rider was announced, then the name of the bull. April recognized the animal instantly. It was Balderdash.

An unexpected hush fell over the crowd at the mention of the name.

"Mom!" Josh said excitedly. "That's the bull Uncle Denver was talking about. The real mean one."

All April could do right then was send up thanks that Denver hadn't drawn the notorious animal to ride. She wasn't at all sure she wanted to watch the hapless cowboy who had that dubious honor.

The crashing and banging coming from the chutes had everyone looking over there. The head of the bull reared up every now and again, his lethal horns stabbing menacingly at the fencing. April's fingers clenched once more as a cowboy hovered over the bucking back, then dropped onto the infuriated animal.

April imagined she saw fire coming out of the bull's nostrils as he plunged from the gate—two thousand pounds of cold, merciless fury.

The man on his back was flipped off in the first two seconds. The crowd surged to their feet as the cowboy hit the dirt, tangled up in the feet of the huge animal. Someone close to April shrieked, as two clowns rushed toward the bull.

Balderdash backed off, lowering his head as he pawed the ground. His massive head swayed from side to side, his eyes rolling wildly to reveal the whites, then he aimed his horns at the helpless man lying still in the dirt.

"Oh, no," April whispered. She grabbed Josh and tried to hide his face, but he wriggled free.

"Wait! I want to see!"

The clown reached the bull and began flapping towels in his face. Balderdash turned toward this new threat, lowered his head again and charged.

One of the clowns darted behind a huge red barrel, while the other dragged the dazed cowboy to his feet and hurried with him, stumbling and tripping, to the fence. Eager hands helped him over, and the clown in the ring skipped and danced over to the gate, where the bull followed him through.

It all lasted no more than a minute, yet April's knees trembled violently as she rested her sweaty palms on them.

"Man," Josh breathed. "That was so cool. I wish Uncle

Denver had ridden him. He'd have stayed on his back—I know he would.''

''I don't think anyone could stay on the back of that monster,'' April muttered, trying to get her stomach back where it belonged.

She felt queasy throughout the rest of the competition, and it was with a great sense of relief that she followed Josh out to the main gates when it was all over. She felt she needed to be in a wide-open space, away from people, away from noise and, above all, away from the horses and bulls.

She no longer had any sensual vibrations about the rodeo. It was violent and dangerous, and the noise, the dirt and the smell of it sickened her. If she had her way, she'd never go to another rodeo again as long as she lived.

By the time she got outside the arena, she was beginning to feel a little better. Shaken by her violent reaction to what had happened, she almost walked by Denver, who stood just beyond the gates, waiting for them.

''Is he all right?'' she asked, as he came up to them. ''The man who fell off Balderdash. Is he all right?''

''Rooster's fine,'' Denver said quietly. ''A few more bruises and a gash or two, but nothing broken. He's used to that.''

Her mind still dwelling on the thought that it could have been the man standing in front of her, she said sharply, ''I wonder if his family is used to it.''

Denver's expression darkened. ''Probably.'' A streak of dust across his cheek made him look all the more formidable, and April felt a tug of dismay. The last thing she'd meant to do was upset him now that they were leaving.

''Can we go see Balderdash?'' Josh asked.

''We don't have time,'' she said automatically. ''If we don't start back now it will be real late by the time we get home.''

"Aw, Mom."

Josh kicked his heel in the dirt, but April ignored the gesture of defiance. "Say goodbye to Uncle Denver."

He obediently held up his arms, and Denver leaned down to give him a hug. "Goodbye, cowboy. Take real good care of yourself, and your mom, you hear?"

His words had an odd ring of finality to them, and April felt a twinge of uneasiness. Deciding that she was overreacting again, she said lightly, "We'll see you again soon?"

He answered her without looking up. "I'll call you."

She felt even more disturbed, and was tempted to ask him when he would call. But before she could form the question, he tipped his hat and strode off toward the camper.

She watched him go, feeling suddenly drained of energy. He hadn't even offered to walk them to the car. "Come on," she said to Josh, who was staring after his uncle like a lost puppy, "let's go get a hamburger before we head for home."

For once, Josh didn't argue.

She went to bed early that night, too tired and dispirited to stay up and watch television. The vision of the cowboy's fall from Balderdash that afternoon kept returning to haunt her, and in the end she gave up the pretense at sleeping and reached for a book.

Maybe, she thought, as she turned the pages, if she could lose herself in a good story, it might just take her mind off things. Maybe she could forget the image of a broken and battered cowboy lying in the dirt. Maybe she could even forget the closed look on Denver's face just before he'd left them standing at the doors of the arena.

Denver sat on the steps of the camper and stared up at the glistening stars above. Jed and Cord had gone to the tavern. He'd told them he'd follow on later. He'd needed some time alone. Some time to think.

A few yards away a group of rodeo people were partying in a trailer. He could hear the soulful strains of a guitar and someone singing the words of a popular country song in a pleasant baritone.

Laughter almost drowned out the music, and he twisted his mouth in a wry grimace. At least someone was happy tonight.

He stretched his legs out in front of him and leaned back against the door, his hat tipped over his eyes. He couldn't ignore the problem any longer. He had to face the fact that the situation was getting complicated and he'd better do something about it.

Hearing Josh tell his friends that he was planning on marrying April had come as a major shock. He could understand why the boy had picked up the idea. It wasn't hard to figure out. Josh had seen them kissing and to a ten-year-old there was a logical conclusion to that. Combine that with a heap of wishful thinking and it all added up.

He just couldn't go on letting Josh, and maybe even April, too, think that he had any plans to settle down. They were becoming too dependent on him. He didn't want anyone depending on him. He couldn't count on being there when they needed him. After all, he was his father's son, as his mother had reminded him more than a few times. Somehow he had to make that clear to them both.

The problem was, the more time he spent with April and Josh, the more they expected of him. And the more rides he lost. Already he was coming dangerously low to the borderline in the standings. If he lost any more rides he'd slip below it and maybe lose his chance at the finals in Las Vegas.

This was going to be his year. This was the year he, Jed and Cord were all in contention for the championship, and all the years of competition between them were finally going to be settled. One of them was going to win the all-around buckle. He was determined it would be him. Maybe then he could feel justified in what he'd done all those years ago when he'd walked out of April's life. Maybe then he wouldn't be like his father, a rodeo man who'd left his family and lost his wife, with nothing to show for it.

He drew his knees up, folded his arms across them and buried his head. He had to put some distance between them all. And he had to do it now. The sooner he made them understand, the better off they'd be. He'd done what he'd promised to do. He'd taught Josh to ride and he'd given the boy something to hang on to. Something to work at and enjoy.

He sat there for a long time, trying to find the strength to make the call. Then, at last, he got slowly to his feet. The two of them would be better off without seeing him so often, he assured himself, as he crossed the street to the tavern.

Without him there to cloud things up, April would have a better chance to find the right man. That's all he could wish for the two of them—that they found a worthy replacement for his brother. For he sure as hell wasn't it.

The shrill peal of the phone startled April, and she dropped the book, her gaze jumping to the green digital figures on the radio alarm. Almost 1:00 a.m.

Immediately her mind flew to Denver. He'd be the only one who would call her at this hour. Her hand shook as she picked up the receiver. "Hello?"

There was a long pause before Denver's deep tones answered her. "Did I wake you?"

"No, I was reading." She took a steadying breath. "Is everything all right?"

Again the long pause, and the feeling of dread began

deep in her stomach, winding its way up over her heart. "Denver," she said sharply. "What is it?"

"There's something I need to tell you, and I thought it best to tell you now." He paused while she waited painfully for his next words.

"April, I think Josh is getting too used to having me around. I've tried to make him understand that I can't be there all the time for him, but I don't think he believes that."

"I don't think he wants to believe it," April said carefully.

"Well, that's kind of my point. I think it would be better if I'm not around as much. You know, let him sort of get used to me not being there."

"What are you saying, Denver?" She knew what he was saying, but she wanted to hear it from him.

"Well, it'll be kind of the way it was before. I'll try to drop by on his birthday—or at least send him a gift—and write now and then."

Just as it was before Lane died, she thought bitterly. He'd given Josh a glimpse of the rose garden and was now slamming the gate in his face. "What about Christmas? Josh really wants you to come visit for Christmas."

There was a long pause, then Denver said awkwardly, "I always reckon Christmas is strictly for family."

"I thought we were family."

"Well, you know what I mean."

The words fell flatly on her ear. Such simple words. Such devastating meaning. "I see."

"April...look, I'm sorry."

"You're sorry." She uttered a mirthless laugh. "Is that all you can say? What am I supposed to tell Josh? That you're sorry, but you don't have time for him anymore?"

"I didn't say that. April, please."

She heard the pain in his voice and made herself lean

back against the pillow, forcing her taut muscles to relax. "You're right. You are entitled to do whatever you want with your life. You have no obligation to watch over your brother's family. None whatsoever. I'm quite sure Lane would be the last one to place an unwanted burden on you."

"It isn't like that."

His voice, still ragged, tore through her heart. She paused, waiting for the spasm of pain to pass. "What is it like, Denver? Why don't you explain it to me?"

"I...damn."

She waited, refusing to help him out. She wasn't handling this well, she thought miserably. Yet she couldn't think of a single word to say right then.

Finally he began speaking, in halting sentences that pierced her like daggers. "The reason I left in the first place was that I knew I couldn't give you what you needed. You were always talking about getting married, having children. A nice solid family life...that's what you wanted. And that's what I couldn't give you."

"I never asked you for that."

"You didn't have to. I knew you'd have to have all that to be happy. You have to understand...."

Again she waited through the long pause, her fingers clenched on the phone.

"I'm not Lane, April. He and I were worlds apart. I'm like my father, a traveling man. The only thing I'm cut out for is the rodeo. It's the only life I know. Without that, I'm nothing. I'd be lost. And it's not the kind of life I can offer a woman and kids. Especially you and Josh. You both need so much more. You deserve so much more."

She couldn't hold back the anger any longer. It was there, boiling inside her. All the grief, all the shattered expectations, all the disappointment, the terrible sense of loss...they all burst like a dam in a wave of fury that more than equaled the rage of the bulls...her true rivals for the man she loved.

"Damn you, Denver," she said fiercely. "You can take your stinking rodeo and you can shove it. Don't you dare patronize me with your whining about your lack of abilities. The only thing you're incapable of doing is building a relationship. As soon as it looks as if someone might actually be getting close to you, you can't handle it. You run away. You've been running all your life, Denver. All your damn life."

"April, I—"

She was beyond listening now. She sat up, pouring all her frustration into the mouthpiece of the phone. "Even your own brother couldn't get close to you. The only time you visited your mother was at her funeral. She was right, Denver. You are just like your father. So go to hell the way he did, and all you'll have to look forward to is a headstone in some lonely graveyard God knows where. And for heaven's sake don't worry about Josh and me. We'll do just fine without you."

She paused for breath, willing herself not to cry.

The silence went on and on, and she wondered if he'd hung up without her hearing it. But then he spoke again, and when he did, he made no effort to hide the agony in his voice.

"You're right. Which is why I'm so sure I'm doing the right thing. Someday you'll thank me. Tell Josh I love him."

The click in her ear sounded like the end of the world. *Tell Josh I love him.* Why couldn't Denver have loved him enough? Why couldn't he have loved her? She turned on her side and buried her face in the pillow.

Vaguely she thought she heard a door close quietly in the hallway, but she was too wrapped up in her misery to pay much attention. She cried until she had no more tears, then she lay awake in the darkness, waiting for the ache in her heart to subside enough to let her sleep.

She awoke with a start, realizing she must have dozed off for a while. A glance at the clock told her it was almost time to get up. Wearily she climbed out of bed and shuffled to the bathroom, where she peered in dismay at her blurry image.

She looked terrible, she thought, fighting the depression that threatened to smother her. Her head throbbed with pain, her red-rimmed eyes felt raw and her stomach behaved as if it would never accept food again.

She splashed her face with cold water, then ran the shower. Somehow she had to repair some of the damage before she woke up Josh. Makeup helped, and she fluffed her hair around her face to hide some of the ravages of the long, sleepless night.

She chose a sage print shirt to wear with her white cotton pants and thrust her feet into a pair of white tennis shoes. Determined to prevent her son from seeing her heartache, she pounded on his bedroom door as she passed and called out, "Come on, sleepyhead, it's time for breakfast."

The delicious fragrance of coffee filled the kitchen a few minutes later and helped to clear her head. She busied herself preparing Josh's favorite breakfast. If nothing else, she thought wryly, the smell of frying bacon should get him out of bed.

She mixed the batter for pancakes and set the syrup on the table, then glanced at the clock. It wasn't like Josh to sleep so late, especially on a bright, sunny morning. He was usually up long before this.

Dismissing her twinge of anxiety, she went back into the hallway and opened the door of his bedroom. "Josh? Are you getting up?"

His rumpled bed was empty. Figuring he had to be in the bathroom, she checked down the hallway. The bathroom door stood open. Just to make sure, she walked down to look inside.

Now the niggling anxiety mushroomed into concern. He could be in the yard, she assured herself. Maybe he got tired of waiting for her to get up. She headed back into the kitchen and opened the patio door. One glance around was enough to convince her he wasn't in the backyard. And neither was his bike.

He knew better than to leave the house without permission. He wouldn't go far until he'd eaten breakfast. *Would he?* He had once before, she reminded herself. When he'd run away to be with Denver.

Warning herself not to panic, she went back to his bedroom and pulled open the door of his closet. A cold hand of fear gripped her throat as she stared at the empty space where his backpack should be. It took her only a moment or two to confirm that some of his clothes were missing, as well as his shoes.

Trembling with anxiety, she peered under the bed. The wooden box his father had given him, and that contained all of his most precious possessions, was also missing. Josh had run away again.

She got to her feet and pressed her fingers against her throbbing forehead. Where would he have gone? Denver seemed the logical answer, but after the things she'd said last night he was the last person she wanted to talk to.

Putting off the inevitable, she called around to the homes of Josh's friends. She received the same reply from each one. No one had seen Josh in days.

The police, she thought, as panic swept over her. Maybe she should call the police. They could call Denver and find out if Josh was there.

No, she couldn't wait for that. All that red tape would take hours. She had to call him herself. Bracing herself, she reached for the phone.

Denver growled as the comforting blanket of sleep was rudely swept away by a rough hand on his shoulder. He opened his eyes, gazed through the mist at someone's blurred face, then closed his eyes again. "Go 'way," he mumbled.

"Sorry, pardner, but this is an emergency. You gotta wake up."

Jed's voice registered in Denver's befuddled brain, and he struggled to make sense of what was happening. The last thing he remembered was stumbling out of the tavern, blinking at the maze of lights that spun crazily around him. He vaguely remembered Cord holding his arm, or was it Jed? He wasn't sure. He didn't remember getting back to the camper or getting into bed.

What he did remember was the reason he'd drunk way too many beers, and that was something he didn't want to have to deal with. Besides, someone was hammering nails into his head. "Go 'way," he mumbled louder. "Leave me alone."

"Denver, listen to me. April called. The boy's missing."

The words sank in one by one, each more painful than the last. Josh? No, he couldn't be missing. With an almighty effort, Denver opened his eyes and heaved the upper half of his aching body upright. "Lordy." He clapped a hand to his head. "Get me an aspirin, someone. Or an ax."

Jed's concerned face swam into view. "You really tied one on last night, pardner. I haven't seen you drink like that since you lost the championship two years ago."

Denver grunted in reply. "Where are my pants?"

"Here." Jed threw a pair of jeans across the bunk. "Your boots are under your bed. I told her you'd call her right back, so you'd better get over there."

The fog was clearing from his mind, though his head still thumped in rhythmic agony. "What did she say?"

"Just that Josh was missing and she thought he might come looking for you."

"Did she say how long ago he left?"

"You'll have to ask her that yourself, buddy. She sounded pretty shook up. I'll go get you some aspirin, though if you ask me, what you need is a hair of the dog. I've got some rum in my locker."

Denver groaned. "Don't even mention the word. Just get out of here and let me get dressed."

He practically fell out of bed, and pulled on his pants and his boots. Then he grabbed a shirt from the pile by his bed and dragged it on, before stumbling down the narrow passageway to the kitchen.

"Coffee," he said thickly. "Good and strong."

"Already poured it."

Jed handed him a mug and he drank it down, oblivious of the scalding liquid burning his tongue and throat. He took the aspirin Jed offered and swallowed them with the last dregs of his coffee, then slapped the mug down on the counter.

"I'll be back soon," he muttered, and stumbled outside, stepping down to the ground with his eyes half-closed against the blinding sunlight.

When he got to the office he found a half-dozen cowboys waiting to register. Deciding that he needed more privacy, he went in search of an outside phone, finally ending up at the gas station across the street. It was noisy, but at least no one was there to overhear.

He heard April pick up on the first ring, and knew she'd been waiting by the phone. "Denver," he said briefly, in answer to her breathless greeting.

"Thank you for calling back."

Her voice sounded cool and brittle, as if it would shatter into tiny pieces at the softest touch. He could imagine how close she was to falling apart. "Look," he said roughly, "he's going to be fine. He's probably on his way here. What time did he leave?"

"I don't know." Her voice quivered, and she paused.

He waited for her to get it together again, wishing passionately that he were there, instead of two hours away.

"He was gone when I got up this morning," April said unsteadily. "He could have left anytime."

He didn't want to ask the question, but he had to know. "Did he say anything last night? About...us, I mean."

"No."

Again she paused, then went on in a voice that broke his heart. "But I think he must have overheard me talking to you on the phone. I heard a door closing after I hung up, but I thought he'd just gone to the bathroom. He does that often in the night...."

"April." The longing to hold her in his arms was so acute he closed his eyes. "Does he have bus fare?"

"Yes. He took his bike, but he could have left it at the station."

"All right. He could have heard me talking about the bus the other day and taken it out here. I'll check with the bus depot at this end. You check that end and see if his bike is there. I'll grab a shower and call you when I get there."

"Thank you, Denver. I'm sorry I had to bother you with this, but I didn't know what else to do. It's just...he probably left in the middle of the night, and I'm so afraid—"

He cut in quickly, before she transmitted her fears to him. "Look, he's going to be fine. He's got a good head on his shoulders and he knows how to take care of himself."

"I wish I didn't have to get you involved. I'm sorry."

He recognized the resentment in her voice and sighed. "We're still family, April. Josh is the important issue here.

Let's just put everything else aside until he's safely back home, all right?''

"All right. I'll wait for your call.''

He put down the receiver and paused a moment to get his mind focused before heading back to the camper.

Jed was waiting for him when he got back. "Cord's gone to check out the grounds,'' he said, as soon as Denver stepped into the camper. "He's gonna get everyone on the lookout for the boy. He won't get far around here without someone seeing him.''

"That'll help.'' Denver brushed past him and headed for the shower, anxious now to get down to the bus depot. He sluiced himself down with cold water, hoping to shock his body into full awareness. It must have worked. By the time he was dressed again, he felt more awake. Even the pounding in his head had begun to ease.

Cord had unhitched the truck the day before, and Denver climbed into the front seat, thankful that he didn't have to stop to unhitch it himself.

"Want me to come along?'' Jed asked, as Denver fired the engine.

"Thanks, but I reckon you'll do more good here.'' He glanced at his watch. "Besides, I might not make it back in time for the ride this afternoon. I'd hate for you to miss yours, too.''

Jed pulled a face. "Good luck,'' he said quietly. "If we find him here we'll try to get word to you.''

Denver nodded, then put the truck into gear and drove out to the street.

It took him fifteen minutes to reach the bus station. He'd scanned the streets on either side of him all the way, hoping to see Josh's thin figure darting along the sidewalk.

To his dismay, the young girl behind the desk informed him that the first bus from Portland had already pulled in.

There had been no kids aboard. The next one was due in an hour, she told him.

Denver crossed the room to the phones and called April. Again the phone was snatched up on the first ring.

"Denver? Any news?"

He told her what the desk clerk had told him. "What about your end? Anyone see him?"

"No. The night shift had already left when I called. They're trying to check for me now. His bike isn't there, but that doesn't mean he didn't get on the bus. He could have left his bike anywhere."

"All right." He studied his watch. "I'll wait for the next bus. If he's not on that, we'll have to assume he didn't take the bus."

"Oh, Denver."

Her voice broke, and he heard the shuddering breath she took all the way down the line.

"Anyone could have picked him up. What are we going to do?"

Right then, he didn't have an answer for her. He closed his eyes, pressing the receiver against his forehead to ease the pain that had returned with a vengeance.

This was his fault. Again he'd messed up. And this time, he could be the cause of something too terrible even to think about.

Chapter 9

April had never felt more terrified in her life. The compelling urge to go out and physically hunt the streets for her son was almost too strong to ignore, yet she could not leave the phone for fear of missing the call that could either end this nightmare or plunge her into a world of unbelievable horror.

Despite her best efforts to prevent them, visions of all the stories she'd ever seen on television about missing children invaded her mind with cruel persistence. Some, she knew, were never seen again. Some were found brutally injured or dead.

On the other hand, some were even found alive and well, she told herself, clutching at any straw to save herself from drowning in a sea of dread.

She sat at the window, her gaze glued to the street outside. Every sound she heard, every movement she saw, sparked her hopes, only to plunge her back into the abyss of crushing disappointment.

Bring him back to me safe and sound, she prayed, *and I'll never complain about him again.*

She rocked on the chair, fighting the cold loneliness that gripped her. She couldn't let herself fall apart now, she thought fiercely. She had to be strong, to face whatever the outcome might be.

The phone rang once more, and she snatched it up, noticing for some silly reason that the table needed dusting. "Hello?"

"Mrs. Briggs? This is Colin at the bus depot."

"Yes!" she said eagerly. "Have you found him?"

"I talked to the night shift. No one saw your son, and the desk clerk is positive he didn't issue a bus ticket to a child last night or this morning."

He sounded dispassionate, uncaring. How could he be so unmoved by the trauma that had suddenly destroyed her world? She remembered suddenly that she'd felt the same way when she'd received the news of her husband's death. The memory plunged her even deeper into despair.

"Thank you," she mumbled, and hung up the phone.

It rang again, almost immediately. She picked it up and whispered, "Hello?"

"Any word?"

Denver's deep voice eased some of the hopelessness. "He didn't buy a bus ticket. They just called."

"I figured that. He wasn't on this bus, either."

"If he'd hitched a ride he'd have been there long ago."

"I've got people looking for him all over the place here. So far no luck."

Her throat closed, and she had to force the words through. "What are we going to do?"

"Wait and see if he comes back when he's hungry. If not, the police are the next step, I guess."

His words sounded so final she began to cry, deep choking sobs that refused to quieten. She heard his voice in her ear, trying to soothe her, but she was beyond pacifying.

"I'll grab a cab—I don't want to leave the guys without the truck—and I'll be there in a couple of hours," Denver said gruffly. "Try to hang on until then."

She heard the click in her ear, but she continued to cling to the phone, as if afraid to lose the slender connection that was all that was holding her together. After a minute or two, it occurred to her that someone might try to call her, and she hung up.

Two hours. It seemed like an eternity.

She passed the time by going through Josh's bedroom, trying to find some clue to where he might have gone. Not that she expected to find anything, but it made her feel better to have something positive to do.

She made numerous trips to the living-room window, afraid to hope but helpless to stop the compulsion that drove her there. When she saw the cab pull up at the end of the driveway, for a moment she actually believed she'd see Josh scramble out.

When Denver climbed out, instead, she almost hated him for not being her son. She willed herself to hold it all together when she opened the door to his ring. The moment he stepped inside the living room, however, she collapsed against him, the sobs racking her body once more.

He led her over to the couch and sat down with her. He held her without saying a word until she'd exhausted herself and her weeping died away.

She pulled away from him, shielding her ravaged face with her hand. "I'm sorry. I promised myself I wouldn't do that."

"I'd have been surprised if you hadn't."

Feeling self-conscious now, she got up and crossed the room to where a box of tissues sat on a bookshelf. She drew out a handful of them and began blowing her nose.

"Have you eaten anything?"

She looked at him, surprised by the question. "No, now that I think about it, I haven't had anything except a cup of coffee. I made breakfast for Josh, but when I realized he'd gone…"

"Take it easy," Denver said gently, getting to his feet.

"I dumped it," she finished weakly, and blew her nose again.

"I think you should eat. It will make you feel better."

It was the last thing she felt like doing. "How long do you think we ought to wait before calling the police?"

"I don't think they'll accept a Missing Persons report until he's been gone for twenty-four hours, but I'll call them now if it will make you feel better."

She shook her head. "No, I'll wait a little longer. Somehow, reporting him missing to the police makes it sound so…" She gulped, unable to finish the sentence. "I keep hoping he'll turn up, that he's staying away just to get back at me and when he gets tired of it he'll come back."

"Get back at you?" Denver shook his head. "I think it's more likely he's angry with me. After all, I was the one who deserted him. I guess he heard enough of our conversation last night to understand what was going on."

She sank onto the nearest chair, her legs unable to support her anymore. "I just can't think about what might have happened to him. The possibilities are driving me crazy."

"I'll get you something to eat." Denver strode purposefully across the room to the kitchen. "You can't deal with this on an empty stomach."

She sat in a dazed stupor, dimly aware of him fumbling around in the kitchen. He came out a few minutes later with a plate and handed it to her. She looked at the sandwich without much interest but took a halfhearted bite of it anyway. He'd stuffed the bread with ham, lettuce and slices of tomato. Considering she had no appetite at all, it tasted good enough to swallow.

Denver made some more coffee and fixed himself a sandwich. "At least we know that Josh won't go hungry," he said, as he sat down across from her on the couch. "He's got money to buy food."

She nodded, trying to take what comfort she could from his reassuring words.

He went on making small talk, and she answered him now and again in monosyllables. Finally, after another hour had passed, she said wearily, "I think we'd better call the police."

"You want me to do it?"

"No, I will." She picked up the phone book and located the number, then took a moment to rehearse what she wanted to say. When she was ready, she dialed the number and waited.

The masculine voice on the other end was quiet, kind and sympathetic. He asked a lot of questions, most of which she didn't have the answers to, then tried to reassure her. "He's probably holed up with a friend somewhere," he said, just before he hung up. "Nine times out of ten kids are just around the corner. We'll send out an APB on him for you. Try not to worry. I'm sure we'll have him back before the morning."

She replaced the receiver, holding her breath when she felt the threat of tears again.

"They're going to look for him?"

She nodded, painfully aware of Denver's worried face. How much worse would it be for him, she wondered, if he knew that Josh was his own son? She hoped she'd have the courage to tell him the truth if something happened to Josh, then shut the thought off when it became unbearable.

"I want to go out and look for him, too," she said, when

another interminable hour had passed. "I can't just sit around here doing nothing."

"All right." Denver got to his feet. "One of us should stay by the phone. Why don't you stay and I'll go look for him."

"I'd rather go myself." She needed to be out there, scouring the streets until she found him.

His face mirrored his concern, and to her dismay he gave a firm shake of his head. "You need to be by the phone in case the police call. Besides, you're in no shape to drive. Give me the car keys, and I'll search the neighborhood. Meanwhile you could call all their parents, just in case his friends are covering for him. One of the parents might have discovered him by now."

"I never thought of that." Miraculously, hope sparked again.

"I'll call every half hour," Denver said, as he got ready to leave. "That way we'll stay in touch."

She got to her feet, and went with him to the door. He looked down at her, his eyes filled with compassion. "You going to be okay?"

She nodded. "Thanks, Denver. I don't think I could handle this alone."

"I won't leave you alone," he said quietly. "I'll be around as long as you need me."

She watched him leave, reluctant to close the door until the T-bird was out of sight. Then she went back to the phone and started making calls. Half an hour later she still had no news of her missing son.

Denver called a little while later. "I've looked all over the school grounds," he told her. "I'm going to try the park next. I'll call back in half an hour."

He didn't know what good that would do, he thought as he replaced the receiver, but he needed the security of knowing she was all right. All things considered, she was holding up pretty well.

Just to satisfy himself, he put in a call to the rodeo grounds. After a lot of waiting around, he finally got Cord on the phone. There had been no sign of Josh out there, Cord told him. But they were still looking.

Denver hung up and returned to the car. He'd been fairly hopeful that Josh would return on his own before now. The longer they waited, the less he could convince himself that the boy was all right.

He was beginning to understand now how April must feel. The thought of something bad happening to the little guy just about tore him apart. He kept telling himself that Josh was ten years old, ''almost grown up'' as he'd said himself. He could take care of himself.

Yet nagging reminders of all the terrible things that could happen to a defenseless child on the streets kept tormenting him, until he thought he would go out of his mind.

The worst of it was, he blamed himself. He was responsible for this. If he hadn't spent so much time hanging around, Josh wouldn't have been so upset by him leaving. And he would never have had that conversation with April.

Echoes of her accusations rang in his head: *You're just like your father. You can go to hell the way he did.* And he probably would, he thought morosely. Especially if something happened to that little boy.

He realized now how very much he cared for his nephew. Josh had become important to him, as important as April was, and he'd let the boy down.

He'd hung around long enough for Josh to get used to having him there, then he'd more or less abandoned him. Josh had already lost his father. Now he was losing his uncle.

No doubt, Denver thought, Josh would feel that loss every time he left after a visit.

Denver was sure of that, because that was the way he'd felt when his own father had done the very same thing. Until in the end he hadn't come back at all.

The alien sting of tears pricked Denver's eyelids, and he blinked hard and fast. He wasn't used to praying. Not since he was a kid, anyhow. He'd never considered himself a religious man, but just this once he made a bargain with God.

If Josh returned safe and sound, he'd get out of their lives for good. It would be hard on Josh at first, but it was better than dredging up the pain every time he came for a visit. It would be the best thing he could do for both of them if they never saw him again.

He cruised the streets for another hour, without much expectation of seeing Josh. Twice he saw a police car turn a corner ahead of him and hoped they would have better luck than he had. After his third call to April, he called the police and was assured that all the officers were aware of the boy's disappearance and were on the lookout for him.

Maybe that news would make April feel a little better, he thought, as he headed back to the house. He wasn't achieving anything, he told himself, and April sounded as if she needed someone with her to lean on.

She opened the door to his knock, and he hated to see the anticipation in her face die when she saw he was alone. She walked straight into his arms, and he held her, stroking her hair, murmuring useless words of comfort.

"The police are looking for him," he told her, when she finally drew back. "There's nothing more we can do except wait. I'll get you a glass of wine. You look like you could use it."

She shook her head. "I want to be clear-headed, in case...." She let her voice trail off, and he winced.

"It will settle your nerves," he said firmly. He went back to the kitchen and found the bottle of wine he'd seen earlier. He poured her a generous glass and carried it back to the living room, where she sat slumped on the couch. "Here, drink this," he ordered, handing her the glass. "You'll feel better."

To his relief, she took the glass and obediently swallowed some. "I called everyone," she said wearily. "Everyone I could think of. I talked to dozens of people. No one has seen him. No one."

She looked so defenseless his heart ached for her. "The police will find him," he said, wishing there were something more he could do to ease her pain. "It's late and you need to eat something. I'll order a pizza."

She stared at him as if she hadn't understood but a moment later said listlessly, "I'll cook something."

"No, I will." He left her sitting there, hoping his meager efforts would help restore some of her energy.

April sat quietly while he fixed the meal. Her initial fear and panic had subsided a little, dulled by a heavy feeling of acceptance. He was right, she told herself. The police were handling it. There was nothing else she could do but wait.

The wine didn't lessen the pain, but at least it softened the edges a little, and she managed to eat a fairly adequate meal later. Denver insisted on putting the dishes in the dishwasher, while she cleared up the kitchen.

She was all right as long as she was busy, she thought. But now darkness was creeping over the sky. Soon it would be night, and she would be gripped in the black loneliness of terror once more. Every hour that went by without her knowing what had happened to Josh would increase the fear.

She walked into the living room and wandered to the window. Orange light from the street lamps spilled out onto the empty street, emphasizing the lonely shadows. Josh was somewhere out there. All she could pray for was that he was unhurt, and that he was with someone who would take care of him. Without warning, the tears began sliding down her cheeks again.

She didn't hear Denver come up behind her. The first she knew of his presence was when he wrapped his arms around her, drawing her back against his chest.

"Go ahead and cry if it makes you feel better," he said gruffly.

She tried to tell him she was fine, but the words wouldn't form. She twisted in his arms, instead, until she faced him, her head buried in his shoulder.

The comfort she drew from his warm, strong body was unbelievable. It spread over her like a soft, cozy blanket, easing the dread and leaving only the dull ache of depression.

She needed his arms right now. She needed his touch, his soft words, his comforting strength. She felt his hands stroking her back, and suddenly, she wanted more.

Shocked by the sudden surge of need at a time like this, she tried to suppress it. The sensation persisted, growing stronger, more acute, more demanding.

It was as if her body cried out, begging him to make her forget, for a little while, the terrible worry and fear. She stirred against him, still struggling with the conflicting emotions that refused to be smothered.

In vain she fought to listen to the instincts that warned her she'd be making a huge mistake. Then again, if something had happened to Josh, her whole life would have been a mistake. Then nothing else would matter. What difference would it make now?

If Denver hadn't moved just then, she might have won the battle raging inside her. But he chose that moment to draw back to look at her, one finger lifting her chin so that he could peer into her face.

Her need must have been reflected in her eyes. She saw

his expression change, disbelief followed by an almost unbearable longing that found an answering echo in her tormented mind.

"April?"

His whisper was a question, and she answered it by reaching up to wind her arms around his neck. "Don't talk," she murmured fiercely, "just kiss me."

She felt his entire body tense as he strained against the pressure of her arms. "Wait," he said hoarsely, "you're upset—you don't know what you're doing."

"I do know what I'm doing." Driven by the demons inside her, she tightened her hold, pulling his face down to hers. "Damn it, Denver, are you going to tell me you don't want me?"

He gazed down at her, his face inches from her, his eyes flashing blue fire. For an instant she felt a wavering of doubt, then he closed his arms around her and muttered, "Hell, no."

She shut her eyes as his mouth captured hers, crushing her lips with the torment of unfulfilled longing. She grappled for the buttons of his shirt, tore them open and dragged the shirt from his shoulders.

Mouths still locked together, hands feverishly yanking off clothes, they stumbled toward the bedroom. They were both naked by the time they reached it.

Denver's swift kick flung the door against the wall. Oblivious of the noise, they fell on the bed in a tangled heap, legs entwined, mouths eagerly searching.

She felt his hands on her—smoothing, caressing, touching, probing—and his mouth hungrily tasting her bare, sensitive skin. Her emotions were at fever pitch, fueled by fear, need, desperation and a love that had refused to die.

Her head swam with the passion that swept her up into a maelstrom of sensations. She swirled into the vortex, welcoming this temporary relief from the agony waiting for her outside.

He rolled over onto his back, then pulled her down on top of him. She rained fiery kisses on his body, with an abandon that shook her soul. Something told her that as long as she poured all her energy and emotion into these moments, she could keep at bay the haunting horror that hovered just beyond the fringe of her sanity.

Her wildness transmitted itself to him, and with a sharp oath, he flung her onto her back, then covered her glistening body with his own.

He was breathing hard, and in the shadowy room she could see the heat burning in his eyes. Now there was no more time. She clasped his hips with her legs as he slid inside her, and at last…at long last…the ancient rhythm rocketed her toward the release she craved.

Faster and faster, harder and harder, she flew, her eyes closed tight and her mind filled with nothing but the driving force of his passion.

They exploded together through the barriers of time, capturing once more this thing that had begun for them so long ago. Only now it was more powerful, more volatile, more thunderous in its supreme dominance of their emotions, and so much more satisfying for the waiting.

Finally, exhausted, they lay side by side, neither talking, neither moving.

Slowly, oh, so slowly, the world seeped back into April's dazed mind. She had never forgotten the dizzy heights his lovemaking had lifted her to all those years ago. Yet it seemed as if this had been the first time, the first exciting discovery, the first tempest of emotions set on fire by an expert touch, loving hands and a tender yet savage mouth.

Almost at once, as if it had been waiting for the chance, the pain poured back into her soul. Josh. Where in God's name could he be?

As though reading her thoughts, Denver said quietly, "I reckon we both needed that."

She nodded. "It helped, for a little while."

He didn't answer, and she would have given a good deal to know what his thoughts were. After a while, she said tentatively, "Are you booked into a hotel?"

"No."

She felt him turn his head, but she couldn't bring herself to look at him just yet. Her emotions were still too raw, her love for him too vulnerable.

"You want me to stay?"

She slowly nodded. "If you wouldn't mind too much. I don't want to be alone."

He moved his hand to clasp hers. "He's going to be all right," he said quietly. "I won't believe anything else. I reckon he ran away because he felt rejected, and right now he's probably wishing he were back in his own home, playing video games."

She nodded, willing the tears to stay away. "I hope you're right."

"I keep remembering something he said to me when he was riding Salty—" He broke off and dragged himself upright. "Damn!"

She felt a cold chill of fear. "What is it?"

"I've just thought of something. Next to the rodeo, what would you say Josh is most crazy about?"

She stared at him, afraid to allow the tiniest flicker of hope. "I don't know—"

"Yes, you do." He leaped out of the bed and held out his hand to her. "Yes, you do, April. It's that damn Salty."

Bewildered, she allowed him to pull her to her feet beside him. She watched him reach for the phone on her bedside table and punch out some numbers.

He waited, the phone clamped to his ear, and in the dim

light from the hallway she saw the hope gleaming in his eyes. At last he spoke. "Caroline?"

Her pulse jumped with anticipation. Now she understood. If only…

"I'm sorry to wake you up," Denver said, drawing April's naked body into the shelter of his arm. "It isn't? Oh, I thought it was later than that. No, I'm at April's house. I wonder if you'd do me a favor. Would you go take a look at Salty for me?"

He paused, then said quickly, "Wrong? No, I'm hoping everything is very right. Josh is missing. I think he might be with Salty."

April heard Caroline's shocked exclamation. She said something else and Denver gave her the phone number to call them back. He replaced the receiver and put both his arms around April's shivering body.

"We'd better get dressed," he said softly. "If I'm right then we'll need to get over there pretty quick."

She nodded, feeling self-conscious now that the flames of passion had finally been extinguished. Leaving the warmth of his body, she walked over to the closet and reached for her robe.

When she turned around he'd disappeared, no doubt to get his clothes. Abandoning the robe, she dressed quickly in warm jeans and a white cotton sweater. Her teeth chattered, more from anxiety than the cold. She felt as if she were on a roller coaster, soaring up one side, only to plunge down the other.

She tried not to hope for too much, yet the anticipation would not be quelled. She longed for the ringing of the phone and dreaded it at the same time.

She combed her hair in the bathroom, then went in search of Denver. She found him standing in the living room, fully dressed, staring out the darkened window.

"Would you like some coffee?" she asked tentatively.

She needed something to do, she thought desperately. She couldn't just sit and wait.

He glanced at her. "If you do."

"I'll make some." She hurried into the kitchen and reached for the coffeepot. The familiar movements comforted her, and after a while the intense shivering died away.

While she waited for the coffee to percolate she picked up the strewn clothes in the hallway and threw them onto her bed. She'd remake the bed later, she thought, or maybe she'd just crawl into it the way it was.

After pouring out the coffee, she carried the steaming mugs into the living room and handed one to Denver. Now that she could see his face clearly, she could detect the lines of tension and knew he was as anxious as she was. The hope faded a little with the knowledge.

She sat on the edge of the couch, staring at the front page of the newspaper, which lay on the arm. The headlines blurred, and she realized she was silently crying again.

She dashed away the useless tears with the back of her hand. Denver must have caught the movement. He walked over to her and sat down.

"Hang on," he said quietly. "It shouldn't be long now."

"I don't think I could bear it if he's not there," she said desolately. "I just can't deal with any more disappointments."

"Let's not—"

He broke off as the peal of the phone shattered the silence around them. She jumped violently, and some of the hot coffee spilled down her arm. The searing pain barely registered. Her heart thumped so hard she thought it might burst. She watched Denver pick up the phone.

His gaze locked with hers, and he said quietly, "Pray."

She did, over and over in her mind, while she watched his face and desperately tried to read his expression.

"Hello? Yes."

His gaze sharpened, and her heart leaped to her throat.

"All right," he said quietly. "We'll be right there."

She stood, tears running freely down her face, still terrified to believe what she saw in his eyes.

Denver replaced the receiver, his gaze still locked on her face. "He's there," he said quietly. "And he's unharmed."

For a moment the room spun darkly around her.

Then Denver said urgently, "April, he's all right. He's frightened, though, and he needs you."

She stared at him, willing her senses to accept what she'd been so afraid to believe. "I'm okay," she said shakily. "Let's go."

She remembered little of the drive through the dark streets and the winding blackness of the country lanes. She only vaguely remembered turning into the drive of the Second Chance Ranch and up into the bright, welcoming lights of the house.

Caroline was on the steps, waiting for them. She ran toward the car as April stumbled out, and grasped her arm.

"You poor thing," she said, her voice tight with concern. "What you must have gone through. Josh told me he left last night."

April nodded, finding it almost impossible to speak. "He's all right?"

"He's fine. But scared of what you'll say to him. He knows he frightened you, and he feels bad about that."

"I don't care," April muttered, as she hurried with Caroline up the steps of the house. "Just as long as he's all right."

"He's in the living room," Caroline said when they reached the hallway. "I put the television on for him. I thought it might calm him down. I gave him something to eat, but he wasn't very hungry."

April heard the words, yet they meant nothing. All her

concentration was focused on seeing her son again. At last she reached the door of the living room, which stood ajar. She could hear the voices and the sound of laughter on the TV. The cheerful noises sounded ludicrous, under the circumstances.

She pushed the door open wider, and her heart stopped at the sight of Josh, his body scrunched up and looking almost lost in the seat of a big armchair.

He turned his head as she walked into the room, and promptly burst into tears.

Abandoning all thoughts of scolding him, she rushed over and wrapped her arms around him. "It's all right, Josh. I'm here now. It's all right." The warm tide of tenderness and relief kept her own tears at bay. She glanced over her son's head at the man who had fathered him.

"Thank you," she whispered.

Denver's eyes were suspiciously bright as he gave her a brief nod.

"Well," Caroline said heartily, "why don't I go get us some coffee. Unless you'd prefer something stronger. You both look as if you could use it."

"Coffee's fine, thanks," April said quickly.

Denver nodded. "Same here."

Caroline left the room, and April fumbled for a tissue in her purse. After finding one, she wiped Josh's tear-streaked face, and made him blow his nose.

Still kneeling in front of him, she asked quietly, "Why did you run away, Josh? Didn't you know I'd be worried about you?"

Josh shrugged. "I guess."

"Then why?"

He sat swinging his foot for a long moment, then blurted out, "'Cause you and Uncle Denver were fighting. You were fighting with Dad that night he went away and crashed his plane."

"Oh, God," April whispered.

Josh started crying again, and his words were interrupted by his heaving sobs. "You told Uncle Denver not...to come back again. I thought...if I ran away, he'd have to come back and help you find me...and then you wouldn't fight anymore...and...he wouldn't get hurt."

April drew Josh's head against her shoulder. "Hush, now, it's all right. We're not fighting anymore."

Her gaze met Denver's again, and the expression in his eyes made her feel cold. She'd seen it before—the uncertainty and apprehension, the fear of being trapped. She knew what it meant. She'd been expecting it, and sooner or later she would have to explain things to Josh. But not now.

"I'll take him home," she said, looking Denver straight in the eye. "You can stay here with Caroline tonight. I'm sure she'll drive you to the bus in the morning."

"April—"

He moved toward her, and she froze, terrified that if he touched her she'd break down and beg him to stay. "We'll talk tomorrow," she said quickly, while she still had the strength to look at him. "Thank Caroline for me. I'll call her later."

His hand dropped to his side, and he stood back, saying nothing as they passed him.

At the door, Josh turned to his uncle. "Goodbye, Uncle Denver," he said, his voice breaking on another sob.

In that moment, April knew that her son understood.

Denver must have known it, too. The agony on his face was almost unbearable to watch. "So long, cowboy," he said, in a husky whisper.

April grasped Josh's hand and pulled him through the door, out to the car waiting silently in the moonless night. He climbed in and curled up on the seat, obeying without protest her command to fasten his seat belt.

She drove fast through the empty streets, longing now to be home and safe in her bed. "How did you get to Caroline's?" she asked, after she'd been driving for several minutes in silence.

"I rode my bike," Josh muttered, sounding immeasurably weary. "I cut across the fields, but it took me a long time."

"I can imagine it did," April said grimly. "Why did you go there?"

"I wanted to be with Salty. He's my friend and I can talk to him."

"You can talk to me, too," April said gently. "Why didn't you try that first?"

Josh shrugged. "You were mad at Uncle Denver. You wouldn't listen to me."

He was probably right, April thought guiltily. She wouldn't have listened to anyone last night. Now it was too late. She'd given in to her desperate need and frightened Denver off for good.

After what they'd done, he'd be even more determined to stay away, for fear she would take what had happened that evening as a sign that he was willing to make some sort of commitment.

He'd practically disappeared from her life the first time he'd made love to her, and now he was all set to do it again.

She'd seen it in his face a few minutes ago, as clearly as if he'd said the words. Josh had seen it, too. They might as well face it, she thought, glancing miserably at her son. Neither one of them was likely to see Denver again for a long, long time.

Chapter 10

Josh fell asleep the moment he laid his head on the pillow. April stood for the longest time staring down at him, reluctant to leave him in case he should disappear again.

After convincing herself that he was too tired to go anywhere that night, she finally closed his bedroom door, though she left hers open just in case he should wake up in the night. In the future if she heard him, she promised herself, she'd investigate.

She had forgotten, for a few brief moments, what had happened between her and Denver earlier. The shock of seeing the rumpled bed when she walked into her bedroom almost destroyed her.

Memories bounded at her from all directions, everywhere she looked. Desperately she locked her mind against them, determined to forget. She gathered up her scattered clothes and dropped them in the laundry hamper. One pillow lay on the floor at the side of the bed, and she picked it up, smoothing it out carefully before she laid it next to its mate.

She went through all the motions automatically, following a pattern set many years ago. She brushed her teeth, combed her hair, put on her nightgown and climbed into bed, keeping her mind totally blank. She would not let herself think about anything tonight. Not Josh, not Denver, not anything. Tomorrow she would face it all. After she'd found some respite in sleep.

She laid her head on the pillow, but the fragrance of Denver's cologne haunted her, and she got up once more and changed the sheets on the bed. Finally, she was able to go to sleep, and much to her surprise slept soundly until the next morning.

Her first thought when she woke up was of Josh. She was about to fly out of bed to check on him, when she heard him come out of the bathroom. Forcing her tense muscles to relax, she showered and dressed at a leisurely pace, then went to the kitchen to start breakfast.

Judging from the sounds from Josh's room, he was playing his beloved video games. She started to smile, then she remembered Denver and Josh playing together, and the ache began.

How long would it be like this, she wondered, before she could feel whole again? She'd barely recovered from Lane's death. Now she had to deal with losing Denver. And this time she had lost so much more.

Losing Lane was like losing a dear and trusted friend. Although she still missed him, she had never felt the tearing kind of pain at his loss that she felt now.

Thank God she had Josh, she thought, as she threw eggs into the pan. At least she wouldn't be entirely alone.

Josh was still subdued when he answered her summons to the breakfast table. He ate hungrily, however, which she felt was a good sign. "What would you like to do today?" she asked him, when he'd cleared his plate.

Her relief to have him back was still so poignantly fresh

in her mind she was willing to grant him just about anything. Besides, she needed to talk to him about Denver, and she needed him in a receptive mood.

"I want to go see Uncle Denver ride in the rodeo," he said, sliding off his chair.

She felt a painful stab of surprise. "I don't think that's a very good idea," she said carefully.

"I want to go see him." He had the familiar stubborn look on his face, and April's spirits sank. The sooner she got things straight about Denver the better, she thought. But she wasn't going to get through to Josh if he was seething with resentment and disappointment.

Much against her better judgment, she said reluctantly, "All right, we'll go back up there. You'd better get ready, then. We'll have to leave pretty soon if we're going to make it in time. It takes two hours to get there."

He rushed for the stairs, and she quickly cleared the dishes from the table and put them away in the dishwasher. The last thing in the world she wanted was to go back to the rodeo. Seeing Denver again would be too painful.

He might even think she was chasing after him, she thought ruefully. Then again, he didn't have to know that she and Josh were there. In fact, it would be better for everyone if she didn't meet him face to face again. It would only delay the inevitable misery.

She'd have her talk with Josh on the way up, she decided. If things went as she hoped and Josh accepted what she had to tell him, then Denver would never have to know they were there. They could see the show and slip away, and there would be no painful goodbyes.

Feeling slightly better now that she had a definite agenda, April called up the stairs for Josh, then went out to the car. Josh came out a few minutes later, slammed the front door and darted down the steps.

April noticed that he had his camera slung around his

neck again. He'd taken several pictures of Salty and Denver with it. He probably wanted to finish up the film, she thought, smiling at him as he scrambled onto the seat.

She wondered if he'd still want to take pictures of his uncle once she'd told him everything he needed to know.

She waited until they'd been on the road a good hour before saying, ''Josh, there's something we should talk about before we get to the rodeo.''

She could tell by the way he held himself that he was bracing himself to hear bad news. She wished she didn't have to be the one to give it to him, but he had to understand about Denver. She just hoped he was mature enough to handle it better than he'd handled the death of his father.

''You have to realize that no matter how much you want things to be different, you can't change people just because you love them. Uncle Denver is never going to change, and there's nothing we can do about that.''

''Why?''

She winced at Josh's mutinous tone. ''Well, as I explained to you the last time we were here, Uncle Denver has to attend as many rodeos as he can if he wants to win the championship. He just won't have time to come and visit us as often.''

''You said he'd come back for Christmas.''

''I said I thought he might.'' She paused, searching for the right words. Nothing came to mind. With a sigh of resignation, she decided to postpone the whole thing until later after all. Why spoil the last time Josh would see his uncle ride?

''Isn't he coming back for Christmas?'' Josh persisted.

''Christmas is a long way off,'' she said, taking the easy way out. ''We'll have to see what happens when the time comes.''

Josh sat back in his seat, but she could tell by his face that he wasn't happy with her stock answer. She'd put the doubt in his mind now and would probably have to deal with his continual questions for a long time. She should be angry with Denver, she thought, but somehow she just didn't have the energy to be angry anymore.

She felt dead inside, devoid of any emotion except her concern for her son. From this day on she'd concentrate on Josh and try to forget that Denver Briggs ever existed, she decided. She could only hope that the memories faded faster than they did the last time she'd told herself that.

Denver sat on the fence in the chutes, watching the calf roping contest, only part of his mind registering the scene in front of him. He was having a heck of a time concentrating on anything today.

It didn't matter what he did—he couldn't get out of his mind the memory of April's beautiful naked body lying beneath him. Nor could he forget the reckless way she'd made love with him. This was a very different April from the shy, hesitant young woman who had stolen his heart and his senses more than ten years ago.

She'd practically seduced him last night. Her wild aggressiveness had driven him crazy, obliterating everything but the two of them locked together in passion. It was the most incredible experience he'd ever remembered, and it was going to take him a very long while to forget.

But forget he must, or he'd go out of his mind. Right now he had to put it all out of his head and concentrate on the ride.

If he won this one it would put him back in contention with Jed and Cord, and from then on they'd have to watch his dust. He was going after that championship and no one was going to get in his way.

He watched the cowboy in front of him leap from his horse and race for the calf. The hapless animal struggled valiantly to free itself from the rope looped around its neck, held taut by the cowboy's horse.

The wrangler reached the calf, then flanked it onto its side. After whipping the rope from his clenched teeth, the cowboy swiftly tied three of the calf's legs together, then threw his hands in the air.

Denver nodded. The wrangler had made good time. He looked at the calf still writhing on the ground, and again a vision of April seeped into his mind. April's naked body, glistening in the light from the hallway, writhing beneath him as he entered her....

A bolt of hot excitement seared up his body, and he shuddered. Not today. Today of all days, he needed his concentration. He didn't need to think about April and how she affected him. He didn't need to think about how lonely his life would be from now on without her, or how much he was missing by not seeing Josh grow up to be a young man.

He didn't need any reminders of all that had happened the past week or two. He needed to forget, to empty his mind of all thought except his coming battle with the bull. To do anything else would not only possibly hurt his chances of regaining his position in the standings but could also be dangerous.

Then again, danger was what he needed to get the adrenaline going in his body. Because right now, he felt dead inside, as if his mind refused to obey his will and his body rebelled against his commands. And he had exactly ten minutes to find the motivation that would keep him on that bull's back for eight long seconds.

April sat way up in the stands, trying to ignore Josh's muttered complaints.

"How come we're sitting all the way up here?" Josh

demanded. "Why can't we sit down there in the front row like we did last time?"

"They didn't have any better tickets than these," April murmured, her gaze on the barrel racer skidding in the dust.

"We can't see the chutes from here," Josh grumbled. "We won't see Uncle Denver until it's his turn to ride."

April preferred it that way. She made a conscious effort to unwind her fingers, before she lost all circulation in them. Part of her couldn't bear the thought of seeing Denver again, yet another part of her—the treacherous, stupid part of her—couldn't wait for the bull-riding competition. She still had the program twisted in her hands. She hadn't even opened it, afraid to see Denver's picture splashed across the page.

The bull riding, she knew, would be in the second half of the contest. She watched the first half without seeing anything except a blur of horses and riders.

The intermission seemed to last for hours, and she glanced hopefully at her watch every few minutes, willing for it to be over.

"There's the cotton candy man again!" Josh exclaimed, jumping to his feet. "Can I have some?"

"You've already had some," she murmured automatically.

"Well, can I have some more?"

"No, honey. It's bad for your teeth."

"Well, can I have a hotdog?"

"Later, after the show."

"I want one now."

She glanced at him, trying to curb her irritation. "We'll miss Uncle Denver's ride if we struggle all the way down to the hotdog stand now. You don't want to miss his ride, do you?"

Josh shrugged. "I don't care."

She frowned at him. "I thought you wanted to see him.

Wasn't that why we came all the way back out here today?''

"He doesn't want to see me anymore," Josh said sulkily, "so I don't want to see him."

April sighed. "Josh, it's not that he doesn't want to see you anymore. You know that. It's just that he has to stay with the rodeos. I thought I explained all that."

"He likes the rodeos better than he likes me."

That was hard to argue with, she had to admit. "The rodeo is his life, Josh. You can't expect someone to give up his life for you."

"Why not?"

She had no answer to that. "You just can't. Here, read the program until the next half starts. Tell me when Uncle Denver will be riding."

Josh took the program from her with a bored expression that had her seriously concerned. It looked as if she was back where she'd started with her son. If so, then everything she'd gone through these past weeks had been for nothing.

Josh leafed through the program, then paused, his finger poised over the page. "The bull-riding contest is next," he said listlessly. "Uncle Denver is riding third—" He broke off, then he looked up at her, his eyes wide. "Guess what bull he's riding."

She felt a shaft of apprehension. "Why don't you tell me."

Josh's voice rose with excitement. "Balderdash! Uncle Denver has to ride Balderdash. Cool!"

April did not think it was cool. All she could think about was everything she'd heard about the ferocious bull. Even Denver himself had admitted that he wouldn't like to draw the infamous bull for his ride.

"Let me look," she demanded, taking the program from Josh with the faint hope that he'd made a mistake. She quickly scanned the page, reading down the list of riders until she reached Denver's name. There it was, in big black letters that seemed to jump out at her with gleeful menace.

Within a few minutes, Denver would be bursting out of the chutes on the back of the most notorious, most dangerous bull on the circuit. Denver was going to ride Balderdash.

"It's almost time," Jed said, perching on the fence next to Denver. "You got your mind together yet?"

Denver gave him a wary glance. "I always have my mind together."

Jed shook his head. "Not today you haven't, pardner. Your head's been up in the clouds ever since you got back from Portland. I don't know what that little lady has done to you, but she sure has taken a piece of your mind away from your work, that's for sure."

Denver scowled at him. "Cut it out, J.C. You have no idea what you're talking about."

"I know enough when I see it. You gotta forget about that woman, Cannon, or you'll be watching Cord and me in Las Vegas from the stands instead of the chutes."

Denver made himself smile. "That wishful thinking, J.C.?"

"Nope, just a friendly word of advice, that's all."

"Uh-huh. You're an expert on women, is that it?"

"Hell, there ain't no man expert on women." Jed shook his head in disgust, then settled his hat more firmly on his head. "A calf with one eye could see you're pining after something, and I'm betting my boots it's that sister'n-law of yours. Mark my words, Cannon, women are bad news."

"Why, that just happens to be your opinion, Jed Cullen," a female voice said.

Denver glanced over his shoulder at the pretty blonde standing behind him with her fists dug into her slim hips.

She wore a wide-brimmed hat that shaded her face, but he could see the fire in her bright-blue eyes.

"You tell him, Kristi," he muttered. "And while you're at it, tell him to mind his own damn business."

Kristi glared up at Jed, who sat grinning down at her. "You just leave Cannon alone, J.C.," she ordered. "You don't know nothing about women, so just leave him be."

Jed chuckled. "Well, Kristi, darlin', and just what do you know about women?"

"A lot more than you do, seeing as how I am one."

Jed threw back his head and laughed so loud he almost fell off the fence. "Is that a fact," he said at last, when he finally caught his breath. "Well, I'm sure glad you let me into that little secret, 'cause I sure as heck wouldn't have known it from watching you."

Kristi tossed her head. "Just because I don't get all prettied up and prance around the dance floor, bumping and pushing up against you, doesn't mean I don't know about women. You're just jealous 'cause I can ride faster'n you can."

"Is that right." Jed eyed her up and down with an insolence that made even Denver squirm. "You wouldn't want to put some of your daddy's money on that, would you now?"

Kristi's mouth tightened. "One day, Jed Cullen, I'll show you. I'll show the lot of you I'm as good as any man out there. And that goes for my father, too." With that, she spun around and marched off.

"My, she does have a wiggle in her hips at that," Jed remarked, chuckling. "You reckon she knows what she's talking about?"

Denver shook his head. "I just can't imagine what she sees in you."

Jed shook his head. "The only thing Kristi Ramsett sees in me is competition." He slid off the fence and brushed the dust from his jeans with the flat of his hand. "She's too busy trying to prove to everyone that she's as good as, if not better'n, the rest of the cowboys out here. I reckon if she wasn't spending all her time working for that father of hers, she'd be busting her britches trying to outride you on the bulls."

Denver nodded. "You could be right, J.C."

"Yeah, well, good luck on your ride. Don't forget you need this one to make it back into the standings."

"I'm not likely to forget," Denver said dryly. "I've been listening to that pesky bull crashing around in there for the past five minutes."

He watched Jed stroll off to join a group of cowboys on the other side of the chutes, then turned his attention back to the ring. The first bull rider was about to take his turn.

The cowboy rode well but just grazed the bull's rear with his hand with a couple of seconds still on the clock. That meant no score for the unfortunate rider. One less to worry about, Denver thought, as the familiar quickening of excitement built in his stomach.

The second rider erupted from the chute, flailed his arm a couple of times, then slid sideways and lost his balance. One of the bull's horns barely missed his thigh as he sprinted for the fence.

It was time. Denver wasn't looking forward to tackling Balderdash; still, the challenge of riding the toughest bull on the circuit had a certain thrill about it. Especially if he managed to hang on for the eight seconds. Now, that would be a real victory.

Denver checked to make sure that both clowns were in the ring, then climbed up onto the chute.

Balderdash was in form as usual, snorting and stamping, shifting from side to side in anticipation of demolishing the foolhardy cowboy who had the nerve to try to ride him.

Denver straddled the fence above the restless animal and

handed the end of the braided rope to the cowboy waiting in the chute. The wrangler took the end of it and passed it under the bull's chest, threaded it through the loop and tightened it.

"All set," he told Denver.

Denver pulled in a deep breath. *Concentrate,* he told himself. *Think only of the bull. Nothing else.*

He waited until his stomach had settled, willing the sounds of the crowd to die away in his mind. Then he lowered himself onto the broad back of the bull.

Immediately, Balderdash's head reared up, and Denver caught a glimpse of a rolling eye. A spasm of adrenaline dashed through his veins. Carefully, he wrapped the rope around his hand, then tightened it around his knuckles. He slid forward, raised his left hand in the air and nodded.

The gate opened, and he was through. The first jolt rattled his teeth. Balderdash leaped in the air, raising all four feet clear off the ground. A second later he hit the dust again with a bone-jarring thud that rang bells in Denver's ears.

Denver gritted his teeth, trying to predict each move of the massive bull, and concentrated on keeping his balance.

Balderdash danced to the right, then jerked sharply left, almost unseating him. When that didn't work, the bull reared up on his front legs, then plunged forward and kicked up his rear.

Denver was ready for him. He jerked his body forward, then back, concentrating on keeping his legs straight out in front of him. The bull danced from side to side in an effort to rock him off. Denver shifted in the opposite direction, keeping a perfect balance.

Furious now, Balderdash spun around in a wicked circle. As he did so, a flash of color caught Denver's eye. Something bright and yellow in the grandstand.

It reminded him of April's shirt the first day he'd taught

Josh to ride. Too bad Josh wasn't here to see him ride Balderdash. Too bad he'd screwed up everything again.

The space of a heartbeat. That was all he'd taken off his concentration. It was enough. He felt Balderdash buck under him, then rear up in front. He saw the horns coming up in his face and knew he was too far forward to pull back.

Balderdash knew it, too. With a snort of triumph, he kicked up his hind legs. Denver felt a flash of fear as he toppled forward.

After that, everything happened in slow motion. He knew he was going over the bull's head and there was nothing he could do about it. He wondered how much time was left on the clock.

It was a moment every bull rider dreads. He knew the chances of escaping the murderous thrust of those sharp horns were slim at best.

Frantically he shook the rope free of his hand, afraid he'd be trapped by it and dragged under the bull's feet. The movement cost him another precious second.

His shoulder hit Balderdash's nose and the bull flipped him in the air. He somersaulted, praying he'd land on his feet. He saw the horns coming at him and knew he wasn't going to make the ground.

The sudden fire in his side told him he'd been gored, but before he could wonder how bad it was, he felt an agonizing pain in his back. The ground came up fast, then disappeared again. He saw the brilliant blue of a cloudless sky as the bull's horns lifted him and tossed him in the air as easily as a softball from a pitcher's hand.

Flashes of red, yellow and blue exploded around him, and with relief he realized the clowns were there. Then he hit the ground again, and the world went black.

April stood paralyzed by fear, unable to believe what she'd just seen. She couldn't think, couldn't breathe, and the sudden hush of the crowd made the roaring in her ears seem even louder.

Josh had gone very still, the camera still held up to his face; it was as if he'd been frozen by the image he'd seen through the lens.

For a moment April had the weird sensation of watching the scene in front of her dissolve like pieces of a jigsaw puzzle scattered around her, then settle back into place.

The clowns had lured the bull back through the gates, but Denver still lay on the ground. Two men were on their knees beside him, and April recognized his travel companions, Jed and Cord.

Denver's hat had landed just a few feet away from him, and one lifeless hand stretched out toward it, as if he were still trying to reach it.

Gazing helplessly at his motionless body, she knew without a doubt that he was beyond reaching for anything.

A wave of nausea caught her unawares, and she sat down hard on the bench. When she was able to look at Josh, she saw he was crying, huge silent tears running unheeded down his face.

She reached for him and pulled him down beside her.

"Is he dead?"

His thin, wavering voice cut her like a knife, and she violently shook her head, desperate to convince herself as well as him. She thought about Caroline, and how she must have felt watching her husband die in the dust and dirt of a rodeo arena.

The announcer's voice echoed from the speakers, and the crowd grew utterly silent in order to hear his words.

"Ladies and gentleman, please be patient while we wait for the ambulance. I will give you news of Denver Briggs's condition as soon as I receive it. In the meantime, Roy Lester will entertain you with his special brand of country singing. Roy?"

The murmuring began again, growing to a loud hum of conversation as the singer's voice poured relentlessly from the speakers.

April couldn't take her eyes off the still figure on the ground. If only he'd move, give her some sign that he wasn't too badly hurt. Though how anyone could have survived that murderous assault from the bull she didn't know.

She felt too hot. The sun burned her face and arms, yet she couldn't stop shivering. She wanted so desperately to go down there, to see for herself how bad it was. Yet she knew she couldn't do that to Josh. She couldn't let him see Denver all broken and bloody, nor could she leave her son in the stands by himself.

It seemed an eternity before the white van rolled slowly into the ring, and once more the crowd fell silent. The two attendants knelt by Denver's still form for a minute or two, then loaded him onto a stretcher.

April held tight to Josh's hand as they watched Denver being loaded into the ambulance, then he disappeared from view and the attendants closed the doors. A minute later the ambulance rolled back out through the gates.

Once more the announcer droned empty words over the speakers. "Denver Briggs, ladies and gentlemen. We wish him well."

Someone started applauding, and the sound spread rapidly, echoing around the arena as the crowd surged to their feet to pay homage to the fallen cowboy.

"Can we go and see him?"

April looked down at the tear-stained face of her son and nodded. "Just as soon as I find out which hospital he's at. Come on."

She led him past the still-applauding onlookers and down the steps to the gate to the chutes. A burly cowboy barred her way, and she said quickly, "I'm April Briggs. Denver is my brother-in-law."

His expression changed at once, and he opened the gate and let them through.

To April's intense relief, she saw Cord standing over by the fence, conferring with a small group of cowboys. She hurried over to him, still clinging to Josh's hand.

His black gaze rested on her, and without changing his expression, he tipped his hat. "Ma'am?"

"How is he?" she asked breathlessly.

Cord's hard gaze softened just a little. "He's alive, ma'am. Just banged up pretty bad. He's tough, though. He'll be all right."

Aware of the rest of the group's curious gaze on her, she asked nervously, "Do you know where they've taken him?"

Cord nodded, then pushed himself away from the fence. Taking her arm, he led her away from the speculative glances of the other cowboys. "Jed's unhitching the truck right now. If you hurry you'll catch him before he leaves. He'll get you to the hospital."

She gave him a wan smile of gratitude. "Thanks, but I have my car. I can drive if you tell me where it is."

"I don't know where it is, ma'am. But Jed does, and it will be a darn sight quicker to go with him than try to find it yourself."

"I guess so. But what about you? Don't you want to go?"

Cord's expression remained impassive. "I'll be along a little later. I've got some things to take care of here first."

"Oh, right." She grabbed Josh's hand. "We'll see you there, then."

With Josh at her side, she hurried through the gate and across the parking lot. Sunlight glinted on the roofs of campers and trailers, and she shielded her eyes trying to pick out Denver's rig.

"There he is," Josh said, pointing off to the left. "He's just climbing into the truck."

"Run," April told him. "You can go faster than I can. Ask him to wait for us."

Josh thrust his camera into her hands and sprinted off across the grass. He disappeared between two campers and April heard the roar of Jed's engine as he started the truck.

She half walked, half ran after Josh, hoping he'd make it in time. She reached the two campers, but Josh had disappeared. Denver's camper was hidden from her view, but she could still hear the engine revving.

Finally she rounded one large trailer, and pulled up with a sigh of relief. Josh sat next to Jed in the truck, waving for her to hurry up.

"Thanks for waiting," she said, panting for breath as she passed his open window.

"My pleasure, ma'am."

His normally cheerful face was creased with worry lines and his mouth looked pinched. Seeing him like that made April all the more frightened for Denver.

She clambered up next to Josh and sat on the worn seat of the pickup. The heat inside the cab was almost unbearable, and the vinyl covering burned her bare legs. For a moment she felt dizzy, and she rolled the window down, gulping in the dry, warm air.

"Don't worry, ma'am," Jed said quietly. "Cannon's tough as nails. He'll pull through this."

She nodded, suddenly afraid that if she tried to speak she'd bawl like a baby.

Jed shifted the gears and the truck rolled out onto the road, then sped up to the first light. Josh sat silent by her side, pressed against her as if for comfort. She put an arm around him and gave him a hug.

He turned his face up to her, and her heart melted when

she saw the thin white trails the tears had left on his dusty face.

"He is going to be okay, isn't he, Mom?"

"You bet he is." She hugged him again, and her eyes met Jed's over her son's head. The grave look in the cowboy's gaze unsettled her again, and she stared out at the road, determined to hang on to the belief that Denver was not going to die.

Buildings flashed by as Jed gunned the engine of the ancient pickup. At long last she saw the hospital signs at the side of the road and knew they were close.

"We're here," Jed muttered.

The truck swerved into the driveway and came to a jolting stop in front of the main entrance. "You go ahead, ma'am," Jed said. "I'll park this crate and follow you in."

Flashing him a grateful smile, April scrambled down from the truck and waited for Josh to jump down beside her. She gave Jed a quick wave, then rushed up the steps of the hospital, with Josh close on her heels.

"Denver Briggs," she said breathlessly, when the motherly middle-aged receptionist asked her if she could help. "He was admitted a short while ago."

"Just a minute." The woman's plump fingers flashed over the keyboard of the computer, then she nodded. "He's in ICU. Are you a relative?"

"His sister-in-law. I'm the only family he has. My husband, Denver's brother, died several months ago."

"Oh, I'm sorry." The woman's face clouded, as if she really cared.

Grateful for the sympathy, April managed a shaky smile. "I'd really like to see him."

The woman tapped the keys again. "If you'd care to take a seat in the waiting room, I'll see if I can get someone out there to talk to you."

"Thanks, I'd appreciate that." April hesitated. "I don't suppose you can tell me anything."

Again the receptionist gave her a sympathetic look. "I'm sorry—I really don't know anything yet."

April nodded. "Thanks anyway."

"Where is Uncle Denver?" Josh asked, as they walked together into the waiting room.

"He's in a room where the doctors can take care of him," April said, checking for an empty seat. The waiting room was comfortably furnished with sea-blue couches set at right angles.

April chose one of the corners, where she had a view of the doorway and the passageway beyond. Josh sat down next to her, looking as if he wanted to run out the door at the first opportunity.

"Why don't you get one of those comics to read," April suggested, nodding at the rack of magazines on the wall.

Josh slid off the seat again and sidled self-consciously over to the rack. He came back a minute later with a comic in his hand, then sat idly turning the pages without paying any attention to what was on them.

April caught sight of Jed's tall figure striding past the door. "Wait here a minute," she told Josh. "I'll be right back. Don't go anywhere without me, you hear?"

Josh gave her a resigned nod and pretended to be engrossed in his comic.

She hurried out to the reception area, and got there just in time to hear Jed arguing with the receptionist.

"I'm the closest thing he's got to family. Me and Cord, that is. Why, we know more about Denver Briggs than that sister-in-law of his could make up."

"He's probably right," April said, coming up to stand next to him. "Jed and Cord travel with Denver on the road. They've been together for years."

Jed sent April an apologetic shrug. "I didn't mean any offense. I was just trying to set this lady straight."

"I understand," April assured him.

"Well, I'm sorry, sir," the receptionist said, in a no-nonsense tone that clearly would not tolerate any argument, "but rules are rules. When patients are in critical condition, it's family only."

April gripped the edge of the counter. "Critical?"

The woman nodded. "That's the status of your brother-in-law at present, Mrs. Briggs. I'm sorry."

"How critical?" Jed asked urgently.

"I'm sorry, sir. That's all I know." She looked at April and her eyes brimmed with sympathy. "It's possible it could change for the better any time soon," she added gently.

April weakly nodded, trying to take comfort from that. "I'd like to talk to the doctors as soon as possible."

"I'll do what I can," the receptionist promised.

"I guess we just have to wait, then," Jed said, as he walked with her back to the waiting room.

Wait, April thought. That was all she ever did as far as Denver was concerned. Only this time, the wait was going to be so much harder.

Just let him be all right, she prayed silently, and she'd stop pining after something she couldn't have. Just let him be all right, and she'd accept whatever part of his life he was willing to give her, and never ask for more.

Just let him be all right.

Chapter 11

Josh looked up expectantly when she walked over to him. "Can we see him now?"

"Not yet," April murmured, her thoughts on the man lying helpless in an intensive care ward. "We have to wait for the doctor. He'll let us know when we can see him."

"Boy," Josh muttered, "this sure is boring."

Jed sat down next to him, looking sympathetic. "Hospitals are not much fun, pardner. Especially if you have to stay in one."

"I guess Uncle Denver won't win the championship now," Josh said, seemingly about to cry again.

Jed exchanged glances with April. "Oh, I don't know about that. Your uncle is a lot tougher than he looks. He'll be back on a bull before the end of summer, I reckon."

"I'll be back in school then." Josh threw the comic down on the table and slumped back in his seat. "I won't get to see him at all."

Jed glanced at the clock. "How's about you and me taking a little ride around this town. See if we can find something fun to do.''

''Oh, that's real nice of you,'' April said hurriedly, ''but Josh will be okay. He'll find something to keep himself amused, won't you, Josh?''

Disappointed, Josh shrugged. ''I guess.''

Jed crinkled his eyes at her. ''Wouldn't be no trouble, ma'am. That battle-ax out there isn't gonna let me see Denver anyway, and it could be quite a while before the doctors let you see him. Josh and I could grab a bite to eat while we're out.''

April looked doubtfully at her son. ''What would you like to do, Josh?''

His young face mirrored his confusion and doubt as he considered the choices. It was obvious he was torn between going with Jed or waiting there to see his beloved uncle.

''I doubt if they'll let him in to see Denver, either,'' Jed murmured.

April sighed. ''You're probably right. Are you sure you don't mind?''

''My pleasure, ma'am.'' He got to his feet, settling his hat on his head. ''You ready, pardner?''

Josh wavered for another moment or two. ''Will I be able to see Uncle Denver when I get back?''

''I'll ask them,'' April promised. ''If I see him before you get back I'll tell him you love him, okay?''

Josh nodded, still unsure of himself.

''You're welcome to come with us,'' Jed offered, glancing at Josh's troubled face.

''Thanks, but I'd rather wait here.'' She smiled at Josh. ''Don't worry, honey. Uncle Denver is going to be here for a while. You'll get to see him.''

That seemed to satisfy him, and he walked out with Jed, looking small and defenseless next to the tall, lanky cowboy.

April leaned back with a tired sigh. She felt so helpless, just sitting there waiting. She tried reading some magazines, but nothing held her attention longer than a few seconds.

She watched people come and go, some smiling and cheerful, some weighed down with anguish. Her own anxiety made her restless and she couldn't stop thinking about Denver's body being flung in the air by those lethal horns.

Maybe she should get a cup of coffee, she thought. It might help to clear her head. She was about to get up, when a dark-haired woman in a white coat hurried into the waiting room.

She peered at the other people scattered about the room, then her glance fell on April. "Mrs. Briggs?"

April nodded, her stomach muscles tightening with apprehension.

"I'm Dr. Shelby. I've been treating your brother-in-law."

April got to her feet and took the woman's proffered hand. The doctor's handshake was firm and brisk, but there was a wariness in the dark-brown eyes, which worried April.

"How is he?" she asked quickly. "Is he conscious?"

"Yes, but he's sedated right now." Dr. Shelby glanced at the other occupants in the room, then said quietly, "I'd like a word with you. Let's go outside."

With an uneasy feeling of foreboding, April followed the doctor's slim figure into the quiet hallway. Her mouth felt dry, and she wished she'd had time to get the coffee. Although questions bounced around in her mind, she couldn't bring herself to ask any of them.

"He has a nasty gash in his side," the doctor said, looking down at the clipboard she carried. "Luckily the horns didn't reach any organs, and the wound should heal up just fine. Your brother-in-law has several bruises and contusions, most of which are fairly superficial.''

She paused, and April had the distinct feeling the doctor was keeping something back.

''There's more, isn't there?''

Dr. Shelby nodded. ''There's a back injury. It should heal, given time. The problem is, your bother-in-law doesn't want to give it time.''

April frowned. ''I don't understand.''

Dr. Shelby flipped the page back on the clipboard and tucked the board under her arm. ''Mr. Briggs is demanding that we release him from the hospital. He seems very agitated, and quite desperate to leave. Do you know of any reason he's in such a hurry?''

''He's probably anxious about his standings,'' April said, trying to curb her irritation at Denver. ''If he keeps missing rides, he'll drop below the top-fifteen moneymakers, which will put him out of the finals.''

Dr. Shelby pursed her lips. ''I think you should know that if Mr. Briggs does not take the time to heal properly, he could easily do some permanent damage to his spine. To attempt to ride a bull in his condition would be tantamount to suicide. He could very well spend the rest of his life in a wheelchair, if he doesn't kill himself first.''

''I see.'' April drew an unsteady breath. ''Have you told him this?''

Dr. Shelby looked grim. ''I've explained the situation, yes. I don't think he understands the seriousness of his injury. Perhaps you can get through to him the importance of resting until his back is fully healed.''

''How long will that take?''

Again the doctor consulted her notes. ''It's hard to tell with a back injury. It could be anywhere from a few days to a few weeks. It depends on how well he rests and how fast his body heals.''

April sucked in her breath. No wonder Denver was upset. This would end his chances of making the finals.

"I have to tell you, Mrs. Briggs," the doctor went on, "I have advised Mr. Briggs to give up the rodeo entirely. His body cannot go on taking that kind of punishment without causing some permanent damage. He's lucky he's basically strong. Many men would be crippled by some of the falls he's had."

Denver had to be devastated by that news. Her heart ached for him. "May I see him?"

"I can give you a few minutes, that's all. He'll be drowsy and may even be asleep. If so, it would be better not to waken him."

"I understand." She followed the doctor down the long hallway to the end, where Dr. Shelby indicated a door on the right. "He's in there. If he is awake, please do your best to convince him to stay at least a few days until we are satisfied with his condition."

April nodded, then walked slowly down to where the door of the room stood ajar. She took a moment to compose her chaotic thoughts, then peered through the doorway at the figure on the bed.

He lay on his back, his eyes closed. One wrist was hooked up to a bottle, from which clear liquid dripped slowly through the thin tube. One elbow was heavily bandaged and dark strands of his hair overlapped a white dressing that covered part of his forehead. He looked oddly vulnerable.

She crept into the room and stood by the side of the bed. Even in sleep, his strong features seemed harsh and unrelenting. He had caused her so much heartache over the years, yet no matter how hard she tried, she could not stop loving him.

She felt an almost unbearable urge to kiss his closed eyelids, his rough cheek. Her fingers ached to trace the grim lines of his mouth, to satisfy herself that he was merely sleeping and not in some deep, unreachable coma.

She knew she had to move away, before she gave in to the urge to wake him. It was so hard to convince herself that he was going to be all right, without seeing his eyes open and recognizing her.

She turned to leave, then froze as he said huskily, "You don't have to creep around—I'm not dead yet."

His eyes were still firmly closed, and she asked warily, "How did you know it was me?"

"Your perfume. The nurses all smell like disinfectant."

She felt a reluctant smile tug at her lips. "How are you feeling?" It was a stupid question, she knew, but right then she couldn't think of anything better to say.

"I'm not feeling much at all at the moment."

"That must be pretty strong medication they gave you."

"Yeah." He opened his eyes at last and looked at her. His gaze seemed a little unfocused, no doubt the effects of the drugs. In spite of that, she saw a defiant rebellion in his face that really worried her.

"I hear you've been giving the doctors a bad time," she said lightly. "What's all this about walking out of here before you're ready?"

"Doctors make too much damn fuss over nothing. All they're worried about is their malpractice suits. There's nothing wrong with me a couple of aspirin won't cure."

April winced. "I'd say a back injury needs a little more than that."

He looked away from her, his gaze fixed on the ceiling above his head. "Did you talk to Dr. Shelby?"

"Yes, I did. She seems very knowledgeable."

"What did she tell you?"

"Just that you've injured your back and need to rest it some before you leave here." If she was hoping to slide by with that she was disappointed.

"What else did she say?" Denver asked, a little too casually.

There was no point in evading the issue, April thought miserably. "She suggested you might want to think about giving up the rodeo."

Denver's mouth tightened. "So she did say it. I was kind of hoping I'd dreamed that part."

"You must know you can't go on riding bulls forever," April said gently.

"I didn't figure on riding them forever. Just long enough to win the all-around championship." For a moment bitterness flashed in his eyes. "I'm so damn close."

"Denver, I know how much the championship means to you. But Dr. Shelby thinks it's possible you could injure yourself permanently. Maybe even have to spend the rest of your life in a wheelchair. When you weigh the chances of that, the championship doesn't seem quite so important, does it?"

The defiance in his face intensified. "It's all I've thought about. All I've fought for. I'm not about to let some pesky bull put an end to my chances. If I don't make it this year, I'll make it the next. Or the next. I'm damned if I'm giving up now."

She searched her mind for the right words to say, knowing that whatever she said wouldn't take away that look of determination on his face. Slowly, in spite of her struggles to prevent it, her resentment burned.

"It means that much to you," she said bitterly, "that you're willing to give up your life for it. Nothing else matters. Nothing and no one."

He refused to look at her but continued to stare at the ceiling, his face harsh and uncompromising. "Yeah, it means that much to me," he muttered.

"Then I feel sorry for you, Denver Briggs. You must be a very lonely man."

He turned his head at last and looked at her. "All right, you want the truth? I'll give it to you. I told you once that the rodeo was my life. It's all I have. The only damn thing I've been any good at my entire life."

He paused, as if gathering strength to deliver his speech. Then he looked back at the ceiling, and his voice was hushed when he spoke again. "Ever since I was a kid I kept hearing about the wonderful achievements of my big brother. The good-looking one, who not only excelled at sports but could pull straight As at the same time. The smart one, who put himself through college instead of bumming around the country like his no-good father. The perfect one, who made his mother proud."

She started to protest, but he went on as if he hadn't heard her.

"Lane was the one who got a degree, who settled down with a wife and had a son, a family. Lane was all success, the man with the Midas touch. No matter what I did, I wasn't good enough to stand in his shadow. I was Denver Briggs, the one who was such a terrible disappointment to his mother. The useless one, who'd never amount to a hill of beans, just like his lousy father."

"Denver, I'm sure—"

"Well, in the end I found something I could do that Lane couldn't. I can rodeo. I can win the all-around championship and be the best of the best. For once I can have something I can be proud of, and damn it, I'm not going to be satisfied until I have it."

Now, at last, she understood. Now that it was too late. "You don't have to prove anything, Denver—"

"Yes, I do. I have to prove something to myself. It's the only way I'm ever going to find any real peace."

"And if you end up in a wheelchair, what are you going to prove then?"

He turned to her, and his eyes burned with his determination. "I promise you, April, I'll either get that championship, or I'll damn well die trying."

She knew it was useless to argue with him while he was in this mood. She moved to leave but paused at the door to look back at him. "Will you at least promise me one thing?"

He shrugged, and she felt a twinge of sympathy for him when he winced. "Depends what it is."

"Josh is very anxious about you. I think it would settle his mind if he could see you. He's not here right now, but I'd like to bring him back tomorrow. Will you at least stay here until he's had a chance to visit with you?"

He narrowed his gaze for a moment, then said brusquely, "I guess another night won't hurt."

"You won't leave before he gets here?"

He raised his hand in a mocking gesture of compliance. "I give you the word of a cowboy."

"Thank you," she said quietly. "It will mean a great deal to him. By the way, he wanted me to tell you that he loves you."

His mouth twisted in a wry grimace.

Satisfied that he would keep his promise, she left him alone. At least she'd bought some time, she thought, as she hurried back to the waiting room. Though probably not enough. Somehow she had to keep him in that hospital bed until the doctors were satisfied with his condition.

After that, she honestly didn't know. If Denver was determined to kill himself to prove something to himself and the rodeo world out there, she didn't know how she was going to stop him. She knew only that if he died, a part of her would die, too.

Josh was in the waiting room, talking earnestly to Jed when she got there. They both looked up as she walked toward them, and she did her best to smile.

"Can I see him now?" Josh asked eagerly.

"He's sleeping right now," she told him.

Josh looked worried, and she sat down next to him, putting a comforting arm around his shoulders. "Well, did you have fun?"

He shrugged. "It's kind of hard to have fun when Uncle Denver is hurt bad."

"How is he?" Jed asked. "Complaining about the service, I reckon. Running those nurses all over the place."

"He seems to be doing okay," April said carefully.

Jed narrowed his eyes, as if sensing there was something she wasn't telling him.

She made herself meet his gaze. "He's not in a very good mood, of course. They're pumping him full of drugs and he's a little drowsy, but otherwise he seems fairly comfortable."

She looked down at her son. "He wants you to visit him tomorrow, so we'll come back then."

"All right!" Josh looked a little brighter. "Maybe I'll bring my video games."

"Well, I don't know if he'll be able to play with them, but we can talk about that later. Right now, I'm ready to go home."

Josh jumped up. "Me, too."

Jed said nothing as they walked out of the hospital together, but as they reached the parking lot he handed his keys to Josh. "Why don't you go ahead and open the door for me, pardner," he said, as Josh stared at him in surprise.

April watched her son race toward the truck, bracing herself for the question she knew was coming.

As soon as Josh was out of earshot, Jed said urgently, "Okay, give it to me straight. How is he really?"

She managed a smile. "He's in pain, but I've been assured by his doctor that he's not at death's door. The gash in his side will heal, and so will his bumps and bruises. It just…might take a little while."

Jed nodded. "I figured as much. Denver won't like that. He doesn't like being stuck inside. Maybe they'll let me see him tomorrow."

"I imagine they will." She was tempted to tell him about the doctor's warning, then decided it was up to Denver himself to tell his travel partners. If he didn't, she might have to take matters into her own hands. If he insisted on taking these terrible chances, she'd need the help of both Cord and Jed to convince him to give up the rodeo.

Josh was quiet on the way back to the rodeo parking lot, and even Jed gave up trying to coax him into conversation.

"Cord will have a wasted journey," April remarked, remembering that he planned on going to the hospital after his ride.

"I called him from the hospital." Jed slowed the truck as they approached the entrance to the rodeo grounds. "Told him to hold off until tomorrow. We'll call first before we go on out there."

"I want to thank you for driving us there today. I don't think I could have found it on my own."

"You don't have to thank me, ma'am." Jed walked with her to her car, then stood holding the door open for her, his unusual golden eyes regarding her gravely. "I just want you to know that I'd do anything for Cannon. So would Cord. Cannon's like a brother to us, and we don't like to see him get hurt."

She had the strong feeling that he wasn't necessarily talking about Denver's physical injuries. "Neither do I," she said evenly. "I think Denver's been hurt enough in his life."

"Yes, ma'am. Glad you understand that."

She thought about those words on the long drive home and wondered exactly how much Denver had told his partners about his past. It was more likely that they had only sensed the pain that drove him.

They were very much alike, all three of them. All apparently searching for self-fulfillment by proving they could rodeo better than anyone else.

Having spent so much time together in that small camper, they should all know one another very well. Yet she couldn't help feeling that each of them had much to hide, and that none of them really knew the others as well as he thought he did.

It was sad to think of the loneliness of such men, unable to share their lives even though they were constant companions. What chance did an outsider have of ever breaking through those formidable barriers?

She felt pity for any woman who would fall for any one of them. Most of all, she pitied herself. For no matter what happened in the future, whether or not Denver rode again, whether or not their lives would merge or separate forever, she would never stop loving him, even though she knew she could never have his love in return.

At least now she knew why. It was Lane who had stood between them all these years. Denver hadn't left her because he couldn't settle down. He'd left her because he couldn't compete with his brother.

He'd been hiding behind excuses all this time, just as she had. While Lane was alive, as long as she was his wife, she had been unattainable to Denver. And now, Lane's ghost still stood between them. Denver couldn't have what Lane had once had. In Denver's eyes, she still belonged to his perfect brother. And so did Josh.

It hit her so hard and so suddenly she jerked the wheel, waking up Josh, who had dozed off at her side.

"Whassamatter?" he grumbled, and promptly closed his eyes again.

April stared at her son's face while the notion grew and spread in her mind. She had to tell Denver the truth. It was the one thing that might stop him from killing himself in a rodeo ring. But how could she, after all these years? He would be angry. Furious with her for not having told him sooner.

And how would Josh take the news that the father he'd adored wasn't his father after all? Would he be able to accept Denver as his father? What was even more important, would Denver now be able to accept Josh as his son?

The questions buzzed in her mind, driving her crazy with indecision. She reached home at last and let herself into the house.

She did her best to put her thoughts on hold while she cooked spaghetti and meatballs for dinner. Josh asked a dozen questions about Denver throughout the meal, and she answered them carefully, wary of saying too much. She could eat little with the turmoil going on in her stomach, and it was with a tremendous sense of relief that she finally tucked her son into bed and wished him good-night.

Alone in the living room, she sat and stared at the blank TV screen. She had to think about the consequences of such a risky move. It would throw Josh's world upside down, not to mention her own and Denver's.

But it could save Denver from himself. If he knew the truth, he might not feel so compelled to prove something that really wasn't necessary anymore. She could give him what he'd been searching for all these years. A sense of self-worth. She could give him something that would lay his brother's ghost to rest in his mind forever—the knowledge that he had given her the son she loved so much.

She slept badly, waking up several times throughout the night with her heart racing and her forehead bathed in perspiration. Part of her mind kept searching for reasons that she shouldn't tell Denver now what she should have told him long ago.

She knew she was still trying to find excuses. She'd used her promise to Lane as an excuse, a promise she should never have given. If only she'd known then the pain that had driven Denver all these years, she might have taken the chance. But it was too late now to think about what might have been. She had to do it now, for his sake. She could only hope that both Denver and Josh would forgive her.

She and Josh drove the two hours back to the hospital the following afternoon. She paid little heed to Josh's constant questions. She needed her strength for what promised to be a harrowing ordeal. She couldn't imagine how Denver would react to the news. Angry, without a doubt. After all, she'd denied him his son all these years. But what else? Would it be worth the risk? Would he give up his dream of the championship?

It was hard to tell, and she was afraid to think beyond that moment in case she lost her nerve. All she could hope was that he would understand why she'd deceived him for so long.

She and Josh hurried into the reception area, where she gave the receptionist her name. When she asked to see Denver, the young woman behind the desk asked her to wait. A few minutes later a nurse beckoned to her from the doorway.

"You can see him now," she said, smiling down at Josh.

April's pulse leaped in nervous anticipation. "How is he?"

"He's feeling a little better, I think. He's very eager to leave us."

"So I heard." April pulled in a steadying breath. "We won't stay too long."

The nurse nodded and hurried off.

April led Josh down the hallway to Denver's room. "You can stay only a little while," she warned him. "We don't want to make Uncle Denver too tired."

Josh looked a little scared, and she hugged him. "Don't worry, he's going to be just fine." She pushed open the door and peered in.

Denver appeared to be sleeping, but as Josh warily approached the bed he opened his eyes and turned his head. The bruise on his forehead had turned a spectacular purple, and his arm was still bandaged, but otherwise he seemed more like himself.

"Hey there, cowboy," he said, giving Josh a slow grin.

Josh studied him for a moment. "Did it hurt bad when the bull gored you?"

April rolled her eyes. Trust Josh to get straight to the heart of the matter.

"To tell you the truth," Denver said seriously, "I don't rightly remember everything that happened. I guess it hurt some, but it's better now."

"Your head's all bruised," Josh announced.

Denver winked. "You should see the rest of me."

April decided it was time to intervene. "Josh wanted to bring his video games," she said hurriedly. "I told him you weren't quite up to that yet, but maybe by tomorrow you'd feel more like it."

Denver flashed a glance at her. "I won't be here tomorrow," he said quietly. "Cord's taking me up to his cabin in the mountains. I'm going to stay there a couple of days before I join up with Jed and him in Idaho."

"You're going to stay there alone?"

"Yeah, alone," Denver said dryly. "I'm not a cripple yet. I just got a sore back, that's all."

"What did Dr. Shelby say about that?"

"There wasn't much she could say."

"Did you tell Cord about her warning?" April demanded, beginning to feel desperate.

"Nope, and I don't intend to. I don't want you telling him, either."

He smiled at Josh, though his eyes looked stormy. She could guess how much he resented her interference.

"Jed tells me he took you out on the town yesterday," he said to Josh, effectively cutting off her questions.

Josh shrugged. "There wasn't much to do. We ate hamburgers and played on the machine where you have to get the claws to pick up a prize."

"Oh, yeah, I used to do that. Win anything?"

"Nah. You have to be real good to win something."

"You just have to keep trying, that's all."

Josh appeared doubtful. "I guess."

April paid little attention to what they were saying. Denver was planning to leave the hospital. Once he was gone there would be little she could do to stop him from rejoining the circuit. And little Cord and Jed could do, she suspected, even if they did know the truth. Somehow she had to find the strength to tell him about Josh. This could well be her last chance to do it.

She let Josh chatter on for a little while, then said gently, "I think it's time we let Uncle Denver get some rest."

Josh looked at him, his face creased in sympathy. "Would it hurt you if I gave you a hug?"

Denver smiled and held out his good arm. "Not nearly as much as it would hurt if you didn't, I reckon."

Making an obvious attempt to be gentle, Josh wound his arms around his uncle's neck. "I love you, Uncle Denver," he whispered.

Over Josh's shoulder, April saw Denver's face pucker up with pain.

"Me, too, pardner," he said softly. "You take good care of yourself, you hear?"

Josh nodded. "I'll miss you. Will you come back and see us soon?"

Denver opened his eyes and looked straight at April. "If I can."

Josh pulled away and looked at him gravely. "I hope you stop hurting soon."

Denver's face was impassive as he ruffled the boy's hair. "So do I," he said gruffly.

"I'll be back," April said, as she drew her son to the door.

He looked uneasy, but she didn't give him time to protest. She nudged Josh into the hallway and walked quickly with him down to the waiting area.

"I have to have a quick word with someone," she told him. "I won't be long, and I want you to wait here until I come back. Then we'll go get something to eat."

To her relief, for once Josh didn't argue. She left him with a pile of comics and hurried back to Denver's room.

His suspicious expression when she entered told her that he was expecting an argument. He was in for a lot more than that, she thought grimly. He was in for the shock of his life.

"No matter what you're about to say—" he started.

But she silenced him with a sharp movement of her hand. "You have to tell Cord the truth about your back," she said bluntly.

"I don't have to do anything I don't want to do. It's my life and I reckon I'm entitled to live it any way I want."

"And you want to live it in a wheelchair?"

"There's only a slim chance of that happening."

"Dr. Shelby told me if you try to leave now you could do some permanent damage to your spine. Or worse."

"I told you, doctors always exaggerate. Besides, I could get killed crossing the street tomorrow. So what's the difference? People take chances with their lives every day." His face was stubborn when he regarded her. "I've been taking chances all my life. It's what I do. I'm not about to stop now."

She lifted her hands in a gesture of defeat. "Why? What

difference does it make now? Lane is dead. Your mother is dead. They'll never know if you win the championship.''

"I'll know." He tightened his jaw. "Believe me, I'll know."

She dropped her hands. "You're being incredibly selfish."

"Yeah, well, how would you know? You've always had everything you wanted. You and Lane both."

Her throat hurt with the effort not to cry. *That's not true,* she protested silently. *I could never have you.*

For a moment the pain in his eyes gave her hope, then he said dully, "Well, you did the right thing by marrying him. You picked the right brother, because he gave you everything that I couldn't. But you knew that, didn't you? That's why you married him."

She took a deep breath. "I married him," she said deliberately, "because I was pregnant with Josh."

His eyebrows lifted a fraction. "Well, well. My brother wasn't a saint after all. I'm glad my mother never knew that. She would have been crushed."

She waited a moment, then said quietly, "Lane never touched me until after we were married."

She could almost see the thoughts working through his mind. He stared at the ceiling for a long time. "Are you trying to tell me Josh isn't Lane's baby?"

"Lane couldn't have children," she said, struggling to keep her voice even. "He was sterile."

His face was set like a stone mask. "I don't believe you."

"Remember that bout of measles he had when he was in college?"

Now she could see the doubt spreading over his face. "How come he never said anything about it?"

"He didn't want your mother to know." She paused, then added lamely, "I guess he didn't want anyone to know. He felt he had to tell me when he asked me to marry him. He made me promise not to tell anyone else. Not anyone.''

Denver's brow furrowed with the effort to accept what he'd heard. ''I can imagine why,'' he muttered. ''That must have nearly killed him. He always had to be so damn perfect.''

She watched his face, waiting for the inevitable question that would change everything. When it came, she was still unprepared.

''If Josh isn't Lane's,'' Denver said slowly, ''how come he looks so much like me?''

She didn't have to tell him after all. He turned his face to her, his expression a mixture of disbelief, shock and anger.

''Mine? Josh is *mine?*''

She nodded.

The color drained out of his face, leaving him so white she began to worry.

''Why didn't you tell me?'' he whispered. His voice rose, ending in a roar. ''Why in God's name didn't you tell me?''

She fought back the tears. ''You weren't there to tell. You left, without letting anyone know where you were going.'' It seemed so lame, such an unforgivably inadequate reason to deny a man his son. She searched for the words that would convey the sense of helplessness, the fear, the utter despair she'd felt back then.

Before she could say anything, however, Denver spoke again. This time there was no escaping the accusation, the terrible bitterness in his voice.

''I know why you didn't tell me. Lane was the better bet. He would make the perfect husband, the perfect father. You chose the perfect man rather than the no-good drifter.

Well, I suppose I should have expected that. He took everything else away from me and you let him steal my son.''

Her own anger was swift and helped restore some of her self-esteem. ''Lane offered me a home for the baby. He gave me what you never could. He gave me security and an unconditional love.''

Denver's face twisted in pain. ''Then I guess you made the right choice.''

''I thought I did at the time.'' She rose to her feet, clutching her purse to her chest like a life belt.

''Does he know?''

''Josh? No, we…never told him. I know I should have told you, Denver. I guess my pride got in the way. I didn't want you to stay with me just because of the baby. I married Lane for Josh's sake. He needed a real father. He still does.'' She walked to the door, then turned to look at him.

He lay unmoving on the bed, his stoic expression carving his face in stone.

''Now you have a choice,'' she said quietly. ''You can accept Josh as your son, or you can turn your back on him, the way you did me. Either way, he will survive. We both will. I'll make sure of that.''

She left him and walked down the hallway, seeing nothing but the emptiness stretching out in front of her.

Chapter 12

He lay for hours after she had left, unable and unwilling to accept the truth. He had a son. Josh was his son. He was torn between love and pride, assailed by bittersweet thoughts of what might have been.

Lane had not been perfect after all. He should feel happy about that, but somehow he couldn't. It must have killed Lane to know that he was unable to give April a child, while his no-good brother had fathered the boy he'd loved as a son. No wonder he'd made April promise to keep it a secret.

Still, it was the worst kind of betrayal. All those years of longing, all those years of loneliness. If only he'd known, he might have lived a very different life. Now it was too late. He'd been on the circuit too long. He was rodeo, and rodeo was his life. He couldn't live any other.

Dr. Shelby visited him later that evening, and reluctantly allowed him permission to leave in the morning. ''You won't be riding any bulls for a while,'' she told him.

"You'll have to take care of that back. In fact, I have to stress again that it would be better for you if you gave up riding those animals altogether. You stand a very good chance of doing some permanent damage, if they don't kill you first. Don't say I didn't warn you."

He thanked her, but her words meant little to him. His entire world had been turned upside down. He wasn't even sure he knew who he was anymore.

Thanks to the medication, he slept well that night, though he awoke with a deep feeling of depression that wouldn't go away. Not even the sight of towering fir trees and mountain peaks helped to lift his spirits as Cord drove him up to the cabin.

Cord said little to him, no doubt aware of his lousy mood. "There's plenty of wood for the woodstove," he told him, as he led him into a dilapidated rustic building buried in a huddle of thick cedars. "You don't need to lift anything heavier than a cooking pot, so you can rest that back."

The musty smell of damp cedar and wood smoke greeted Denver as he looked around the sparsely furnished living room. Tattered books crammed the shelves of a bookcase, and a couple of faded armchairs sat in front of the woodstove. A battered electric range stood in one corner, with a stained sink next to it, and ratty curtains hung at the dusty window.

A door in the back wall obviously led into a bedroom. Denver wondered what kind of shape the bed was in. He was probably going to need the drugs the doctor had given him.

"It ain't much," Cord acknowledged, "but it sure is quiet and peaceful. No one will bother you up here."

Denver looked out of the window, to where a sliver of shimmering water glistened between the thick green branches of the trees. "What do you do up here all alone?"

"Some fishing, hiking, reading, mostly meditating. You'd be surprised how clear your thinking is after being here for a week or two." Cord carried Denver's bags though a door into the bedroom and dumped them on the floor.

He came out again and squatted in front of the stove. "You probably won't need this during the day, but it gets chilly at night." He pulled the flap down and peered inside. "It's all set to go—you just have to put a match to it."

He got to his feet and gave Denver a long look. "You gonna be all right up here alone?"

"I'll be just fine," Denver assured him. "I've got medication, a comfortable chair and plenty of books to read. A couple of day's rest around here and I'll be a new man."

"I sure hope so." Cord ambled over to the door. "Just in case, I left my cell phone on the bed. There's an old-timer lives about ten minutes from here. He's your closest neighbor. There's a campground about twenty miles away, but there's no knowing who's around. The phone numbers for both are in the cupboard over the sink."

Denver eyed the two cabinets hanging loosely on the wall. "I don't reckon I'll need them, but thanks."

"We'll pick you up Monday on our way back through here."

Denver lifted his hand in a salute. "Much obliged, pardner."

Cord gave him a brief nod and left.

Denver heard the sound of the truck fade in the distance. Fishing, hiking and meditating. Well, he wasn't much up on fishing and he didn't think he would be hiking too far, but he sure had a lot to think about.

He hadn't done any real thinking in a very long time. But if he was going to make the kind of choices that faced him now, he couldn't have picked a better place to do it. Just him, the trees and the critters of the forest.

He spent the afternoon exploring his immediate surroundings. The pure joy of being out in the open air again kept him on his feet until his aching back forced him to return to the cabin.

He lit the stove and heated the stew and beans he'd brought with him. Then, settled in front of the stove, he opened the book he'd picked out to read.

The silence was broken only by the spitting logs on the fire and the rustle of the pages as he turned them. It was a mystery and should have held his attention. When he read an entire chapter and still didn't know what the story was about, he gave up and put the book aside.

The fire had begun to burn down, and he got up to put more logs into the stove. He paced the room and peered out the window at the blackness of the night. Finally, he could not keep the thoughts at bay any longer.

He sat down, buried his head in his hands and let them take over. He thought about his childhood and the devastating day his mother told him his father wasn't coming home.

He thought about all the times he'd been in trouble at school and how Lane had lit into him for it. How bitterly he'd resented his brother.

How he couldn't wait to be free, dependent on no one but himself. How April had nearly changed all that. And might have done if she hadn't belonged to Lane first.

He didn't want to think about April. He didn't want to remember how her laugh could brighten his day, how she could make him tremble inside whenever she was near. How the touch of her hands set his very soul on fire. How the memory of their lovemaking intruded on his dreams and scrambled his mind in the waking hours.

He thought about Josh, instead. Josh, his son, whom he'd learned to love, even though he'd belonged to Lane, too.

Josh, who wasn't Lane's child at all but had been created with his own genes, his passion, his lifeblood.

Josh, his son. He said the words out loud, tasting them as they left his lips, listening to them echo in the empty room, striving to understand what they meant to him. *His son.*

Except that Josh didn't know. To Josh he was just the uncle. Josh had always believed that Lane was his father. Lane, the man who'd held him as a baby, nurtured him, disciplined him, taught him to ride a bike and taken him to ball games.

In Josh's heart, Lane would always be the father he'd loved and lost. And there was no way on this good earth that Denver Briggs could ever take that away from him.

He sat there for a long time. Long after the last flickering flames of the fire had died. Long after the cold had seeped through the cabin walls. Until he'd faced his demons and knew what they were. Until he knew, at last, the path he must take.

"When is Uncle Denver coming back to see us?"

April snapped the pruning shears shut and closed her eyes. If Josh asked that question one more time, she thought wearily, she'd scream.

She'd been promising herself she'd prune the rosebushes for weeks and had finally found the energy to do it. She'd hoped that working out in the warm sun would help lift her spirits, but Josh would not allow her to escape the pain.

In another week, she told herself, Josh would be in school and she'd be starting her new job at the bank. It had been a good many years since she'd used her accounting skills, but she was reasonably sure she'd be able to handle things, and she was looking forward to it.

She'd even managed to arrange her schedule so that Josh would be alone for no more than an hour after school. He seemed so much more well adjusted than he had been at the end of the last school year, and she had high hopes that everything would work out for them now.

There would still be some hills to climb—she had no doubt about that. The biggest of which was Josh's refusal to let go of his expectations about Denver.

No matter how much she cautioned him, no matter how much she impressed upon him how remote the chances were of Denver coming to see him any time soon, Josh insisted on asking every single day.

She couldn't go on this way, she thought, as she bagged up the cuttings from the rosebushes. Every mention of Denver's name was like a knife plunged into her heart. It was bad enough that thoughts of him kept her awake at night. She couldn't take these constant reminders every day, as well.

She couldn't go on thinking about him, living in terror that he might fall again and never get up. She had to put him out of her mind if she was to have any peace, and that meant putting him out of Josh's mind, too.

Sooner or later Josh would have to realize that Denver wasn't coming back. She'd had no word from him since the day she'd seen him in the hospital. It was obvious he'd chosen not to acknowledge his son.

She could understand why. He could never forgive her for what she had done. He would never forgive his brother. She kept remembering what he'd said that day: *You let him steal my son.*

Every time he looked at Josh he'd be reminded of that. The ultimate betrayal. As far as Denver was concerned, Josh had always been Lane's son, and Denver would never see him as anything else. Just as he would never see her as anyone else but Lane's wife.

She had to accept that. Josh would have to accept it, too, even if he never knew why.

She chose that night to talk to him, knowing that the longer she put it off, the tougher it would be. She waited until he was in bed, then sat down next to him, praying that she would find the right words.

"I don't think we should count on seeing Uncle Denver again," she said, her heart breaking at the look of anguish in her son's eyes.

"Why not?" Josh's bottom lip trembled. "Did he die?"

April felt a cold chill. "Oh, no, honey, he's just fine. I expect he's riding the bulls again by now."

"Then why doesn't he want to see us again?"

"It isn't because he doesn't love you, Josh. Because I know that he does." She'd told him that so many times, but now she believed that with all her heart. She'd seen it in Denver's face that last day. If only Denver could have loved her, too. It might have been enough for him.

"Then why isn't he coming?"

Tears glistened at the corners of Josh's eyes, and April held out her arms.

She rocked his warm, thin body and rested her chin on his soft hair. "One day, Josh, you'll understand. Denver isn't like your father. He can never stay in one place. He has to keep moving from one place to another. It's something deep inside him that won't let him rest."

"But he said he'd come back. He said I could ride Salty with him again. He said he'd come back for Christmas." The last words ended on a wail.

April closed her eyes. "I know, honey. He meant it at the time. But sometimes things get in the way of what we want to do, and we have no choice. Uncle Denver has to follow the rodeo. He doesn't have any other choice. He's not coming back, Josh. I'm sorry."

Josh was sobbing now, his wet face pressed against her shoulder. His voice was muffled, but she heard the words, and they sank into her soul like burning coals.

"I don't love him anymore."

She held him until he fell into an exhausted sleep. Tomorrow, she decided, she'd take Josh back to Caroline's ranch and ask if he could continue with the riding lessons. It might help take his mind off losing Denver.

She slept fitfully, as she always did nowadays. She could control her thoughts during the day, but at night, in the hazy world of half sleep, Denver's voice and the memory of his warm hands on her bare skin tormented her unmercifully.

Her treacherous body longed for him, in a way that far surpassed the yearnings she'd fought while with Lane. The memory of his passion was still too fresh in her mind, and she could not escape the tendrils of need that coiled inside her and would not let her rest.

As she expected, Josh was subdued and sulky the next morning. He sat at the breakfast bar, toying with his cereal, and wouldn't answer her when she asked him if he wanted more fruit.

"You have to finish your breakfast," she said lightly, "if you want to come out with me this morning."

"I don't feel like going out," Josh muttered.

"You might if you knew where I was going."

He shrugged. "So where are you going?"

"I'm going to see Caroline at the Second Chance Ranch."

She thought she saw a flicker of interest, but he stubbornly refused to look at her.

"I thought you might like to ride Salty."

She waited a long time for his answer. Finally he asked cautiously, "By myself?"

"Well, I was thinking of asking Caroline to take you for a lesson." She tried to ignore the treacherous thought that Caroline might know how Denver was doing. If she had to cut out her tongue, she decided, she was not going to bring up Denver's name.

"Okay," Josh said, picking up his spoon.

His response was a long way from enthusiasm, but it was better than the sulky silence she'd endured. She cleared away the breakfast dishes and dumped them in the dishwasher, then put in a call to Caroline.

"I'd be delighted to take him on," Caroline assured her. "Bring him over this morning and we'll see how well he's doing. Then I'll know better which class to put him in."

To April's intense relief, Caroline didn't mention Denver's name. With any luck she could avoid conversation about him. If Caroline brought up his name, she told herself, she'd just have to change the subject.

Caroline greeted them at the door, smiling down at Josh with genuine pleasure on her face. "I've missed seeing you around here, Josh. It will be fun to have you join our classes."

Josh sent a wistful glance in the direction of the stables. "Will I be able to ride Salty?"

"Well, bless your heart, of course you will." Caroline gave April a wide smile.

She'd had her dark hair cut, April noticed. The short flip suited her.

"Let's have some coffee," Caroline said, leading them into the sitting room. "Then we'll take Salty out and give him some exercise."

April winced as the painful memories invaded her defenseless mind. Memories of Denver sitting in that armchair, eating a Danish, smiling at Josh while he told him about Balderdash.

As if reading her mind, Caroline said casually, "I saw Denver the other day. It's good to see him looking so well. He says his back is just fine now."

She was leaning over the small table, pouring out the

coffee. April was glad her own face was hidden from the perceptive woman.

Josh glanced at his mother, then looked away, his mouth pulled down at the corners in an expression she dreaded.

Apparently unaware of the sudden tension in the room, Caroline straightened. "Josh, there's some milk for you. Have a donut. I got them fresh this morning."

She handed the coffee to April and waved her onto an armchair. "I was happy to hear that Denver is back on the circuit again. I can't imagine him doing anything else, can you? I really don't know what the poor man will do when he's forced to retire—" She broke off and peered at April's face. "My dear, are you all right? You're positively ashen."

April shook her head. "Just a rather bad headache, that's all. I'll be fine once I get out in the fresh air." So it had all been for nothing, she thought miserably. She had risked everything and lost.

"Then we won't sit around here too long. Can I get you an aspirin?"

"Thank you," April said, a little too loudly. "But I took some earlier."

"You'll be back in school soon, Josh," Caroline said, offering him a donut. "Are you looking forward to going back and seeing all your friends?"

Josh took the donut with a shrug. "I guess."

Caroline smiled at April. "Isn't that just like a boy. They hate school when they're there and then wish they were back there when they are grown up and have to go to work."

April nodded. "I guess none of us realize what we have until we don't have it anymore."

"Oh, isn't that the truth." Caroline then launched into a story about her days as a barrel racer, and much to April's relief, Denver's name wasn't mentioned again.

She stood at the fence later and watched while Caroline ordered Josh and Salty to walk, trot and finally canter around the paddock. Josh seemed a little more nervous than when he was with Denver, and looked almost relieved when Caroline announced it was time to give Salty a rest.

"I think you're ready for the intermediates, Josh," Caroline said, as he climbed down from the horse's back. "We have about a week and a half to work with you before summer vacation is over, so I'd like you to come every day."

She looked over at April. "Does that sound all right with you?"

"That's fine. I don't start work until next month, so I can bring him every day. How long will the lessons take?"

"Most of the morning. They actually ride for about an hour, but we spend time harnessing up, then grooming the horses afterward. It teaches the kids how to take care of their horses. Have him here around ten and you can pick him up at noon."

April thanked her and left, relieved to know she wouldn't have to wait around for Josh every day. She had things that needed doing in the house before she started work, shopping to do, school clothes to buy, anything that would keep her from thinking about Denver and how long it would be before he died in the dust of a rodeo arena.

It was on the third day of Josh's lessons that she decided to wash all the blankets and hang them out to dry. It was the perfect day for the job, clear and sunny, with a warm breeze that would dry them off quickly.

She was out in the yard, struggling to peg the last corner of the wet blanket, when she heard a car door slam. She paid little attention to it, thinking it must be a neighbor, but then she heard the faint chime of her doorbell.

Frowning, she pushed the peg down on the clothesline and hurried back into the house. She tried to remember if she'd ordered anything from the catalog that hadn't yet arrived as she pulled open the door.

The world spun, then jolted to a stop.

"Hello, April," Denver said quietly.

She stood like a fool on the doorstep, just staring at him.

He shifted from one foot to the other. "Aren't you going to ask me in?"

"Of course." She felt the warmth flood her cheeks as she stepped back. "I'm sorry. Please, come in."

She watched him walk into the living room and glance around. She couldn't believe he was actually there, in her house, looking even more rugged and heartbreakingly attractive than she remembered. *Why was he there?*

The questions plunged through her mind as she stared at him. Questions she dared not ask, dared not think about. "J-Josh isn't here," she stammered, thinking he must have come to visit his son. It would be the first time they'd seen each other since Denver had discovered the truth.

"I know."

He turned to look at her, and his expression took her breath away. She saw uncertainty, forgiveness, and something else she didn't dare analyze.

"I was out at Caroline's. I needed to pick up something. I saw her out in the paddock with the kids. Josh was there, so I figured this might be a good time to come and talk to you."

"Did you speak to him?"

"No. I wanted to talk to you first."

Her heart started thudding, and she dropped her gaze. "Would you like some coffee? A beer? I have some—"

"Sit down, April."

There was a note in his voice that made her instantly obey. She sat on the edge of her couch, gripping the seat on either side of her with tense fingers.

"I've been doing a lot of thinking," Denver said, taking

the armchair opposite her. "I think it's time we talked this out."

One hand strayed to her throat as she looked at him. "All right."

Denver stared at his hands, clasped in front of him. "I thought about a lot of things after you left me that day at the hospital," he said, his voice barely above a husky whisper. "I was angry at first. I felt betrayed, by my own brother and by the one woman I'd ever loved."

She put her hand over her mouth as a strangled sound escaped.

He flinched but didn't raise his eyes. "I was angry that Lane, who'd had it all, had taken the only thing from me that rightfully belonged to me. My son."

She started to say, "I'm so sorry—"

He lifted his hand. "No, let me finish. I can understand why you couldn't tell me. You thought I'd left because I didn't care about you. That the rodeo meant more to me that you did. That I'd be miserable if I was trapped with a baby, and I'd make you miserable, too, isn't that it?"

She nodded, relieved that he'd understood so well.

"I can even understand why Lane did it. He didn't trust me to take care of you. He loved you enough to take you and the baby, even though it must have destroyed him every time he looked at Josh. For the longest time I managed to convince myself that I was doing what was best for you. I figured I'd only end up hurting you, the way my father hurt my mother, Lane and me. I just couldn't admit, even to myself, that it was jealousy of Lane that was driving me all this time."

He paused, and the torment on his face made her long to go to him. "You know what's really ironic?" she said softly. "Lane was jealous of you. Jealous because you had the ability to give me a son. Something he couldn't do."

"I figured that, after I thought some more about it. It

must have been tough on him. I realize that now. I guess I don't have anything to prove anymore.''

She wasn't sure yet what he was trying to tell her, and she was afraid to hope for too much. ''He cared a great deal about you, Denver.''

Again Denver's face twisted in pain. ''Yeah, I guess he did.'' He cleared his throat and looked up at the ceiling. ''Maybe I didn't deserve to have Josh then. Maybe Lane *was* the better man to be his father.''

Her pain matched the agony on his face. ''Denver—''

''But Josh doesn't have his dad around anymore, and although I know I'll never take my brother's place, I'd like to hang around and kind of watch my son grow up.'' Again he cleared his throat. ''If that's okay with you.''

She could feel the tears slipping down her cheeks. ''Oh, Denver, of course that's okay with me. It what I've always wanted.''

''I'll try not to step on your toes too much—''

''Denver—''

''But I think you should know that I'm going to be around a lot.''

''I'd like that.''

He looked at her then, and her heart soared at the passion in his eyes. ''I've never stopped loving you,'' he said softly. ''No matter how damn hard I tried.''

She was crying in earnest now. ''I've always loved you, too,'' she whispered.

He gave her the slow grin that could always melt her heart. ''Then come here and kiss me, woman. I've waited too damn long as it is.''

With a cry of joy she went into his arms, returning the hot, frenzied kisses he smothered over her mouth, her throat, her neck—anywhere he could reach.

It seemed so right, after all. She felt his fingers tugging at the hem of her sweater and tore it off herself. She fumbled at the buttons of his shirt, desperate to touch his naked skin.

He rose to his feet, his mouth still locked over hers. More clothes fell to the floor, and he lifted his head. "The bedroom," he muttered hoarsely.

Ridiculously, she got an attack of decorum. Wondering if the neighbors could possibly see them through the window, she said breathlessly, "I've washed all the blankets. Besides, it's the middle of the morning." She gasped as he bent his head to trail wet kisses over her breast.

"So what's your point?"

"Josh. I have to go get Josh. I can't just—"

"Yes, you can. Caroline will keep him until you get there. I left her a note."

She gasped again. "You told her you were planning this?"

He lifted his head and looked at her. "Hell, no. I wasn't at all sure you'd be happy to see me. I was kind of hoping, though."

"What would you have done if I'd thrown you out?" She placed her hands on his bare chest and pushed herself away from him.

"Hung around until you'd come to your senses." Ignoring her attempts to keep him at arm's length, he pulled her back against him and kissed her until she was fighting for breath. "I let you get away from me once," he muttered. "I wasn't about to let that happen again."

"What if I didn't love you?"

"I would have made you love me somehow. Besides, after the way you seduced me, I figured there had to be some feelings there."

She pretended to be shocked. "Seduced you? I did no such thing."

"Yeah?" He smiled lazily at her. "Then what do you call it?"

"I call it answering a need. I was pretty shook up at the time, if you remember."

"Sweetheart, I haven't been able to think about anything else since it happened." He kissed her again, so thoroughly she locked her knees together.

"Denver—"

"If you don't quit asking those fool questions, I'm gonna have to carry you in there myself."

She gave up, as she always knew she would, and let him lead her into the bedroom. This time there was none of the frenzied rush of the last time. No quiet desperation, no frantic need to shut out the world.

This time the world was a glorious place, full of promise and expectations, joy and dreams fulfilled. They took their time, trailing kisses down each other's bodies, touching, exploring, taking, demanding and always, always giving.

When he finally could wait no longer, she took him inside her, welcoming him with a passion that matched his own driving need. She soared with him to the heights where only he could take her, and rested with him afterward in a blissful peace that left her drowsy and wholly content.

The question that had hovered in the back of her mind, however, would not let her rest for long. She had to know, before she could truly let go of her fears.

"What about the rodeo?" she asked him. "Will you have time for that as well as Josh?"

He lay on his back, the sheet carelessly tossed across the lower half of his damp body. "The rodeo," he murmured. "Oh, yeah. I was coming to that."

She rolled onto her side and gazed at him. She would never tire of watching his strong profile, she thought in quiet enjoyment.

"I'm giving up the rodeo," he said, staring straight up at the ceiling. "I figure it's time."

"Caroline said you were back on the circuit," she said

unsteadily. "I was so afraid you were going to get hurt again."

"I told her that because I didn't want to answer any of her questions." He stretched his arms above his head. "I know a lot of guys who ride the circuit and have a wife and family at the same time, but I'm not one of them. I've been checking out acreage. Come January I'm going to open my own rodeo school in eastern Oregon."

She barely heard the last part of his statement. She was too busy concentrating on the wife and family part of it. Did he mean what she thought, hoped and prayed he meant?

"I don't know how you feel about moving out there," Denver went on, apparently oblivious of her confusion. "I know you're starting a new job soon, but I thought it might be nice if you could kind of take care of things for me at the school. I'm going to need someone to handle the accounts."

She stared at him. "You're offering me a job?"

He finally looked at her, and there was love and laughter in his eyes. "I'm asking you to marry me. You and Josh. I never was good at making pretty speeches."

"Denver, my gorgeous, wonderful love, that's the prettiest speech you'll ever make." She flung herself on top of him and showered him with kisses, ignoring his laughing protests until she was out of breath herself.

"Now I have to tell Josh," she said, sobering at the thought.

She saw his expression change and immediately amended that. "Maybe you should tell him," she said quickly. "I think he'd like that."

His ice-blue gaze sought hers. "Honey, I've been thinking about that. I'm not sure it would be such a good idea to tell him about me. Maybe later, when he's had time to become used to things, but not now. He's still getting over the loss of the man he loved as his father. I don't want to take that away from him. Not yet.''

She thought she couldn't ever love him more than she already did. She'd been wrong. ''You won't mind if he goes on thinking of you as his uncle?''

Denver shook his head. ''I'll know I'm his father,'' he said quietly. ''That's enough.''

''You know something, Denver Briggs?'' She touched his nose with her lips. ''You're going to make one heck of a father.''

He grinned. ''Something tells me you're gonna make one heck of a wife.''

''I'm certainly going to try.'' She caught sight of the clock on the bedside table and gasped. ''Oh, Lord, look at the time. I have to go get Josh.''

He grabbed her before she could slide off the bed and pulled her down on top of him. ''One more kiss, lady, and then we'll both go get our son.''

Half an hour later Denver sat behind the wheel of the T-bird, marveling at how much his life had changed in a few short weeks. He'd gone from a lonely, embittered cowboy without a home to a prospective groom and a father. He had the woman he loved beyond reason at his side, and he was on his way to collect his son. *His son.* He still couldn't get used to those words.

''How are Jed and Cord?'' April asked, stirring his body again as she leaned against him. ''Are they going to make the finals?''

''I reckon Jed will.'' Denver braked, slowing down for a light. ''That's if he doesn't waste any more of his time looking for some glamorous blonde to play make-believe wife for him.''

April stared at him in astonishment. ''Why in the world would he want to do that?''

''He has this fool idea about winning the all-around

championship, then he wants to rent a big fancy car and ride into his hometown waving the gold buckle in everyone's face. He figures that if he has a knockout wife sitting next to him, she'll give him more respectability and all the men will envy him. Since he has no intention of ever getting 'hooked,' as he calls it, he just wants to find someone who'll pretend to be his wife.''

April looked amused. ''I wish him luck.''

''Yeah, well, so far, he hasn't had any luck at all.''

''I'm not surprised,'' April said, grinning. ''What about Cord? Isn't he after the championship, too?''

Denver sighed. ''You bet he is. But right now he's holed up in his cabin with a busted arm. He reckons he'll come back in time to make the finals. I wouldn't be surprised if he does.''

''Amen to that,'' April murmured. ''Never underestimate a cowboy—I know that for certain.''

Denver couldn't answer her. He had turned into Caroline's driveway, and he'd just spotted Josh sitting on the front steps of the house.

Josh jumped to his feet as the car pulled up in front of him. Caroline must have told the boy he'd be with April, Denver realized, seeing the eager look on his son's face. A feeling of tenderness curled inside him like a gentle fist.

He braked, then switched off the engine. Now that it was actually time to meet his son, he felt almost nervous, as if this were the first time they'd met.

''You go ahead,'' April said gently.

He gave her a tight nod, grateful for her understanding. This was a very special moment for him. He wanted to handle it on his own.

He climbed out of the car and walked around the hood to where Josh waited with a mixture of excitement and uncertainty chasing across his young face.

Denver wondered briefly what Caroline had told him.

How much she'd guessed from his brief note. He hadn't known himself quite what to expect when he'd gone to ask April to marry him. He'd just hoped like mad, and had told Caroline he'd be back to see Josh.

Now he was here, and nothing in his life would ever be the same again. He paused at the foot of the steps and gazed at the boy who looked so much like himself. The boy who would one day grow into a man and make him proud, no matter what course in life he took. His firstborn, because he hoped to have others.

"Hi, Josh," he said awkwardly. "I've come to take you home."

Josh took a hesitant step toward him. "Are you going to stay this time?" he asked, his eyes brimming with hope.

Denver smiled. "I'll be home for Christmas, and I won't be going away again."

Josh's face shone with such joy it almost dazzled Denver. He held out his arms and the boy bounded down the steps and flung himself into them.

"I love you, cowboy," Denver said, unashamed of the tears clinging to his eyelashes.

"I love you, too," Josh's muffled voice answered.

His heart too full to speak, Denver turned and, with his arm about his son, walked back to the car.

April watched them walk toward her, the big man and the small boy, so much alike. She and Lane had denied Denver so much, she thought sadly, but she had the power and, God willing, the time to make it up to him. And she would spend the rest of her life doing just that. Somehow she knew that Lane would approve.

The door opened, and Josh scrambled into the back of the car. "Uncle Denver says he's going to be home for Christmas, and he's going to stay," he said, his voice breathless with excitement. "Is he going to be my new dad?"

"Yes," April said, smiling at her handsome husband-to-be. "He's going to be your new dad."

Denver leaned in and kissed her full on the lips. "And your mom's going to be my new wife."

"All right!" Josh bounced up and down. "Now we can play video games all the time."

"I should go up and see Caroline," April said, glancing toward the house.

"We'll call her." Denver eased himself into the seat and switched on the engine. "Right now I want to take my new family home."

April had no argument at all with that.

* * * * *

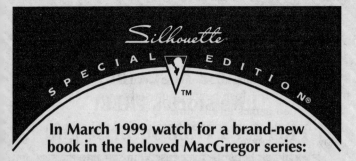

If you enjoyed what you just read,
then we've got an offer you can't resist!

Take 2 bestselling love stories FREE!

Plus get a FREE surprise gift!

This March Silhouette is proud to present

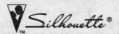

INTIMATE MOMENTS®
Silhouette®

*invites you to join the Brand brothers,
a close-knit Texas family in which each
sibling is eventually branded by love—
and marriage!*

MAGGIE SHAYNE
continues her intriguing series

with

THE BADDEST BRIDE IN TEXAS, #907
due out in February 1999.

If you missed the first four tales of the irresistible
Brand brothers:
THE LITTLEST COWBOY, #716 (6/96)
THE BADDEST VIRGIN IN TEXAS, #788 (6/97)
BADLANDS BAD BOY, #809 (9/97)
THE HUSBAND SHE COULDN'T REMEMBER, #854 (5/98)
You can order them now.

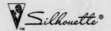
Silhouette®

Available at your favorite retail outlet.

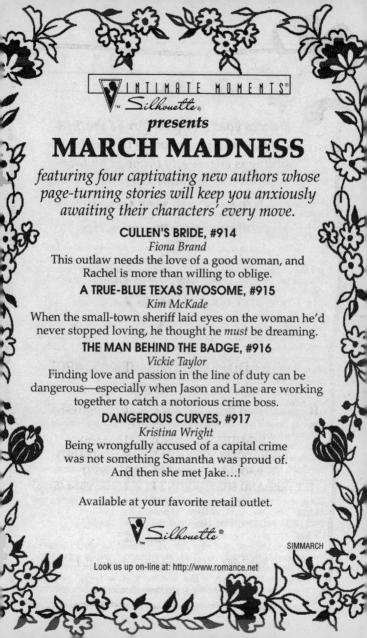

INTIMATE MOMENTS®

Silhouette®

presents

MARCH MADNESS

featuring four captivating new authors whose page-turning stories will keep you anxiously awaiting their characters' every move.

CULLEN'S BRIDE, #914
Fiona Brand
This outlaw needs the love of a good woman, and Rachel is more than willing to oblige.

A TRUE-BLUE TEXAS TWOSOME, #915
Kim McKade
When the small-town sheriff laid eyes on the woman he'd never stopped loving, he thought he *must* be dreaming.

THE MAN BEHIND THE BADGE, #916
Vickie Taylor
Finding love and passion in the line of duty can be dangerous—especially when Jason and Lane are working together to catch a notorious crime boss.

DANGEROUS CURVES, #917
Kristina Wright
Being wrongfully accused of a capital crime was not something Samantha was proud of. And then she met Jake…!

Available at your favorite retail outlet.

Silhouette®

SIMMARCH

Look us up on-line at: http://www.romance.net

COMING NEXT MONTH

#913 ROYAL'S CHILD—Sharon Sala
The Justice Way

Royal Justice knew he would do anything to make his daughter happy. So when she insisted that a lone hitchhiker needed *their* help, he went against his better judgment and told Angel Rojas to climb on board. After that, it didn't take long before his two favorite females were giving him a few lessons on how to live—and love—again.

#914 CULLEN'S BRIDE—Fiona Brand
March Madness

Sexy Cullen Logan thought he had no chance for a happy family—until he met Rachel Sinclair. She was everything he'd ever wanted in a woman, and now she was about to have his child. Cullen knew that being a father was a full-time job, but given his dangerous past, was he qualified for the position?

#915 A TRUE-BLUE TEXAS TWOSOME—Kim McKade
March Madness

Toby Haskell was perfectly content with his life as a country sheriff. Until his one true love, Corrine Maxwell, returned to town. Losing her had been hard—and accepting it even harder. Now she was back, and he knew he had a second chance. But was his small-town life enough for a big-city girl?

#916 THE MAN BEHIND THE BADGE—Vickie Taylor
March Madness

The last thing FBI agent Jason Stateler needed was to get too close to his sexy female partner. But Lane McCullough was part of the case, and he knew she wasn't going away—and, secretly, he didn't really want her to. Tracking down a criminal was easy—it was their unexpected passion that was going to be the problem.

#917 DANGEROUS CURVES—Kristina Wright
March Madness

Samantha Martin knew she was innocent of murder—she'd just been in the wrong place at the wrong time. And so was Jake Cavanaugh, because he had been foolish enough to pick her up when she was making her escape. But now there was no turning back, and before long she was trusting him with her life…but what about with her heart?

#918 THE MOTHER OF HIS CHILD—Laurey Bright
Conveniently Wed

The moment Charisse Lane most feared had arrived: her child's father had found them! More disconcerting was her immediate, intense attraction to the tall, dark dad—an attraction Daniel Richmond clearly reciprocated. But Charisse knew that a legacy of lies—and secrets—could very well prevent the happily-ever-after she wished could be theirs….